Love
and the
Perfect Match

Colin Henderson

Author's note.

The story is set in the early 1970s. Schools, teaching and probably teachers have changed over the last fifty years. The daily use of, and familiarity with, computers and modern technology have changed our lives, both in and out of the classroom. Many of the situations in which the main characters in this story find themselves could, and would, have been avoided if they had only possessed mobile phones.

Main Characters

Roddy Amport	A young graduate
Suzy Johnson-Little	A school mother
Philip Pipe	The Headmaster
Dottie Pipe	His snobbish wife
Rosie Pitchworth	An attractive young lady
Angela Bailey	A senior teacher
Derek Drinkall	A 'know-all' teacher
Edwin Stevenson	An eccentric pupil
Norman Stevenson	Edwin's eccentric father
Wesley Berkshire	A unusually grown-up pupil
Kate McNally	A film star
'Fee'	Kate's oldest school friend

ACKNOWLEDGMENTS

Huge thanks to those who read, suffered and corrected my early drafts. In particular, all my family, Robin Nordgreen, and Alan Cameron. Fortunately, Susan Wyatt's initial observations saved me from straying into dangerous waters.

Freddie Millburn-Fryer kindly helped me and provided some vital computer expertise. Without the generous time, patience and technical skills of Ben Dixon, a published author, my efforts would still be a scruffy Word document.

My wife, Clare, has tirelessly provided help, advice and encouragement. Her own editorial experience has been absolutely invaluable.

Polly Murray produced the cover, patiently tolerating my frequent indecision. And finally, many thanks to RW and 'Skipper' for allowing me to use the photographs of them on the cover.

CHAPTER 1

Summer 1971: The first mother to spot Roddy
The young, attractive and fashionably dressed Mrs Suzy Johnson-Little had a keen eye for a good-looking man. However, she hardly expected to be made to jump by one as she filled her Volvo estate car with petrol at her local service station. She was startled when an elderly Austin 1100 ghosted down the slope onto the garage forecourt having run out of fuel only seconds earlier.

The driver, twenty-three year old Roddy Amport, had managed to freewheel his vehicle alongside the vacant petrol pump immediately behind Mrs Johnson-Little. The silent approach and sudden appearance of the Amport Austin made her jump. Holding the filling pump, she turned, issuing a surprised gasp. "Oh!" she gulped, appearing a little flustered. "You gave me a shock. I didn't hear you coming." She apologised as if it were her fault and hoped her embarrassment was not too obvious. She also immediately observed that the young man in front of her was unusually handsome.

"That's the trouble with these Austin engines," said Roddy, trying to keep a straight face. "They're so quiet that people don't hear them."

The woman looked puzzled. As she stood upright,

Roddy admired her trim figure. He then noticed a boy, aged about ten, sitting in the Volvo's passenger seat, listening to this verbal exchange.

"You mean…that car is…silent??" continued the woman whom Roddy now guessed was in her early thirties.

"Smooth and silent," continued Roddy. "Not unlike me," he added with a grin.

He was about to tease her further but the ten year old intervened:

"Mum, Mum," he called from the open car window. "He's having you on. That car's an old banger. The engine was probably switched off."

The woman hesitated, then gave an embarrassed smile.

"That's not fair," she complained, "taking advantage of a woman's ignorance. Not very gentlemanly!"

"Oh, I'm no gentleman," replied Roddy, in an accent which proved that he was actually the product of many generations of good breeding.

The woman turned to go and pay, placing the payment on her husband's business account. When she returned, she passed Roddy who could only afford to feed the Austin a few pounds' worth of fuel. She paused and her pale blue eyes stared into Roddy's, admiring his dark, good looks.

"Smooth and silent? Hmm! I'd like to get my own back one day," she said, frowning slightly and inadvertently straightening a lock of blonde hair. "Do you live round here?" she asked.

"No. But I am hoping to. I am on my way to an interview – for a teaching job nearby.

"Really? Which school?" asked Mrs Johnson-Little casually.

Roddy had to think for a moment.

"It's called Whitsborough. I think most of the boys there are boarders."

The woman called to her son who was busy searching for sweets in the car's glove box.

"Did you hear that, Taylor? This…," she paused for effect, "*gentleman,* is going for an interview at Whitsborough."

Taylor turned quickly, to give Roddy a longer look.

"Well, good luck with your teaching," said Mrs Johnson-Little, fixing Roddy with eye contact before entering her car. The Volvo engine sprang to life and she gave the suggestion of a wave as the car moved off.

Roddy's eyes followed the car. It appeared to have a personalised number plate which he read: 'SJL 2'.

"**S.J.L.**? **S**eriously…er…. **J**aunty??…**L**ady," he mumbled as he searched for some coins in his pocket.

"Mum, I hope you didn't tell him…where I go to school," said Taylor as they drove away.

"Of course not," she replied, glancing in the car's rear-view mirror, but already she was casting her mind forward in enthusiastic anticipation of Taylor's next term, at Whitsborough School.

Whitsborough: The interview

Easy-going Roddy Amport was now late for his interview. His rusty Austin 1100 was speeding along Whitsborough's shingle drive towards the steps of the front entrance. At the same time, Budget, the Headmaster's beloved black labrador, was waddling out of the front doors, heading for the shade of the oak tree in the centre of the lawn. Braking heavily, and thus slewing sideways to avoid a canine collision, Roddy realised that this was not the ideal way to create a good first impression. The loud crunching as small stones were sprayed onto the front lawn, and the disagreeable sound of a worn exhaust pipe, served notice of Roddy's arrival. However, Budget's senses had failed to register his own 'near death' experience.

Chance was a major influence on Roddy's life and, with no particular career path in mind, it was his mother who, using a family connection, had arranged the interview. Inside the school, originally built as a large Victorian country retreat, the Headmaster, Philip Pipe, and his wife, Dottie, were waiting. They were both in their early sixties and Philip's fragile health continually worried Dottie. They were seated in the large drawing room which was only used for formal occasions, such as interviews and the visits of prospective parents. The furniture needed updating but the school's finances were precarious, which was one of the reasons why the Pipes were keen to appoint Roddy Amport as a new teacher: just out of university and in his early twenties, he would be cheap.

Roddy parked the ten year old car on the empty drive, adjusted his tie and reached for his sports jacket on the back seat. Budget, unaware of his recent dice with death, wandered over to demand a friendly pat from the new arrival.

"Well, hello, Roddy," called Dottie as she strode out of the front entrance towards him and delivered a firm handshake. She took a pace back, observing that he had grown into a fine-looking young man.

"Am I allowed to say that you have grown even more since I last saw you…at your parents' twenty-fifth celebrations?"

"Yes. I think you must be right," replied Roddy, relieved that they had shaken hands and that he did not have to suffer an embarrassed kiss on both cheeks.

"Thanks for coming. I see that you have already met Budget."
Roddy refrained from explaining that, only moments earlier, Budget had been close to meeting his Maker.

"Right, do come in. Philip will be delighted to see you again but don't be surprised if he looks a little older. He's had a few health problems since you last saw him."

Several days earlier, Arnold Percival, a long-serving resident teacher at Whitsborough, had resigned impulsively. He had suffered a fit of pique when the headmaster informed him that he would have to move out of his school accommodation. His rooms were to become part of a plan to provide a 'recreation area' for the boarding pupils. Later the following day, Percival had calmed down and he attempted to withdraw his resignation. But he was too late: Philip Pipe had already informed the school governors of Percival's resignation. Percival's teaching had become increasingly ineffective and the Pipes considered that he was 'overpaid.'

The resignation proved a blessing in disguise and it was Dottie who suggested contacting her old school friend, Patricia Amport. Dottie knew that Patricia's son, Roddy, had recently left university but had no clear, future plans. She had known Roddy since his birth and witnessed his development. She felt sure that Roddy's pedigree and sporting strengths alone would justify his appointment. One look at Roddy, as he attempted to smarten himself up, seemed to confirm the likely accuracy of his mother's description: "He's a pretty useful all-round sportsman."

Dottie had periodically observed Roddy cheerfully rough-and-tumbling through his childhood. 'Easy-going' and 'laid back' were terms frequently used to describe him. As he had no particular plans or aspirations when he left university, his mother jumped at the idea that he should try teaching. Arranging for him to drive to Whitsborough for an informal 'chat' with the Pipes was easy. Teaching represented uncharted waters but the regular involvement with sport provided Roddy with an attractive incentive.

The 'chat' with Philip proved to be little more than a formality. Roddy had always liked and respected the Pipes. The interview was just a friendly conversation.

"Now, let's get down to a few details," said Philip. "What exactly did you read at university?"

"Well, History was the main subject but I also spent a year reading some French Literature. I speak pretty reasonable French and would be keen to teach it."

Dottie frowned slightly as she caught Philip's eye.

"Ah, well... our 'French lady,' Angela Bailey, runs a pretty tight ship and she really likes to cover all the French lessons herself," explained Philip.

Dottie saw Roddy look a little disappointed and intervened:

"But I am sure we could have a word with her and...."

Philip did not wish to raise this as a problem.

"Good," he said, "History. Hmm? So that means you could also cover English ...and if necessary a little Geography? We all have to be adaptable here,"

"Yes, I understand," agreed Roddy.

"And then of course," continued Philip, "there's all the sport. I know you are a strong all-rounder. Main sports?"

Roddy paused: "Rugby, Cricket, a bit of football - and I once played tennis for the school when they were short. And I swim fairly...er...buoyantly?"

Philip smiled at the joke but Dottie frowned at the mention of swimming. There was, alas, no pool although a few brave souls were, on very hot evenings, permitted to swim with the resident mallards in the large pond.

"Sport's a very important part of the day for us. We'd expect your full participation on a daily basis."

"Of course, and I'd really look forward to that."

Philip exchanged an almost imperceptible nod of agreement with Dottie. Roddy pretended not to notice it.

"Excellent. Well I take it that you'd be happy to join us in September? Many of the boys are boarders so there are various activities to organise in the evenings. I can promise you one thing for certain: you won't be bored!"

"That's fine with me," replied Roddy.

"Now, I've asked Angela to show you round. She'll give you plenty of the nitty gritty information. She's about to disappear for the holidays and we are driving up to Scotland as soon as we can get away. I'll send you a formal letter in the next few days... with the salary scale, health checks, that sort of thing. Have you got any interesting holiday plans?"

"Just cricket really. There's the annual old boys cricket week which I always go to. It's a good standard of cricket, there's plenty of humour and perhaps a pint or two of good beer."

Philip smiled. "Sounds most agreeable but a bit too hectic for me these days. We prefer the midges in Scotland."

Dottie scowled at the mention of this perennial menace. Briefly, Roddy considered asking a few questions. He would like to have known the ages the boys would be in the classes he would teach and which sports but…Philip stood to signal the end of the interview and he moved towards the door. He held out his hand.

"I look forward to seeing you in September, Roddy."

Roddy stood, shook hands and thanked Philip. He then turned to thank Dottie.

"Goodbye and thank you, too…er…" Roddy was unsure whether or not to continue to call her 'Dottie.'

"I think it had better be 'Mrs Pipe' from now on - otherwise other members of the Common Room might think …."

"Of course. I quite understand… Mrs Pipe!" said Roddy with a smile and a slight, affected bow.

Dottie opened the door just as Angela Bailey was about to knock and enter.

"Ah. Angela," said Dottie. "Perfect timing! This is Roddy and as I predicted, he'll be joining us in September. If you'd be kind enough to show him round and answer any questions…. that would be very kind."

"Yes, that would be great, thanks," said Roddy with a smile. He nodded to the Pipes as he closed the door and left Philip's study.

"Well, that's one matter sorted out," commented Dottie.

"Yes," Philip agreed. "We've got the staff but the finances aren't looking good. The governors keep asking me about future numbers. Both the Jenkins boys are leaving at Christmas and Hugo Martin is off with his family to New York at half term. Next year, things could be critical. We may even have to….."

"Oh, don't get depressed about it," urged Dottie. "I'm sure that Roddy will be good news for the school. Let's look on the bright side."

The tour with Angela Bailey

Angela Bailey was a tallish woman in her early thirties. Wearing a green jumper and a thick grey skirt, she held out her hand in a hearty fashion.

"Hello. I'm Angela Bailey. Welcome to Whitsborough."

They shook hands and exchanged friendly smiles. Roddy was not quite sure whether he found her attractive or not but there was something definitely interesting about her. Perhaps it was her eyes…or her dark hair….?

"Philip asked me to come and say hello - and show you the ropes."

Roddy observed the confident use of the appellation, *Philip*. He guessed that Angela was a member of the inner circle of senior teachers and he wondered how many other members there were.

"I hear Dottie and your mother are old friends," said Angela. Roddy felt this sounded rather like an accusation but he simply answered that they had been at school together - 'years ago, of course' - and had always 'kept in touch.'

"Ah, I see," replied Angela, "and so you came here for an interview. And that has obviously gone well?" There was another mildly accusatory tone in the question, which Roddy chose to volley.

"Well…yes. Otherwise, I suppose you would not now be about to show me around."

Angela looked a little irritated by this reply. Roddy's agreeable nature was being tested and he thought it would be good idea to alter the course of the conversation.

"And have you been here long...er...Miss er Mrs..?..."

"*Angela* is fine," she answered firmly, "and yes - I've been here for seven years. Time races by and it's not a bad place to work." She hesitated thoughtfully and then provided the glimpse of a smile. Roddy decided that she was certainly not unattractive.

"Come on. I'll give you a proper tour. Be prepared to see the 'warts and all'.

Angela led the way along a rather dimly lit corridor. As the tour progressed, the verbal exchanges became warmer. Roddy noted familiar items from his own school days: the red blankets on the dormitory beds, the rows of classroom desks, the long wooden dining room tables and the playing fields, worn in patches and requiring attention.

"I gather you are a keen sportsman, Roddy. We need some young blood on the pitches. Coaching not playing!"

"Yes, I am certainly looking forward to doing some coaching. It's rugby next term, I believe."

"And what about in the classroom? Parents do tend to expect a spot of academic stuff, you know. It's not all sport," said Angela with a grin.

Roddy appreciated the dry humour.

"Yes. It's a pity about that. I read History, but I think I may have to teach other subjects…English, and perhaps Geography. Actually, my French is pretty reasonable and I'd like to teach that, if possible."

When Angela did not reply immediately, Roddy remembered that Angela was, in Philip's words, his 'French lady.'

"But of course, I realise that may not be possible…to start with," Roddy added diplomatically.

Angela looked at him sternly. "No, I don't think it would."

She answered his questions about the daily routine, weekend duties and the other members of the Common Room. However, as the tour soon ended, Roddy sensed that Angela had now become a little less friendly. She led him round to the front of the building.

Roddy's Austin 1100 looked a little unloved and the exhaust pipe appeared rather insecure. He was aware that there was a messy jumble of sports gear on the seats.

Budget waddled over from his slumber on the front lawn, wagged his tail gently and received another friendly pat from Roddy.

"Well, thank you for the tour," he said, offering to shake Angela's hand. "I imagine it is all very different when the boys are around."

She gave him a half smile as they shook hands.

"Yes, very! I expect Philip will send you details but the staff are expected to arrive a couple of days before term starts. There's plenty to do then."

She stepped back, nodded and walked away. Roddy surveyed her not unappealing rear view as he started his car and drove off slowly. He winced as the exhaust chose this moment to emit a brief, unhealthy belch.

Driving home, Roddy considered his future. This was not something he did very often. Provided he avoided any unforeseen disasters, it seemed as though he would be teaching at Whitsborough for at least the next year. He sensed an element of uncertainty about the school's prospects; he had noticed that there were areas of the school where fresh paint and new woodwork were needed. The fact that the Pipes were keen to appoint him so quickly was also rather puzzling. But, he reminded himself, he was only twenty-three; time was on his side. His father, a doctor, had been a late starter at his medical school. Roddy would take things as they came. Chance always played a large part in determining the course of his life. Besides, he was looking forward to the week's cricket at his old school. Runs, wickets, beer and banter represented an enticing brew.

CHAPTER 2

Roddy: From undergraduate to schoolmaster

As he drove to his Cricket Week, Roddy ruminated over the fact that currently, and rather unusually, he did not have a girlfriend. At university, providence often seemed to dictate his life and relationships. His striking looks, of which he seemed unaware, ensured that girl friends were not hard to find. During his first year, the lovely Lucinda Camford had ensnared him; she stage-managed a collision with him in a students' pub when her handbag was supposedly 'knocked' to the ground. Apologetically, Roddy picked up the bag and, as Lucinda had planned, he was obliged to buy her a drink. This simple ploy initiated an evening's conversation and some not very subtle exposure of Lucinda's enviable legs. A few hours later, Lucinda lay back in her bed with an exhausted Roddy asleep beside her: mission accomplished!

This mutually satisfactory relationship lasted for nearly two years when, with an eye to her journalistic career aspirations, Lucinda stage-managed another successful collision; this time it was with the undergraduate son of a well-known and influential publisher. Roddy was not unduly worried about 'losing' Lucinda as he had noticed other desirable fish in the university pond.

In his final year, he was assigned to a young History tutor, Emily Chesterman, who was only a few years older than he was. Although she was a high-flying academic, she was surprisingly inexperienced with men, having spent most of her life studying books in various libraries. However, Roddy's weekly History tutorials soon spawned a mutual attraction. Thus, during the year, Emily found herself exploring areas of knowledge of which she was largely unaware. Drawn towards her handsome student, she learnt rather more from Roddy in her bedroom than he learnt from her about Tudor History.

When Roddy graduated at the end of his final year, Emily was leaving to become a lecturer at a prestigious Scottish university. They parted as friends and Roddy returned home with nothing planned for the rest of his life except a few games of cricket and many pints of beer.

Rosie Pitchworth

The Cricket Week, which took place in view of the South Downs, was something of a throwback to earlier days: striped club blazers were worn for lunch and a feature of 'The Week' was the mixture of ages to be found; many players and several former players slept in one of the huge, thirty-bed dormitories. Post-pub high jinks were evident. The good-natured President of the club, in his late seventies, was frequently woken after midnight only to endure the arrival of golf balls being chipped onto his bed from the far end of the dormitory. Over the years, girl friends came to 'The Week' and on the outfield of a nearby pitch, the ritual of 'family' camping and barbequing developed. Children with bats, balls and bicycles swam in the school swimming pool and played endless chasing games.

One evening, Roddy was ordering his third pint of Turtle Bitter half an hour after arriving at the local pub. He had to bend his head low as a row of decorative tankards hung above the bar. A woman in her early twenties appeared by his side at the bar. Wearing a pair of shorts of tasteful length and a checked, slightly masculine shirt, she gave Roddy a controlled nudge with her shoulder. This was accompanied by a warm smile.

"I gather you're the man who allowed my grandfather to steal all the glory in the game today," she beamed.

"Grandfather?" Roddy was not at his sharpest; he was wondering what lay beneath the girl's checked shirt which was almost level with his hand and his newly purchased pint of Turtle.

"Yes, you were batting with him," the girl explained.

Roddy's mind had strayed elsewhere - actually, it had not strayed very far at all; the woman was lovely and her face radiated charm and friendliness.

"Geoff? Geoffrey Pitchworth!" said the woman. For a moment Rosie Pitchworth thought the Adonis she was blatantly attempting to chat up was going to be a huge disappointment.

Roddy understood, just in time.

"Oh, Geoff P. Pitchworth. Of course. That was fun today. He's your grandfather, is he? I see!" Roddy paused as he looked into the blue eyes which were staring at him and sending out inviting messages.

Roddy noted that the attractive proposition in front of him did not have a glass.

"Forgive me. You don't have a drink. What would you like?"

"Oh…" she hesitated, "…a half of what you've got, please. And by the way, I'm Rosie Pitchworth."

"Pitchworth! Yes," responded Roddy who was now concentrating; there was something very appealing about this woman.

"I'm Roddy Amport."

"Yes, I know," replied Rosie as they shook hand and exchanged positive eye contact.

Roddy carried Rosie's beer and steered her between a

noisy group of players, many still wearing cricket whites. Several of them smiled at Rosie as she edged between them and the team captain, a successful barrister, tapped Roddy knowingly on the shoulder as he passed. He gave Roddy a wink of approval. They sat at a table by the wide glass doors which opened onto a busy courtyard garden.

Rosie explained that her family was one of the first families to camp on the school playing fields during The Week. She had made annual visits to the Cricket Week.

"Tennis, though, is really my game," said Rosie before pausing with obvious effect. "But I enjoy all sorts of games," she added, staring unblinkingly into Roddy's eyes.

Roddy began to realise that this was possibly going to be an eventful week *off* the cricket pitch and, by the way Rosie was looking at him, his next innings might take place rather sooner than he expected. But there was a sudden interruption.

"Come on, Amport. If you want a lift back to school, you'll have to come now. And since you're on the Cocoa Run this evening, you have no choice."

It was Philip Matthews, a jovial doctor who treasured The Week as a sane escape from the bedlam of General Practice.

The Cocoa Run, an evening trip to the school kitchens to collect mugs of cocoa for those in the dormitory aged over sixty-five, was another prized ritual. As luck would have it - and Rosie would not - Roddy was 'on duty' that evening and it was forbidden to swap or avoid this task.

Roddy stood up and downed the remaining Turtle Bitter in his glass.

"Forgive me. I've got to go...."

Rosie gave a brave but disappointed smile, as though her Fighter Pilot boyfriend had been hastily summoned back to his Spitfire.

"Yes, of course, all part of you 'Old Boy's re-living the past, I suppose."

"I'm sorry...." Roddy turned to go and then spun round

again with a sudden thought.

"Tennis? Tomorrow morning? You say it is your game. I'll borrow a racket. I can just about get the ball back over the net and I'll bet you have got some kit with you."

Rosie's disappointment dissolved immediately.

"But won't you be playing cricket?"

"It's a midday start tomorrow. There's plenty of time. 9.30? On the courts by the old open air pool. No one really uses the courts in the holidays."

"Right. It's a date. And I'll show you how to play the game properly." Rosie lifted her glass and waved it at him in salute as Roddy walked towards the car park and the soft burble of Dr Matthews' green MGB.

Tennis and swimming with Rosie

Having had an excellent breakfast under the high ceiling of the school Dining Hall, Roddy borrowed a suitably old tennis racket; he rejected the offer of a modern and expensive one, preferring to present the 'gifted amateur' image; an old one was more his style – a racket that he could pretend could serve as a fishing net.

He walked past the sturdy, flint-walled Chapel, down the slope to the tennis courts. Rosie, wearing some blue shorts and a bright yellow T-shirt was about to practise a serve. The ball struck the net but Roddy, who was a better player than he was prepared to admit, noted that this was the service action of someone who was not a novice. Unaware of Roddy's presence, Rosie's second serve blistered impressively across the court.

"Out!" called Roddy with a huge grin.

Rosie turned to see Roddy in his baggy old track suit trousers and flannel cricket shirt.

"Rubbish," smiled Rosie. "I'm obviously going to have to teach you the rules...as well as how to play the game."

After a slightly awkward formal handshake, the pair began to knock up. Roddy was able to return the ball effectively but in an inept manner reminiscent of a table tennis player attempting to play 'lawn' tennis for the first time. Meanwhile, Rosie's skill and elegant style soon became apparent.

Keen to impress, Rosie wanted to start the game. After about twenty minutes, she was leading 4-0. It was as she was serving in the fifth game that Roddy returned one of her faster serves with a stylish flourish. Rosie stopped. She was surprised. She paused for an unusually long time before delivering her next serve. This was to Roddy's backhand but the ball came fizzing back, across the net, with a degree of top-spin. Rosie advanced to the net, summoned Roddy to come forward and then stabbed him firmly in the chest with her index figure.

"I don't play very often," replied Roddy apologetically.

"Hmm!" was Rosie's disbelieving reply. For a moment she just glared at Roddy.

Was there a hint of venom in the glare, he wondered or was it just her competitive spirit? Roddy returned the stare innocently. Beside the tennis courts, the sun sparkled on the swimming pool.

Rosie broke the silence.

"Right. We're going to start again - and this time *you* are going to play properly. I will *not be* patronised. Understand!"

Forty minutes later, with the score at 4-4, both players were hot and sweating. A teasing drop shot brought both players to the net but Roddy over hit his attempt to return the ball. He collided with the net itself – and this brought him close to Rosie. He smiled:

"You're too good for me. I've had enough. I surrender."

Rosie pretended to be cross.

"But we haven't finished the set. You may still win."

"I know when I'm beaten." Roddy looked into her eyes and nodded in the direction of the pool.

"Swim?" he suggested and, without waiting for an answer, headed for the shower basin at the far end of the pool.

Roddy let out a series of gasping protests about the coldness of the shower. This first sight of the Amport body certainly satisfied Rosie's expectations and she noted the ample layers of wet hair channelling the water down his chest, which now appeared to be modelled on the delta of the River Ganges. It was the faded and appallingly baggy swimming shorts that prevented this from being a vision of a Mediterranean Adonis. The shorts represented what Roddy termed 'style'.

While he was commencing his third length of leisurely crawl, Rosie stripped off her tennis clothes and tackled the shower. Anticipating a swim, she was already wearing a bikini.

She timed her dive into the pool precisely. As Roddy emerged from a turn at the deep end and as he was opening his eyes to re-orientate himself, he had a pleasant surprise. Rosie's well shaped legs and neatly pointed toes disappeared under the water in front of him. Having briefly halted to avoid a collision, he continued his swim towards the shallow end. Here he stopped because he felt his legs being tugged. He attempted to make his way towards the wooden steps but now a pair of arms encircled the Amport midriff, preventing his exit.

"Oh no you don't. You won't let me beat you at tennis so I am going to race you to the other end," insisted Rosie, with water streaming down her face.

"But that's not fair. I'm exhausted already."

"Nonsense! You have an advantage because you have already warmed up," replied Rosie.

It was soon clear that Rosie was a fast and graceful swimmer; Roddy had never tried to swim fast in his life, except to make up numbers in the house relay competition.

Halfway down the return length and leading effortlessly, Rosie slowed, turned and allowed Roddy to catch up - almost. She then swam the last few strokes to victory while Roddy veered across the pool towards the steps.

"I'm a bad loser," he mumbled as he was about to haul himself out of the water.

"Hey," protested Rosie, "you might at least shake hands with the winner."

She grabbed Roddy round the waist, pulling him back into the water. As he turned to remove her arms, she released them and wrapped them instead around his neck. The resulting kiss was not a brief one and it led to some gentle exploration of the exposed parts of each other's bodies.

"Not here..," garbled Roddy as Rosie's enthusiasm became apparent.

"All right," replied Rosie.... "over there."

She grabbed Roddy's hand, pulled him up the steps and over to the far side of the pool where a bank sloped away from the school towards open fields. During the term time, boys would revise for exams and sunbathe here. Now, the grass grew high and two bodies could lie there unseen. Rosie drew Roddy down onto the bank. He remembered that he had once become painfully sunburnt while revising for a History exam near this very spot, but Rosie soon provided other distractions.

Thus, some twenty minutes later, on the bank beyond the swimming pool, an area of flattened grass betrayed the amorous activities of Roddy Amport and his recent opponent on the tennis court. The delightful moments of post coital tenderness were, however, foreshortened because, once the summit of their activity had been reached, both participants gradually became aware of the scratchy grass on which they had been lying. Roddy jumped up as a sharp prickle attacked his shoulder. As he did so he realised that he and Rosie were no longer alone near the pool. Roddy immediately disappeared once more into the grass; he had neglected to don his swimming trunks.

Oliver Goodish, another Cricket Week regular, had arrived to play tennis with his young daughter, Jemima.

Rosie, who had hastily refastened her bikini, stood and waved innocently.

"Hi Rosie," yelled Jemima waving enthusiastically.

As the two lovebirds gathered their tennis gear and passed the tennis court, Oliver asked Roddy if he was playing in the match that day.

"Yes, I think so," replied Roddy. "What about you, Ollie?"

"No. It's family 'duty' for me today. Spot of tennis and swimming - with the children."

"What have you two been doing?" asked Jemima.

"Oh, just tennis… and we had a swim," replied Rosie.

Roddy caught Oliver's eye. Oliver said nothing - but his knowing grin spoke volumes.

"I'd better get going," said Roddy, "it's nearly half eleven. The game is supposed to start at twelve."

Roddy placed his arm round Rosie's shoulder as they walked back up the path towards the chapel. They parted with a quick kiss and a brief 'see you later'. Roddy returned Rosie's cheery wave as she returned to her campsite. As she disappeared, Roddy paused. There was something a little different about this girl. Whatever it was, he found it unusually engaging, but the noisy arrival of many cricketers' cars, cheery greetings and the unloading of old cricket bags soon drowned these thoughts. Roddy made a quick trip to his dormitory nearby to grab his own kit. He then returned to the pavilion to change.

He lunched in the pavilion with the players while Rosie joined the families' barbecue with the campers. She was looking forward to seeing Roddy again when the match was over and was excited by the prospect of spending a whole evening with him. Sadly, she knew she would have to leave for London the following day because she was due to move into a friend's flat. Her new job started a few days after that.

However, during the barbecue, Julian Wheeler, a pleasant old boy whom she had known for some years offered her a lift back to London. He lived near her and the offer was too convenient to refuse. It would also save her an expensive train fare.

Disappointed about abandoning her plans for that evening, but confident that she would see Roddy again soon, Rosie managed to catch Roddy's eye on the cricket field. He was still batting but, at the end of an over, she waved desperately and mimed writing on her palm. She then pointed towards the car park and mimed placing hands on a steering wheel. This indicated that she would leave a note, and her address, on his car windscreen. Roddy seemed a little puzzled at first, but had time to wave a gloved hand to signal that he had understood the message.

Julian Wheeler had a formal dinner to attend that evening and was keen to depart. Standing by Roddy's disreputable vehicle, Rosie wrote her new address neatly but did not yet know the telephone number of her new flat. Roddy's car's windscreen wipers were loose but, instead, Rosie managed to slip her note through the top of the passenger's window which was not fully closed. The hastily written details fluttered on to the passenger's seat and she felt sure Roddy would be in touch, probably when 'The Week' was over. She was very much looking forward to seeing him again and spending more time with him.

When the match finished, Roddy showered and then returned to his car, accompanied by several other jovial cricketers who had reminded Roddy that it was his turn to drive to the pub that evening. Simon Webster, a tall fast bowler, plonked himself on the passenger's seat. He brushed the note, the cricket magazine and the shrivelled apple lying there, onto the floor. He jokingly complained to Roddy that he was not accustomed to being given a lift in a dustcart. The important note, bearing Rosie's address, was then inadvertently 'scrunched' beneath Simon's massive feet. The evening's jollifications in the pub, which included some hearty singing of rude songs and a game of hide-and-seek in the pub garden (later halted at the insistence of the long-suffering landlord) temporarily deferred all Roddy's immediate thoughts of Rosie Pitchworth.

CHAPTER 3

The school numbers problem

For several years, Whitsborough had been battling to maintain a viable number of pupils. Financially, it was vital to recruit boarders. However, numbers of both boarders and day boys had declined in recent years. Unfortunately, it was Dottie Pipe herself, the headmaster's wife, who was largely responsible for this. Dottie was a snob. For some prospective parents, whom Dottie regarded as 'unsuitable', a school tour with her left them in little doubt that they were regarded simply as a necessary evil.

Philip Pipe had been an excellent Headmaster for over twenty years but latterly he had developed a heart condition. This had required a major operation. Warned that he must take things more gently, it was, therefore, Dottie who now showed prospective parents around the school. This had a most significant and detrimental impact on school numbers. Dottie possessed degrees of warmth and kindness but she was unashamedly 'old school.' As far as she was concerned, many parents were simply to be tolerated as an inconvenience. Boarding, she believed, was the only 'proper' way to educate a boy.

Most parents were impressed by Philip, during their

initial chat with him in his study. However, by the time Dottie's tour was over, during which she had expressed her outmoded views on contemporary parenting, Whitsborough was often firmly crossed of their list. Regrettably, Philip remained unaware of the effect his wife was having on school numbers.

The day after Roddy's interview

From across Whitsborough's parched August lawn and gravelled drive, it looked as though a young zebra was attempting to climb into the boot of a large, ageing Vauxhall. In fact, the heavily patterned black and white striped skirt, of impressive thickness, was worn by Dottie Pipe. In front of the main school building, she was loading ancient suitcases, wicker baskets and fishing gear into the car. With Philip, she would soon set off for North West Scotland. The trek to the tiny rented croft - 'nearest village: 10 miles; nearest midge: 10 millimetres' – was imminent. But there was a last-minute hiccup.

A few minutes earlier, the telephone had rung while Dottie had been discussing her final holiday details with the school's long-serving secretary, Fiona. Fiona had answered the call with her usual quick efficiency but her accent soon moved smartly up the social ladder. This was a signal that it was a parent on the phone and - even more importantly - a prospective one.

After a perfunctory exchange of questions and answers, Fiona asked the lady on the other end to wait a moment while she consulted the Headmaster's wife. Dottie was listening keenly nearby. Fiona carefully covered the microphone.

"It's a woman whose family have just returned from the Middle East....husband is still working out there......the school they had chosen has let them down at the last minute...something about being over-subscribed...do we have any places? Could she come and look round Whitsborough...this afternoon?"

"Ridiculous," replied Dottie. "I am not waiting here for the sake of one child. Probably only a day boy anyway. Just tell her that....."

Fiona urgently tried to hush Dottie; her response was being uttered too loudly. Fiona placed the palms of her hand together, making a sleeping gesture against her cheek. Dottie looked puzzled; she was in no mood for charades.

Fiona had not been understood so she mouthed the magic word:

'Boarders!'

Dottie was startled: "Boarders? Plural??" This represented an exciting and potentially lucrative enquiry.

Fiona nodded and raised three fingers.

"Three??" Dottie looked stunned. "Boarders?" This, indeed, was gold dust. Dottie nodded enthusiastically at Fiona.

"Would 2.30 suit you, Mrs...?" Fiona paused for an answer....

"Berkshire."

The appointment was confirmed and Dottie was about to find Philip and inform him that they would have to delay their departure. She paused and turned to Fiona as she headed for the door.

"Oh?" she hesitated to check that no one was listening. "Did she sound...er...well-spoken??"

Fiona smiled conspiratorially. She sensed the imminence of a further snobbish question and so she continued, deliberately. "Right, I'll stay on this afternoon. Make the school look more professional."

"Thank you, Fiona. What would we do without you? *'Professional!'* - I know exactly what you mean but I do hate the use of that word in schools."

An 'unsuitable' mother's school tour with Dottie.

At 2.20pm that afternoon, a large blue Ford saloon swept up the school drive. Seated in their drawing room, Dottie and Philip were just finishing their tuna and cucumber sandwiches, purchased by Fiona from the local petrol station.

"Oh, Lord! Why are people so rude? Arriving early is so unnecessary. It's not as if the school has to catch the tide and is going to *sail* at 2.30 pm," moaned Dottie.

"Now do be calm, dear," urged Philip. "The woman must be desperate for places for her boys. Remember to make it *seem* as though we are full. I'll chat to her when you have shown her round."

Dottie was gawping at the arrivals from behind the heavily curtained window frames. She noted a boy, aged about nine, immediately emerging from a rear door. The lady driver, Mrs Berkshire, then got out and moved to the other rear door. It was evident that the occupant was reluctant to leave the car. The woman was wearing a yellow dress with a number of random blue spots on it. She was a little overweight and the hem of the dress rode a little too high above her sturdy knees.

"Well, I've seen worse," mumbled Dottie.

"Remember, we need them. Just don't let them know it…Three boarders!" advised Philip.

At that moment, the remaining passenger was catapulted out of the car; even an ejector seat would not have accounted for the velocity of this exit. Mrs Berkshire's powerful forearm had generated this remarkable momentum as an even younger boy landed and skidded to a halt on the Whitsborough gravel.

"This does not look at all promising, Philip," said Dottie shaking her head and brushing a few crumbs off her dress." She headed for the door but Philip caught hold of her hand as she passed his chair. He held it and squeezed it. He glared into her eyes.

"Remember. *Three* boar...."

"Yes. I know," interjected Dottie, "Three bloody boarders!"

As she approached the Berkshire car, Dottie braced herself. Gritting her teeth, she extended a welcoming hand.

"Hello, I'm Dottie Pipe. Philip, my husband, is the Headmaster."

Mrs Berkshire was still trying to get the younger child to stand still and stop complaining. She finally turned.

"I'm Mrs Berkshire. I'm pleased to meet you."

"And these are....?" Dottie glanced at the boys with a false smile.

"Conrad, he's eight and Jordan who's nine." Jordan half nodded but Conrad twisted his head to avoid eye contact.

"But I, er, understood that there were *three* boys?"

"Oh yes, There's Wesley as well...but he didn't want to get out of bed."

The vibes Dottie was receiving were less than encouraging.

"Well, let me show you round. We're lucky with the weather aren't we? Such a beautiful day."

"I'm cold," whined Jordan.

"He's used to the heat in Abu Dookah," explained Mrs B, "it was 35 degrees out there."

Dottie remembered the complaints the school had received during the previous winter. One boarder had smuggled a thermometer into the North Dormitory. It had registered just two degrees above freezing and the boy's mother initiated a number of angry parental letters, forcing Philip to turn on the radiators. An 'unnecessary expense' thought Dottie.

She led the Berkshires, as prospective customers, round to the 'good side' of the school where the lawns had recently received their monthly trim. They then reached the playing fields which had not been tended during the summer holidays.

Jordan seemed unimpressed.

"The grass hasn't been cut!" he noted.

"And he's used to air-conditioning in the classrooms," added Mrs Berkshire, looking towards Dottie in the hope that she would confirm that the school was, indeed, air-conditioned. Dottie, however, batted away this question cleverly.

"Of course. It's a *condition* that the air is always allowed to circulate in all our classrooms...and dormitories. Tell me, did you have your own lake to swim in?" she asked, neatly changing the subject.

"We had our own swimming pool," boasted Jordan.

"Long enough for the Olympics," added Mrs B.

"Indoors," added Jordan.

"Oh what a pity!" countered Dottie. "So stuffy."

"We had an outdoor one as well," Jordan continued, "and of course we could also swim in the sea."

Dottie was in danger of losing her self-control. She whisked the family into the most recently decorated classroom and up the stairs to the one dormitory boasting two radiators. She was beginning to dislike the family intensely and just managed to resist the temptation to show them the dormitory where there were no radiators at all.

'Three boarders', Dottie kept thinking: 'gold dust'.

It was a moral dilemma. The school, and Philip, needed their fees. Could she really risk turning them away?

As they descended the stairs, Philip intercepted them and, relieving Dottie, took them into his study. From a drawer of his well-worn desk, he produced a tin of very large humbugs. He had learnt that these sweets were often a novelty for young boys and, more importantly, kept them silent and busy chewing for at least fifteen minutes - the amount of time he usually allocated to prospective parents. The Berkshire boys were soon dentally occupied and silenced.

Philip had already decided to go on the attack. He made it clear that the school had a full complement of boarders for next term. However, it was possible - with 'a certain amount of logistical reorganisation' - that space *might* be found; he would have to consult the Bursarial department (Fiona) and see what they could come up with. In the meantime, he wished Mrs Berkshire ("Oh please call me

Chuselle") the very best of luck. He was himself hoping to grab a few days (three weeks) annual leave in Scotland.

"When will you be able to let me know if you have places? My husband decided to send us over here at such short notice. I've got so little time," pleaded Mrs B.

Philip stood and steered them out of the door.

"The Bursar will be in touch with you once we have assessed whether we can fit your sons in."

"But Mum, Mum, I don't want to play rug......" insisted Jordan, but at that moment the remains of his humbug dropped out of his mouth, onto the floor and skidded under a large table in the hallway.

"Don't worry", said Philip, grateful for this distraction. "Budget will find it and eat it."

"Budget?" queried Mrs B.

"Yes. He's our dog, a black labrador. He loves eating sweets and...," he looked down at Conrad who was nestled beside his mother, "young boarders!"

Philip smiled kindly but Conrad nervously tightened his grip on his mother's hand. Even Chuselle Berkshire felt unsure whether Budget really was a man-eater.

The two boys seemed extremely keen to get back into the car and Mrs Berkshire was a little bewildered by the whole experience. As the car crunched along the Whitsborough drive, she wondered whether her third son, Wesley, had bothered to get out of bed yet.

"Mum, I thought that Dottie woman was scary," commented Jordan.

Conrad spotted something black, stretched out sleepily on the lawn.

"Look! The dog! Do you think it really eats boys?"

"I doubt it. But you know what this school's got?" his mother announced as she started the engine. "Class."

Mrs Berkshire may have driven away feeling satisfied but Dottie entered Philip's study in a state of frustration.

"Philip, we really can't! They were awful. The two boys certainly did not want to come here. The older one moaned and complained about everything. They've obviously been completely spoilt and the eldest couldn't even be bothered to get out of bed to come here."

Dottie sank down in the old armchair opposite Philip's desk. Philip smiled at her sympathetically. He had already made up his mind. He decided that humour was the best way to address the problem.

"Well I thought they were charming."

Dottie stiffened:

"Charming??"

Philip held his wife's glare.

"I thought the boys behaved perfectly. They sat quietly while...."

Dottie interrupted:

"Yes, the old humbug routine. Really! What does that tell us about them?"

Philip continued, timing his next revelation perfectly,

"And I thought the mother was delightful. I am sure Chuselle and I...."

"Chuselle?? Her name is Chuselle??" Dottie jumped to her feet. "Chuselle! Philip, we can't possibly have a mother here called...."

Philip smiled. He knew the name would light a fuse but was determined to settle the matter.

"We simply cannot run this school as dinosaurs. The world has changed. We must accept pupils of all faiths and social backgrounds. I have already told Fiona to send Chus...er... Mrs Berkshire, a letter," Philip continued, "telling her to request full fees for all three boys, in advance. She will explain the unusual circumstances of their late entry and the various changes we will have to make to accommodate them."

"But – Chuselle!" winced Dottie, shaking her head.

Philip decided to change the subject:

"When we return from Scotland, we will have the pleasure of having your young friend, Roddy, in the Common Room. It'll be interesting to see if he proves a useful addition."

Neither of them could possibly have known just how significant Roddy Amport's appointment would prove to be.

The Pipes return from Scotland: More financial worries

Philip and Dottie's three weeks in Scotland had been only partially successful. The weather had been hot - too hot. The midges had been overactive and the fish were reluctant to accept Philip's teasing flies.

At times, conversation inevitably returned to school matters. Dottie was still annoyed that Philip insisted on accepting the three 'unsuitable' Berkshire boys. One other bone of contention concerned Roddy Amport. Dottie felt strongly that, being Patricia Amport's old friend, she was responsible for employing him. This meant that she wanted Philip to grant him his request of teaching at least *some* French lessons. Philip rejected the request by saying that Angela was a school stalwart. He did not want to upset her: since she willingly performed all sorts of unspecified tasks. She had even been known to act as a matron, cook, gardener and cleaner.

It was while they were returning from Scotland, sitting in yet another motorway traffic jam that Philip finally succumbed to Dottie's badgering. He would allow Roddy to teach a couple of French lessons.

When they reached Whitsborough, Philip sank into an armchair with a large whisky. Dottie opened the post which included an ominous letter from Ashley Stilton, Chairman of the Governors. Philip felt his body tense; something told him that the news would be bad. Ashley Stilton had called an informal meeting of the Governors to discuss the school's finances. He had expressed concern about them for some time as Philip already knew. However, Philip had not fully realised that the governors were so acutely worried. The letter simply stated that unless the number of boys in the school increased - or at least the *future* numbers appeared to be favourable - the governors would have to consider taking action to close the school at the end of the next academic year.

"But that's only in three terms time," complained Dottie.

"I had an informal chat with Ashley in April and he was very concerned about numbers. I didn't want to worry you about it," said Philip.

Dottie moved close to him and placed a hand on his shoulder.

"Well, perhaps it's a good thing we agreed to take those awful Berkshire boys," she said. Philip's sense of humour rarely deserted him. He replied:

"I wonder if, by any chance, your friend Chuselle Berkshire has any *more* sons?"

CHAPTER 4

Roddy arrives at Whitsborough: The start of term

Roddy arrived at the school two days before the start of the 'Autumn Term. Budget lay on the front lawn in the shade of his favourite tree but it was too hot for him to rise to greet Roddy. Roddy parked near the main door and wandered into the cool of the unlit Entrance Hall. He noted the slight smell of recently polished wood. Dottie Pipe spotted him from the drawing room overlooking the drive. She was tidying the drawing room, used on formal occasions to impress the parents. She hurried to intercept him.

"Roddy, there you are. How lovely to see you again." She avoided giving him a hug and offered a handshake. "I do hope you had a good summer. I am afraid things will soon become a little hectic here."

"Yes, of course. And how was Scotland?" asked Roddy. "And the midges?"

"Frightful. Almost worse than the parents here. But Philip loves it up there. Somewhere where he really seems to relax." Dottie paused. "Before you do anything else," added Dottie, "would you mind moving your rather noisy car away from the front of the school? You can park it round the back, near the rear Fire Escape by your flat which is at the top of the steps. You can't miss it and you'll probably find Angela Bailey there…you met her before. She's checking it's all in order."

"Right. Thank you."

Roddy sensed Dottie's not-so-subtle change of manner; their relationship had changed. Roddy was already being seen as an employee rather than as an old friend. He walked to his car and winced as the Austin's engine returned to life. The noise caused by the rusting exhaust pipe caused him a moment of embarrassment and he hoped *Mrs* Pipe was not listening. He drove round to the side of the school, past an area which might have been deemed a playground, and parked near the fire escape where there was room for a couple of cars. He grabbed his old suitcase and his duvet and climbed the steps. There was a large area of flat roof running beside the steps and he spotted an ancient tennis ball dying in a gutter; a small plastic aeroplane appeared to have crash-landed nearby.

The door was open and the flat was a little larger than he had expected. The bedroom looked out over the flat roof, towards the playground area. Fortunately the bedroom window sill was quite high, otherwise he might have been seen when dressing. There was a large, green armchair in the study which looked a little newer than the other, rather tired looking one. He sat in it and was testing the springs when there was a knock on the internal door. This door led from a corridor on the first floor of the main school building. It opened before Roddy had a chance to react and Angela Bailey appeared, carrying a large bath towel and a crimson bed blanket.

"Well, hello again. So you've arrived, ready to face the enemy?"

Roddy was not quite sure what this meant. Angela paused and looked straight at him.

"The boys: the enemy!" explained Angela.

"Oh, of course!" Roddy feared that Angela might think

he was a little slow on the uptake.

"Come on. Let's have a walk around. Stretch your legs after driving that noisy car of yours."

"Oh. You've heard it too, have you?"

"Well, who hasn't??" Angela gave him a friendly smile.

She had seemed a little frosty when they had previously parted and Roddy was relieved to return her smile. He was not quite sure what it was but there was something definitely interesting about her. Perhaps it was her eyes...or her dark hair....?

"Dottie asked me to come and say hello - and show you the ropes."

Once again, Roddy observed the confident use of the appellation, *Dottie*. Clearly, Angela was an important member of the Common Room.

Roddy's longer tour with Angela

Angela led Roddy past several dormitories. Beside each of the beds was a stout wooden locker, some in obvious need of repair. The corridor led to a wide, creaky staircase. Paintings of various military heroes hung on the walls.

"You've obviously been through the system," she commented. "Come on, let's get some fresh air."

Outside, Roddy remembered the games' pitches and the lake on the far side.

"Ah, yes. The lake. Boys are not supposed to swim there. Dottie told me," said Roddy.

"No. Not officially. But I do. Preferably when the boys are in bed." She turned to look into Roddy's eyes.

"Do you enjoy swimming, Roddy?"

Roddy remembered with a satisfying smile, the last time he swam. It was with Rosie, during the Cricket Week. He had been disappointed, and rather surprised, that she had not, as promised, left her contact address for him. Angela repeated her question as Roddy appeared distracted.

"Er, oh yes. And it would be fun to swim in the lake. Is it reasonably clean?" asked Roddy.

"Well **I** have swum there and have survived so far. You will have to join me sometime," Angela replied with another look lasting just long enough for Roddy to interpret it as a possible invitation to further shared experiences.

"Oh dear!" Angela nudged Roddy. "Here comes trouble."

A waving figure was approaching enthusiastically along the side of the building, carefully avoiding an open window. It was a man in his late forties, wearing grey flannel trousers and a checked shirt with the sleeves loosely rolled up. Angela introduced him with a marked lack of enthusiasm.

"Roddy, this is Derek Drinkall. Known to all as... "
Derek interrupted:

" 'D.D'. You can probably guess why! Good to meet you." He held out his hand and they exchanged a firm handshake. "You're a sportsman, I hear. That's good. We need some young blood on the playing fields."

Roddy did not realise that this comment was primarily a dig at Angela who took little part in the boys' games' programme.

"Well, rugby and cricket are really my sports," said Roddy modestly although he was a very competent all-rounder.

"Yes, cricket and rugby – that's excellent- but we do play football here too," added Derek.

"Derek is very keen on football. He supports Portsmouth." Angela knew very little about football - except that the Portsmouth team regularly suffered its share of ups and downs.

Roddy was unsure whether all this was just verbal banter or whether it betrayed a genuine animosity.

"What do you teach, Derek?" asked Roddy.

"Oh, Physics, Chemistry, Biology..."

"That means General Science," explained Angela, keen to deflate Derek's misleading C.V. "Basically: bangs, smells and tadpoles. Isn't that right, Derek?"

Roddy sensed that his suspicions of hostility might be

correct.

"And of course I coach the 1st XI football team," insisted Derek.

"Which," countered Angela, "is the *only* football team and it only has one fixture. Isn't that right, D. D.?"

Derek felt he was losing this exchange but in a moment of inspiration grasped a hopeful nettle.

"I gather you are going to be teaching some French lessons, Roddy. I'm sure Angela is delighted about that," he said with no attempt to hide the intended sarcasm. Roddy was now convinced that this was open warfare and attempted to duck the crossfire.

"Oh, I didn't know that I was going to be teaching French. I thought..." Roddy felt awkward about it and looked at Derek who knew that he had just scored a bull's eye.

However, Angela parried Drinkall's attack smoothly:

"Yes, Philip and I agreed that it would be a good idea to let Roddy teach a couple of my lessons each week. I'll be keeping an eye on him, of course..." There was the briefest of glances at Roddy, "...and it will be useful for me to have a couple of *spare* lessons each week - to do some marking and lesson preparation."

'Spare' lessons represented highly valued currency. Most Whitsborough teachers had only one 'spare' each week. Derek, as Angela knew very well, had none. 'Gobsmacked' was not a word that Angela would often use, but it did perfectly describe the jealousy expressed on Derek's face as she triumphantly led Roddy away.

"Well, I suppose you really ought to come and see the classrooms," said Angela.

Roddy smiled weakly at Drinkall as he followed Angela from the battlefield.

They passed the windows of the school dining room and Philip Pipe's study. They then rounded a corner where there was a building that looked rather like a 1930s suburban villa. Inside, several walls had evidently been knocked down to form larger classrooms. The old school desks were squeezed together in long rows. Their lids, which could be raised, showed evidence of graffiti which had only been partly erased.

Angela took Roddy up the stairs. The paint on the walls was scored and scratched.

"This is my classroom. I expect you'll be able to teach your two French lessons in here." Sensing that teaching French might be a sore point, Roddy did not pursue this issue.

Similar 'traditional' desks were in use but they were well spread out and in much better condition than in the other classrooms. The window at the front had a delightful view to the fields and hills beyond the school.

"This looks like a very pleasant classroom. Lots of space and light. I'll bet the other teachers are envious," commented Roddy.

Angela took this as an accusation of favouritism and offered her defence rather tetchily:

"Well, I help Philip out with a lot of admin so I need somewhere like this."

Feeling that he may have unintentionally touched a nerve, Roddy took a small thin French grammar book from a shelf.

"Ah, good old Gillette. I used this book at school. I think I may even have my own copy somewhere." Roddy fingered his way through several pages of verbs and tenses while Angela calmed down, having realised that Roddy had not actually intended any ill will.

Suzy Johnson-Little's dreams

Ever since her brief encounter with Roddy at the petrol station, Suzy Johnson-Little, the driver of 'SJL 2', had been wondering what happened at his interview at Whitsborough. However, her son, Taylor, was not particularly looking forward to the new term.

With a friend, he had cycled and swum regularly in rural

France while his parents, Suzy and Gerald, had lazed by the pool of their newly purchased French villa. Gerald drank copious amounts of the local wine and slept in between meals, while Suzy spent hours acquiring a deep sun tan – turning over and applying suntan oil at regular intervals. She was desperately hoping that the handsome young man she had encountered at the petrol station would have become a teacher at Taylor's school.

Suzy's husband was much older than she was but she had ensured that he had certain attractive qualities when she married him: his wealth, and his willingness to let her spend considerable amounts of it. She was always flattered when Gerald's friends flirted with her but they were too old to be of interest to her.

Her suspicions that Gerald was not entirely faithful had arisen when he began to spend nights at 'his club' in London. She was not unduly worried or jealous as Gerald was not a particularly satisfying bedmate. However, she did begin to feel that she might like to try a little fishing of her own, in more stimulating waters.

Her brief meeting with Roddy had remained in her mind. She often cogitated over this as she honed her tan. If the young man had indeed become one of Taylor's teachers at Whitsborough, the new term might, she hoped, prove unexpectedly interesting.

The evening before term starts. Roddy gets to know Angela

It was customary for the Headmaster and his wife to entertain members of the Common Room to a buffet supper in the dining room on the night before a new academic year started. Philip usually gave a brief chat about matters of importance before it began. Any new members were introduced and on this occasion Roddy was the only one. It was also unofficially expected that the serious drinkers would adjourn to the Huxton Arms after Philip called the buffet supper to a close in time for the members of the Common Room 'to have an early night.'

Roddy, who had never been known to turn down the opportunity to sink a pint or two, followed Derek Drinkall's car in his noisy Austin. Amidst some pleasant countryside, the Huxton Arms was perfectly situated. It was a couple of miles from Whitsborough, set beside a clear, fast flowing stream. According to the photographs on the walls, fine trout had been caught nearby. Derek Drinkall, the instigator of the session, had brought with him Angela Bailey and another master, Leslie Kent, who also lived in the village nearby. Leslie was a quiet but pleasant teacher, well-respected by the boys.

Having found a vacant booth in a corner of the pub, Roddy found himself seated on a bench next to Angela. She soon engaged in some good-natured banter with Derek Drinkall - whom everyone seemed to call D.D. It wasn't clear to Roddy if this was cheerful banter or whether there really was some deep, underlying animosity.

D.D. seemed happy to hold forth on a number of subjects. When not teaching at Whitsborough, Roddy learnt that D.D. could be found 'dealing' in cars. By just visiting the car auctions, he boasted that he could earn 'upwards of several hundred quid or more' (wink, wink) in an afternoon. The fact that he regularly drove to school in a variety of cars was, apparently, testament to his boasts.

He informed his fascinated audience that he had often bought a car at an auction in the morning. Having given it the Drinkall treatment – washing and valeting it - he had then sold it profitably, shiny and gleaming, at the same auction, in the afternoon. Roddy was intrigued by this. Angela and Leslie were less impressed by D.D's stories as he was always rather full of himself.

Angela was still kicking herself years after spending a weekend in Devon with Derek Drinkall. Drinkall's marital status was a mystery and he was believed to be either divorced or to have an estranged wife. Angela had, however, once agreed to spend a half term weekend with him walking on Dartmoor, provided there was 'no funny business'.

The walking was rather unsatisfactory because the mists had descended over the Devon tors. Unfortunately, Derek became drunkenly amorous after supper on the second evening. Angela liked to think that the slight limp with which Derek now walked was as a result of the kick he had received that night in response to his earlier advances.

As the second round of drinks was nearly completed, it was Leslie who turned the conversation to school matters.

"Could be an interesting year," he began drily. "School numbers are going to be important."

Leslie turned to Angela. She was known to be close to the Pipes and would surely be aware of any such issues.

"That's old news. School numbers, especially boarder numbers, are always important," Angela replied. She was respected for her discretion but she always did her best to avoid any form of lying.

"Well," continued Leslie, "a neighbour of mine in the village is very friendly with one of our school governors. Heard it from him. There's talk of a big housing development in the area."

Leslie got up at this point, leaving the matter unresolved.

"Right, it's my round. Who's for another?"

Roddy hesitated as he was driving and his noisy car was an obvious magnet for police checks. However, Angela intervened:

"I'll need a lift back to school. Leslie and Derek live in the other direction. I'll just have a tonic water and then I can drive you back in that ghastly car of yours, Roderick. Go on - have another pint; your prison sentence commences tomorrow."

"O.K, thanks," beamed Roddy as though a maiden aunt had just slipped him a birthday fiver. He was a little puzzled by Angela's use of his full name. Only his father ever used that name - and that was only if he was cross.

Was this, he wondered, a slightly flirtatious gesture? He had already decided that Angela did indeed possess some attractive qualities.

She drove him back from the pub at considerable speed but with impressive skill. When she invited him to her rooms for 'coffee and a chance to get to know each other', Roddy was unsure what this meant. However, as Angela had kindly driven him back, he felt it would be churlish to refuse. When he had hesitated briefly, Angela had taken his hand firmly and led him to her lair, a pleasant first floor flat at the far end of the school.

At first, Roddy was not quite sure what Angela had in mind or, indeed, what he himself had in mind. Angela disappeared so he sat on the sofa, noting a large collection of books and several framed photographs of a younger, slimmer Angela riding ponies. One winner's photograph recorded Angela's age and the year of her success. Angela must be thirty-two computed Roddy.

He got up to examine the various photographs more closely and he noticed a small silver framed photo behind the others. It was a wedding photograph. The young bride, clearly Angela, and perhaps only in her early twenties, was clutching the bridegroom outside a church, surrounded by a cheerful group. So Angela had been married – but where was the husband now? Dead? Divorced? Roddy had no time to speculate; Angela had already planned Roddy's immediate future.

She returned from the kitchen with two mugs of coffee, two large glasses of whisky and two buttons of her blouse undone. If Roddy still had any doubts about Angela's intentions, they soon became apparent. She sat next to him and suggested that they should drink "to the new term." Her shoulders moved close to his and her hand rested just above his knee.

"Now drink up - and tell me about the real Roddy," she purred.

Roddy could drink many pints of beer and yet still be in

control of his actions, but he had rarely drunk whisky, and never neat. The warm, amber fluid soon began to work as Angela planned. Briefly, Roddy felt obliged to resist her advances. He felt uncomfortable: a new job; involvement with a senior colleague; but Angela had trapped her prey.

"Let's just say that this is a one-off. A payment – a payment for the fact that you have stolen two of my favourite French lessons. Now I am going to give you a lesson!"

She moved close to him and Roddy had no opportunity to formulate a reply. Consequently, he did not manage to reach his own bed until after 2.00 am.

CHAPTER 5

The first morning of the term

Angela and several other teachers were already eating breakfast when Roddy wandered into the dining room looking lost. He prayed that the effects of the painful hammering in his head could not be noticed, or even heard, by anyone else. Acting with professional friendliness and with no hint of their recent intimacy, Angela instructed him to help himself to the various items on offer. He struggled with a bowl of cereal and some coffee and attempted to respond to several polite conversational overtures.

Philip and Dottie had both woken at dawn. They were early risers in term time anyway but they both shared the feeling that this might be the last time they were beginning a new school year. The thought, however, was unspoken. As he entered the dining room to say good morning, Philip was determined to appear normal and positive. A few other members of the Common Room had now joined the others to snatch a cup of coffee.

"Good morning everyone. I trust you are all ready for a return to the battlefront. Ah! Roddy, our new boy. I hope you had a good night's sleep in your new bed." Philip's words sounded more like a command than a question but it was Angela who coolly intervened.

"I'll look after Roddy, Philip, and show him to his class after Assembly. I've allocated him to Lower Five. I am sure he will be able to handle a class of young gentlemen, won't you, Roddy?"

Roddy's mumbled affirmation was drowned out by the chattering of a group of boys passing the door. The noise prevented Roddy from hearing someone enquiring in Angela's ear:

"Won't Edwin Stevenson be in Lower Five this year? Could be an interesting challenge for our new comrade!"

"Right. Time to go!" said Philip.

Angela led Roddy through the corridors. Fortunately for Roddy's aching head, there was no opportunity for conversation as the noise of start-of-term chatter was deafening. Roddy was taken to the back of School Hall, a large room that also served as a makeshift gym. Wall bars and a few climbing ropes represented rather bleak decorations. By now, the boys were filing in and the noise of wooden chairs scraping on the floor exacerbated Roddy's hangover. He took his place with other members of the Common Room, most of whom he had not met before. He exchanged a few brief introductions and handshakes before sitting down. Many boys nudged each other and turned to glance at the new master. To Roddy, it seemed like only yesterday when he, too, would have been carrying out the same schoolboy inspection.

The Assembly did not last long as Philip Pipe welcomed the (few) new boys, reminded the old hands of the school's high expectations of their behaviour and wished them all good luck for the next year.

"And probably their last one here," whispered Derek Drinkall to one of the other teachers, a rather intense looking middle-aged man in a badly fitting brown suit.

Ten minutes later, and much sooner than he expected, Roddy found himself alone - with his head still pounding - standing in the classroom, beside his own desk, facing the enemy.

Roddy's first lesson

It was a view Roddy would never forget: sitting quietly at their ancient desks, many with their arms folded, there was expectation, keen anticipation. Rows of faces. He was on stage. The audience was waiting for the show to start. Adrenalin was coursing through his blood. He determined to ignore the dull the hammering in his head. Very well, he thought, let's *have* a show.

He breathed deeply, paused for one moment, and then asked:

"Is anyone here a good runner?"

Sixteen twelve-year-old boys raised their hands in response. One rather overweight boy, looking embarrassed, declined as did the much thinner specimen beside him.

"Well, I want someone who will take a little time over my request and won't run too fast."

Choosing a fat boy, Roddy surmised, would have been indelicate so he selected a thinner one who stared at him with a challenging grin.

"Please. I can run very slowly, Sir!" offered another voice. Roddy noted the first use of 'Sir' with an inner glow. He was encouraged; the enemy was complying.

"Well I can run even slower than Clements, Sir! I'll just run backwards!" added another boy who earned giggles from the back of the room.

At least, Roddy noted, his audience was awake. Perhaps they weren't hostile.

"Yes, thank you, but this chap will be fine."

Roddy moved to stand in front of the thin boy.

"And your name is...."

"Stevenson, Sir. Edwin Stevenson".

There were a few moans from the class.

"Sir, he's not just slow. He can hardly even walk!"

Roddy silenced the laughter with a stern look and was

surprised that this proved effective.

"Right, come here, Stevenson...er...Edwin." Roddy was as yet undecided about the use of first names.

He led Edwin to the window. Outside was the main playing field and an area that had obviously been a cricket square in the summer. A glass-panelled door at the side of the classroom led outside.

"Now I want you to run to the cricket square. Quickly. But no need to sprint. Then I want you to *walk* round it and await further instructions. Have you got that?"

"Yes, Sah!!" replied Edwin with a grin and a salute. Clearly he had a sense of humour and Roddy managed a smile despite his aching head.

Edwin set off, across the grass, rocking from side to side on his skinny legs. There were a few shouts of encouragement and Edwin responded with a dismissive wave.

"Not a pretty sight, is it, Sir?" commented one voice.

Before reaching the cricket square, Edwin held out his hands, as though gripping a steering wheel, and then executed a series of strange movements with his right hand. Roddy was puzzled.

"He's just changing gear, Sir. He thinks he's a car," called a voice.

"Yes, he often does that, Sir. You watch him in the dining room, steering his plate between the tables. He's mad, Sir. Should be locked up," said a boy in the front row, shaking his head in despair.

Roddy was beginning to enjoy this good-natured banter.

Having reached the square and walked round it, Edwin applied his handbrake and stood to attention in his best military manner and dutifully waited for Roddy's next instructions.

By now the whole class was crowding by the windows.

"Now," called Roddy, "I want you to run here, as fast as you can - backwards!"

There was a roar of laughter and Edwin put his hands on

his hips in mock protest. However, he appeared to select reverse gear, adjusted his hands on his imaginary steering wheel and set off. Although he stumbled several times, he made good progress.

"Sir, Edwin's faster backwards than forwards!"

Half way back, Roddy called, "Now stop! Face us... and do five press-ups!"

There were more roars of laughter.

"Sir, he won't even manage two!"

Edwin knelt. Paused. Twitched his shoulder muscles for effect and then began.

The class began to count:

"ONE...TWO..........THREE?................FOUR???......"

Edwin was pacing himself.

"FIVE... SIX...SEVEN??"

The counting became louder and louder. Edwin continued, oblivious to Roddy's call that he could stop now.

"SEVENTEEN......EIGHTEEN......NINETEEN......TWENTY!"

The form was delirious and cheered as Edwin drove back into the classroom. Roddy did not notice that the Headmaster, Philip Pipe himself, was outside in the corridor, peering into the room through the little porthole in the door. Pipe had heard the noise and seen Edwin performing his gymnastics from his study window. Had Amport lost control already? And what was he trying to teach them?

On Edwin's return to his desk, and having received congratulatory pats on his back, the class quietened.

"Tell me, er, Edwin, how do you manage to be so fit? I doubt if any of the others could do twenty press-ups so easily." Roddy looked round at the others who were nodding their heads in agreement. "And I certainly couldn't."

The pounding in his head seemed to have eased - but at the thought of straining to do press ups, his brain reminded him that there was still life left in his hangover.

"Well, Sir, I've been doing lots of training?" Edwin explained.

"Really? What for?"

"Well my father's very keen for me to earn a place in a school team. I've never played in a match for the school and he thinks there's a chance that I might make the 3rds for rugby." Edwin paused. "So he's been making me train to get fit...all through the holidays...running long distances... carrying heavy weights..."

"You poor chap!" Roddy suddenly felt aware that he must not be thought to be indirectly criticizing Edwin's father.

"Anyway, he's certainly done a good job of getting you fit. Those press ups were astonishing. I'm sure you'll deserve a place in a team."

There was a gentle knock on the door and Philip Pipe now entered. The boys all jumped up.

"Everything all right, Amport?" Pipe cast his eye around the room.

"Er, yes, I think so thank you. I've just been providing the class with some essay material. They are all just about to start an essay for me - although they don't know that yet. They've all got lots to write about. The essay will be entitled:

'A most unusual lesson' and they will be finishing it for their English Prep."

Philip backed away with a satisfied nod to Roddy. He was a little mystified but, nevertheless, mildly impressed.

"Well...er...good. Excellent. Do carry on."

After his first three lessons, Roddy was ready to have a cup of coffee in the Common Room during morning break.

"Well, you seem to have survived so far," said Derek Drinkall.

"Yes. Ok, so far, thanks. I have already come across some interesting characters. Is Edwin Stevenson a little unusual?" asked Roddy.

"The chap who thinks he's a motor car? Oh, yes. Harmless - but bonkers. Mind you his father – Norman - is a bit odd too. Very intense."

Roddy felt peckish and realised that his head was no longer pounding. Drinkall, he observed, had already secured a number of chocolate fingers but Roddy was unable to locate any. Drinkall continued through a mouthful of crumbs:

"You probably haven't yet come across a boy called Wesley Berkshire. Another oddball. He's new this term, looks older than twelve and talks like an eighteen year old senior prefect."

"Ah, yes. Wesley," agreed Angela, who had sharp ears. She lowered her voice. "One of three new brothers. Dottie did not want to have them here but Wesley's going to prove an interesting customer. Very grown-up."

She offered Roddy a biscuit from the plate she was holding but was careful to keep it out of Drinkall's reach.

The first afternoon: The cross-country run

On the first afternoon of the term, the whole school went on a so-called cross-country run. There was not much 'country' about it. However, it did include a circuit of an adjacent field, most of which was a Public Footpath. An elderly lady who was walking there was briefly forced to join the run as her excited spaniel insisted on dragging her along with the runners.

This whole-school start to the new term's games programme was necessary because the pitches had not yet been marked. Derek Drinkall was left in charge of some teachers whom he 'volunteered' to inflate the balls and mark the main pitches.

Roddy, whose head had at last ceased to throb, was instructed to stay with the front runners. 'Front runners' he quickly discovered, was a rather misleading term for those who were furthest from the back, where the majority was massed and barely moving. Of those who were actually making an effort to move with any speed, Roddy noted with a smile the skinny boy with the sporting ambition: Edwin Stevenson

"Well done, 'Mr. Press-up'," yelled Roddy encouragingly.

Last to return from the run was the unusual new boy, a complaining Wesley Berkshire. He had made no effort whatsoever to move at a speed faster than a walk. He sat heavily on one of the benches in the changing room, his head almost hidden by a pair of grey trousers hanging from a peg above him.

"I really cannot understand the value of such a meaningless exercise. I am sure that if Nature had intended us to walk, Evolution would have provided us with wheels," he complained.

"Well you would need tractor tyres to get you through the mud, Berksted" retorted a boy who was struggling with his shoe laces.

Again, assuming a rather superior air, Wesley replied:

"My name is Berk*shire*. Wesley Berkshire. *Wesley* as in John Wesley: the Methodist theologian and preacher. I am sure you are familiar with him."

Several number of boys exchanged baffled looks and raised eyebrows:

Who *is* this fellow, Wesley Berkshire?

Day Four: Roddy is congratulated

During Morning Break, two days later, Angela approached Roddy with a knowing smile and the offer of a Bourbon biscuit.

"I hear your lessons have been going down well. You've made quite a hit with the boys already."

Roddy was a little surprised but was grateful for some feedback.

"Are you sure they mean me?" he replied with a questioning frown.

"Oh yes," replied Angela. "They mean you all right," she

added, giving him a longer look than was necessary. "I have spies everywhere. Something about making a boy do press-ups on the games' field? Where did that idea come from?"

"Ah, well, I always remember one of my masters starting a new term by getting us all to hop through the school on one leg. But I thought that might be rather noisy."

Derek Drinkall joined them, armed with more than his fair share of fig rolls.

"How's it going, Roddy? Taken any prisoners yet?" he asked, spraying fig crumbs across the floor.

"The lad's doing well," answered Angela.

"This new boy, Wesley Berkshire, is proving interesting," said Drinkall. "He speaks in a very adult manner. Can't think what he's doing at Whitsborough....but the more the merrier if the rumours about school numbers are true."

"Well make sure you don't upset him. There are two other Berkshire brothers in the school now and they are also boarders. Gold dust," added Angela.

"Must be some big money in that family then," observed Drinkall.

"Could be very big, I believe," replied Angela. "Comes from the Middle East - Abu somewhere or other."

"Oil, then - not gold," observed Drinkall, giving Angela a warning nudge; Philip Pipe had just entered the Common Room. He exchanged greetings with several people, poured himself some coffee, and noted that the biscuit plate was already empty.

Rosie Pitchworth in London

Rosie Pitchworth had been very disappointed that she had had to leave the Cricket Week so soon after her first most satisfying liaison with the handsome Roderick Amport. She regarded her session on the bank by the swimming pool as 'unfinished business.' Indeed, she anticipated that this most pleasurable episode would be the start of a long and fulfilling journey. It was, she believed, a foregone conclusion that Roddy would make contact with her. He had briefly mentioned that he was 'going to have a shot at teaching' but most of their brief association had been concentrated round exploring the physical nature of their relationship. It had never occurred to her that Roddy had never discovered her address, posted through his car window.

Once back in London, she was busy. There was all the hassle of moving into a new flat. Her new flat was owned by an old friend, Melissa Stacey. Melissa had a flat, a new Fiat and a rich father. He had bought the flat partly as an investment and partly to encourage Melissa to settle down to a permanent job in London.

Rosie was thrilled to be offered a room in the flat in Redworth Square. She was a hard-working and conscientious researcher for ITB Television. She had worked hard at University, unlike Melissa who had only lasted one year. Melissa had spent her year - 'mattress testing'. When asked to leave, she spent a year drifting around Australia and the Far East before finally agreeing to attend an expensive finishing school in Kensington. Melissa's parents were delighted that Rosie was keen to share a flat with her. Rosie was regarded as a well-balanced and sensible friend whom they hoped would be a good and wise influence on Melissa.

Melissa obtained a job in a private bank near Mayfair. Acting as a Personal Assistant and carrying out some undemanding secretarial tasks. She came into contact with some wealthy clients and was happy to accept invitations from them to the theatre, major sporting events and expensive restaurants. Often there were spare tickets and Rosie was invited along but she repelled any 'advances' because she felt sure that it was only a matter of time before Roddy contacted her. However, the weeks passed and Rosie had no idea that Roddy, too, was disappointed that their relationship had not progressed.

CHAPTER 6

Roddy settles in.
During a quiet moment in the Common Room, Roddy had questioned Drinkall about Angela's marital status. Drinkall, who thrived on gossip, readily informed Roddy that Angela and her husband had arrived together to teach at the school. Apparently the marriage had soon fallen upon the rocks and Angela's husband had, mysteriously, not returned to the school after the first year. Rumours of his infidelity with one of the temporary matrons were rife but inconclusive. However, Philip had once, inadvertently, referred to Angela's divorce. This had all happened several years before Drinkall came to the school but he was certain that Angela was now, indeed, divorced.

By the end of the second week, Roddy began to feel part of the furniture. Accustomed to a school life of lessons, bells, timetables, dining rooms, books and games, Roddy was simply giving rather than receiving: standing on the other side of the desk. The territory was familiar. There were, however, occasions when he had to learn to restrain his own laughter, even though he knew that he would enjoy recounting an incident to his colleagues in the Common Room.

In his second week, during the last lesson of the day, Roddy was reading a story to a group of eight year olds. Encouraging them to relax and enjoy 'story time', the boys had gathered round him, seated on the floor, while Roddy was enthroned on a rather dilapidated padded armchair. As he was reading, a small, bespectacled and innocent-looking pupil, Robert Hughes, was holding a miniature plastic chicken. This realistic toy was being bounced onto the arms and then the shoulders of several boys seated nearby.

It was beginning to cause irritation among the boys and this was distracting Roddy. He gave Hughes and his chicken a meaningful, warning look. However, as Roddy continued reading the story, the chicken strutted up the arm of another boy, paused, and then pecked the boy's ear. The boy winced audibly. Enough was enough. It was confiscation time. As he continued to read, Roddy simply held out his open hand for the chicken to be taken prisoner and then pocketed: confiscation.

The guilty Robert Hughes dutifully obliged and the chicken was placed in the centre of Roddy's outstretched palm. As Roddy was about to transfer the confiscated item into his jacket pocket, he realised what had happened: the plastic chicken was not in his hand. Instead, on his open palm, he saw that the small plastic chicken had simply laid a small plastic egg.

Angela roared with laughter when Roddy recounted this episode in the Common Room. Derek Drinkall, however, was more circumspect: he had once found an adder on his desk which was beside an open window. When he entered the classroom, the boys were cowering behind their desks and calling him to remove the dangerous reptile. Sangfroid is not the correct term to describe his reaction. Drinkall's feeble, nervous attempts to edge the reptile into a wastepaper basket with a ruler proved useless. When he eventually realised that the snake was dead, as all the boys already knew, his status was severely diminished. However, he refrained from punishing the boy responsible -

splendidly named Noah - as he thought this would have brought him even greater discredit and notoriety.

"Never let them think you're a soft touch," warned Drinkall, who regarded the presence of pupils in his classroom as a necessary evil. "If they think you've got a weak spot, a chink in the armour, they'll exploit it."

"Oh come on, Derek," argued Angela, whose powerful voice and good-natured competence was respected by the boys. "We're not in the trenches now. And after all, they are our customers."

"No, they're not. The parents are: they pay the fees. And we all know how much Dottie *loves* parents," added Drinkall with heavy sarcasm. "She'd ban them from the school if she could....and I'd support her!"

Roddy's 'Also-Rans' of the 3rd XV. .

By the end of the second week the boys aged over eleven had been finally sorted into groups for Games. Roddy was placed in charge of Game Two which was, unofficially, known as the 'Also Rans.' These were the boys who would make up the 3rd XV for their one and only match, against Poppleford Court. There were only eighteen boys in the group and this made selection awkward: who would be left out? Furthermore, it made practice even more difficult. They could only have practice games in teams of nine. In fact, it was usually fewer than nine as one boy suffered from asthma and rarely appeared.

Nobody initially informed Roddy that the 3rd XV had lost their annual match with Poppleford Court each year since 1960, eleven years earlier. The referees had even been known to lose count of the points conceded by Whitsborough.

Undaunted by these statistical challenges, Roddy discovered an enthusiasm for coaching the game. He wanted the boys to enjoy the sessions at their own level. Each session began with chasing games, games of 'he' or bizarre hopping or crawling races. Roddy kept up a noisy running commentary during these sessions and the boys delighted in earning nicknames which became badges of honour: Edwin Stevenson was quickly known to all as 'Press-up' and he would cheerfully oblige whenever Roddy, himself, claimed to be out of breath:

"I'm not fit," Roddy would gasp. "Edwin, do ten press-ups for me, would you?"

"Yes, Sah," would be the grinning reply as Edwin knelt, delivered a quick vehicular 'Broom, broom" and then burst into action at knee level.

As the days went by, the team began to take shape. Skill levels had improved and, on one glorious autumn afternoon, Roddy's loud, congratulatory commentary was so euphoric that the boys began laughing and Budget was heard to bark in the distance. Edwin even wrote home about it. However, it was Edwin's tackling that clinched his selection for the team. Edwin simply tackled anyone in range furiously.

He spent much of the time wrapped around boys' knees. Roddy roared Edwin's praises when he scythed down a startled Peter Jenkins, but pointed out that Edwin would be more effective by tackling boys who weren't on his own side. Roddy advised him, in future, to note the colour of the opposition's shirts before going nuclear.

Wesley Berkshire joins Roddy's game

It was the demotion of Wesley Berkshire from 'Top Game' to the 'Also-Rans' which first suggested to Roddy that the result of the Poppleford Court fixture might not, after all, be a foregone conclusion. Though not unusually tall, Wesley was solid and probably stronger than most boys of his age. His presence in a school rugby team would prove invaluable, even if he did not move very fast. It might take several boys to tackle him.

Wesley appeared one afternoon, soon after Roddy's coaching session had begun. Game Two, the Also Rans, were practising their passing.

"Hi, Wes!" called a number of players as a fed-up looking Wesley approached. He had become a popular figure with many of the boys, but his adult manner unnerved several of his teachers. Wesley intended no malice but they seemed to think he was being condescending. He was usually dressed impeccably; his trousers and jacket were well-pressed, his shoes were polished and his tie was proudly knotted and centred in his collar.

"Forgive me for interrupting your training session, Sir, but Mr Briton on the Top Game deems it unlikely that I will be of benefit to either of the teams he is preparing. He therefore requested that I should present myself to you - and offer my services."

Several boys giggled at this peroration but most of them were puzzled. Roddy, who had begun to see the many dramatic opportunities offered when small boys are the audience, answered grandly,

"Indeed, Lord Berkshire. Your presence will lend great...er...." Roddy paused for effect, "...weight," (many giggles) "to our endeavours. It will be an honour to behold your presence. Right. Let's get on. What position do you play, Wes?"

"I'll bet he's a forward, Sir," called Clesham.

Wesley took a deep breath:

"I feel that I should make it clear that I have never participated in this game before. I do not understand it and I do not intend to engage in any unnecessarily violent physical activity. I have no expectation of making contact with the ball, any other player or, indeed, the ground. Having made this clear to Mr Briton, he finally abandoned his ambition to make me a forward, a backward or even a sideways."

Wesley's authoritative statement held the boys spellbound. No boy spoke to a master like this. However, he did not appear to be being deliberately discourteous and his reference to 'a sideways' brought some nervous giggles.

Even Roddy smiled.

"Very well, Your Lordship," replied Roddy, affecting a tone that might have been well suited to the debating chambers of Westminster, "We'll adjourn the discussion for now while I continue coaching this rabble" - (more giggles). "In the meantime, you may observe my attempts to turn them into skilful and successful rugby players."

He then whispered conspiratorially into Wesley's ear, "Which may take rather more than a miracle!"

As Roddy was about to issue further instructions, Wesley tapped him on the shoulder.

"Well, Sir," he said with a twinkle in his eye, "didn't a carpenter's son once turn water into wine?"

Suzy Johnson-Little encounters Roddy ....again

One morning, Roddy's first lesson should have been French with some nine-year-olds. However, he was frustrated to discover that this lesson had been cancelled. He was rather fed up about this because he enjoyed teaching French and playing silly language games with the younger boys. Unfortunately, the local GP - grandly termed the School Medical Officer- was making a rare visit to the school and was addressing all the boys on the subject of 'Health and Personal Hygiene'.

Hands in pockets, Roddy was walking off his frustration with a circuit of the school buildings. As he rounded a corner which brought him to the front of the school, he almost collided with a mother who was carrying a bag of school games' kit.

"Gosh, sorry. I didn't see you there," apologised Roddy.

"So we meet again," replied the woman with a smile that would have made her dentist proud.

Roddy, although nonplussed, was immediately aware of the woman's attraction. Neatly and expensively dressed, she might have been the envy of some of the other mothers or, indeed, the subject of their husbands' dreams.

"Yes," she continued confidently. "You are Mr Amport.

Taylor has told me all about you."

"Taylor?"

"Taylor Johnson-Little. You teach my son. But *we* met in the holidays...when you were buying petrol for your little car....with the *silent* engine?"

Roddy noticed a smart estate car parked in the drive bearing **'SJL 2'** on the number plate. **SJL?? ..** Now he began to remember. **S**eriously...**J**aunty?....**L**ady? The words surfaced from his memory.

"Ah, yes, of course. I remember now. The filling station. I had just run out of petrol.''

"Or..." corrected the woman coquettishly, "your *car* had."

Roddy, smiled at the jest, held out his hand and Mrs Johnson-Little awkwardly transferred Taylor's games' bag to her left hand and returned the handshake.

"I'm Roddy Amport."

"And I'm Suzy," and then added, "Johnson-Little," as if it were a slightly embarrassing irrelevance.

Roddy noted that Mrs J-L seemed to hold his hand for a second or two longer than necessary. Her pale blue eyes seemed to sparkle during this exchange.

"And how are you getting on here? I gather that the boys like you. Taylor says you are fun."

"Well, it is quite fun – teaching. The boys seem to respond to a spot of humour and..."

Mrs J-L interrupted: "Being younger than most of the other teachers, they can relate to you better."

"Er, I suppose so. I hadn't really thought of that."

"And you'll probably find that you relate better to the younger parents."

Roddy wondered how old Mrs J-L was but she seemed to read his mind.

"You'll find that there are a lot of parents here who are in their late forties and fifties - and a couple of fathers look even older than that." She managed to make this sound as though it was almost sinful.

"I suppose I haven't come across many parents yet,"

replied Roddy, who was beginning to feel that he must tread carefully. He knew, from Common Room gossip, that certain parents should often be regarded as the enemy and that conversation with them could be potentially awkward.

"Well some of us are barely out of our twenties," confided Mrs J-L rather boldly.

It struck Roddy that she was speaking rather like a teenage girl who was admitting that she was part of the 'naughty' group who visited pubs or secretly smoked cannabis. Roddy, somehow, had always thought of parents as being members of a different species, like his own parents... always about thirty years older than you were and had an unblemished past. However, this parent not only looked young but appeared to challenge his views on parenthood. He was not quite sure how to extricate himself from this increasingly delicate conversation but, fortunately, Mrs J-L changed tack.

"So what are you doing now? Shouldn't you be in the classroom? I think Taylor said you teach English."

"Ah. A bit of a sore point at the moment. I do teach English most of the time - but I also teach two French lessons a week, which I really enjoy."

Roddy paused. Should he vent his frustration on a parent? Would that be unprofessional?

"And....?" Mrs J-L waited. Her smiling blue eyes demanded an answer.

Roddy weakened.

"One of my two French lessons – which I should be taking right *now* - has been cancelled because the whole school is having a medical talk from the local doctor. So no French lesson. And nobody told me. Not that I could have done anything about it." Roddy sounded, briefly, like a little boy who has just had just been informed that his birthday party had been cancelled.

Mrs J-L switched into maternal mode.

"But that's awful for you." She put a sympathetic hand on

his shoulder. She hesitated but her hand remained on Roddy's shoulder. She appeared to be thinking and considering what she was about to say.

"Well, you could always give *me* French lessons."

Roddy was shocked. He could not believe that this very attractive woman was making such a blatant suggestion. He had always understood that 'French lessons' was a euphemism for a certain intimate physical activity.

"What? Now?" said Roddy with undisguised astonishment.

Mrs J-L was genuinely embarrassed and removed her hand from Roddy's shoulder. She realised what Roddy must be thinking.

"Oh, Heavens! No!" She endeavoured to recover her dignity. "Not now!"

It was now Roddy who felt embarrassed. However, their mutual embarrassment was saved by the bell: a school bell sounded loudly nearby. They both jumped as it blasted out.

"It's just that Gerald, my... husband" (she gave a slight cough in an effort to 'lose' the word husband) "bought a little place in France last year and we've talked about taking French lessons....but have never really got round to it."

"Oh, I see," said Roddy, partly relieved and yet somehow a little disappointed. After all, Mrs Johnson-Little was very attractive. Perhaps the 'French lessons' double entendre was not what he had imagined – yet had possibly hoped.

"Would you consider giving some private lessons? You must have some free time surely. And teachers never get paid as much as they deserve."

Roddy looked at his watch. He could hear boys moving through the school.

"Look. Forgive me but I must go," he apologised.

"Yes, of course. And I must hang these clean clothes on Taylor's peg. If he sees me here he will be terribly embarrassed." She grabbed Roddy's arm as she searched for her card in her handbag. Roddy thought he caught the whiff of some rather pleasant scent.

"Now, make sure you phone me! I'm keen to learn...and we'll pay well," she said, thrusting the card into Roddy's hand.

"Oh, it would be you *and* your husband then?" Roddy tried not to sound disappointed.

"Well, we'll see," she replied and then added, after a significant pause, "and by the way, remember: I'm *Suzy*. Do forget the Mrs Johnson-Little bit."

She turned and broke into a brisk walk as she headed for the boys' changing rooms. Without turning round, she raised a hand over her shoulder, wiggling her fingers in farewell.

"*Jaunty*. Yes, that's the word," thought Roddy: "Seriously Jaunty Lady".

Prepositions follow Suzy's proposition.

Roddy spent most of the rest of the morning teaching English and enjoyed one lesson in particular. Attempting to explain what prepositions were, he explained that most of them linked a noun or pronoun to another word in a sentence. He used 'the chair' as the noun and then selected the largest boy in the class, James Harrison, as his stooge. Harrison was a good-natured fellow who usually had a large grin on his face.

Roddy invited Harrison to join him at the front of the class where a chair held centre stage. The class looked on expectantly; Harrison was known to enjoy the limelight. The grinning, willing Harrison was then informed that he was about to demonstrate the use of various prepositions. Thus, he was instructed to sit *on* the chair (easy), *by* the chair (easy), *under* the chair (many giggles), and *inside* the chair (chaos).

Harrison later returned *to* his desk *from* the front *of* the class. The lesson proved uproarious and also instructive. When it ended, Roddy gave Harrison an appreciative slap on his back

"Thanks, James. You acted as a fine stooge."

James turned towards Roddy, puzzled: "A *what*, Sir?"

"A stooge: Someone who is prepared to be made fun of. For instance in a theatre or in a comedy sketch," explained Roddy.

James paused. He had half-understood: "Does that mean I should be paid, Sir?"

Roddy adopted a deep, theatrical voice:

"Paid?? Paid!! You should pay extra to be taught by *me*!" Betraying a grin, he raised a hand as if to strike the boy.

James ducked and took several steps backwards.

"And if you hit me *on* the head," laughed James, "you would be using a *preposition*, Sir."

Roddy rewarded the departing James with an emphatic thumbs-up sign. The realization that teaching could be a form of acting was beginning to dawn on Roddy. He was discovering genes - or talents - he never knew existed. Chance, again, was dictating the course of his life.

CHAPTER 7

Norman Stevenson: His dream for Edwin

Edwin Stevenson, whom Roddy had warm-heartedly nicknamed 'Press-up', suffered from having a father who had unrealistic expectations of him. Aged forty-seven, Norman Stevenson had been hopeless at sport during his own school career. This had been a source of great frustration for him. He had longed to be one of those boys who was cheered on madly on the games' field but his body was not designed to fulfil his aspirations. Like many failed sportsmen, therefore, Norman's greatest hope of success lay in the reflected glory of his only child, Edwin.

Norman was aware that his own genes were not likely to provide Edwin with a head start on the Whitsborough sports field. Nevertheless, he believed that his wife, Cecilia, possessed sporting genes which would compensate for this. Cecilia had, after all, not only played in two tennis matches for her school's Under 15 'B' team but she had also once played in goal for the school's - only - hockey team. Since leaving school, Cecilia had played badminton in the village hall and attended 'heavy yoga' classes. Norman was, therefore, convinced that his wife's outstanding sporting genes would have been passed on to

Edwin. Edwin would be a sportsman - or so Norman believed.

However, despite Norman's fruitless attempts at genetic engineering, Edwin had no apparent aptitude for sport. Edwin's greatest enthusiasm was for cars. He liked the odd, quirky ones: wartime Citroens, Morris Marinas, or vast 1930s' American cars. Hence the reason he spent much of his time 'driving' between classrooms.

Edwin Stevenson's enforced fitness regime

Before the start of his final year at Whitsborough, Norman had plans for twelve-year-old Edwin. This was the year when Edwin *had* to earn a place in a school rugby team. 'Had to': there was no option. Norman would not contemplate failure.

He had studied the school lists and had calculated that, with very few boys in his age group, Edwin might earn a place in the 3rd XV rugby team. Norman was determined that Edwin, at the start of term, would be one of the fittest boys in the school. His training would commence during their annual Cornish holiday based in a bungalow overlooking the vast, sandy beach at St Verow.

Norman was up early on their first morning in Cornwall but there was no sign of Edwin; his bed was empty. With his high powered binoculars, Norman swept the horizon as if he were looking for the forbidding sails of the Spanish Armada. He finally spotted a familiar figure at the far end of the beach, crouched amongst the rock pools, armed with a large bucket and a small net. It was to be the last visit that this small unfortunate, figure would make to the rock pools that week.

Edwin's protests were quickly scotched and his arduous training commenced. Edwin's week on the sands at St Verow could fairly be compared to the training undergone by members of the SAS on the Brecon Beacons. Edwin had to perform shuttle-runs from the rock pools across the beach to the lifeguards' post; timed sprints between the cliffs and the tideline, and carry large buckets full of sand along the beach, thigh deep in the briny. Edwin complained of blisters, a damaged Achilles tendon and possibly a broken leg. Unfortunately, Norman ignored these excuses, being well aware of Edwin's fecund imagination. The reward for success, as Norman repeatedly told his struggling son, would surely be selection for the 3rd XV. Edwin would play in a school match: he would be a member of the elite – a sportsman!

When the Stevensons returned home, Norman introduced a large number of press-ups to Edwin's training schedule. At first, this was one of the tortures that Edwin most dreaded but as the days past, he found that this exhausting activity became somewhat easier. Perhaps he was becoming fitter after all. Edwin was, however, desperately looking forward to his return to boarding at Whitsborough. He needed a rest.

Wesley's speed is revealed

Soon after Wesley Berkshire had joined Edwin's game, Roddy discovered, by chance, that Wesley could run fast; so fast that avoiding a heavy defeat against Poppleford Court was now a possibility. One afternoon, Roddy was side-tracked and arrived late to supervise his game. The mighty Wesley was having trouble with a boot as Roddy approached. The boot was lying beside Wesley and just as he bent down to put it on, Neil Clements randomly kicked it. The lone Wesley boot shot towards Harvey, who picked it up and threw it across the pitch. Wesley's response was immediate, electric and dramatic.

With one powerful shove, Clements was knocked to the ground. Wes then accelerated like a sprinter out of the starting blocks towards Paul Harvey, who made a desperate, unsuccessful attempt to avoid capture. Wes's chase was conducted at an impressive speed. No one had previously seen him move so fast. Wes then carried the captured, struggling Harvey over to the boot, whereupon he was dumped on the ground and then instructed to fit the boot onto Wesley's foot.

This brief episode held the spectators spellbound. Roddy watched, fascinated. He was now convinced of one point: he had discovered the weapon - the mobile heavy artillery - which he now needed to harness and use against Poppleford Court. It was Edwin who articulated Roddy's very thoughts.

"Cor, Sir. Did you see that? If we could just get him to move like...."

"Yes. Thank you, Press-up. I know exactly what you are going to say."

Roddy paused. Harnessing Wesley's unexpected speed required subtlety. To encourage Wesley now to use this speed on the pitch, Roddy, decided to offer an incentive. He remembered how one of his own teachers had used 'fruit gums' as an incentive to learn Latin vocabulary.

"When we start the game today, I'll buy a tube of fruit gums, for the first person to score two tries and….." Roddy wanted to encourage *all* the players "...and a tube for the best tackle of the game."

There was an immediate buzz of enthusiasm although one boy claimed this was unfair as he only liked fruit pastilles. By the time Roddy blew his whistle to end the game, Wesley had just scored his third try after a blistering run through the opposition defences. His speed and power had proved eye-opening. Very few boys even managed to grab his shirt but Edwin held on to him manfully on one occasion when the two collided in midfield. With the help of three others, Edwin doggedly prevented Wesley blasting his way to another score.

Roddy announced that he would be delighted to buy fruit gums for both Wesley – for his speed - and Edwin, for his brave tackling.

"Much as I appreciate the incentive of receiving a tube of fruit guns, Sir," said Wes, "I should like to share the prize with the members of my team."

There were some approving cheers from his team and more cheers when Edwin said that he would share his fruits 'guns' with *his* team as well.

"You know, with your power and acceleration Wesley, I think we might give Poppleford Court quite a surprise," said Roddy before ending the session.

"Who is *Popel-for-cor*?" asked Wes. He had no idea what Roddy was talking about.

"Poppleford Court is a school," explained Roddy, "and they are the opposition, in our one match this term. Whitsborough hasn't beaten them for hundreds of years."

"Opposition? Is that the same as an enemy?" asked Wesley, who then paused briefly before adding:

"I don't like enemies!"

Roddy nodded.

"Very well, Sir," replied Wes after some thought. "Let's beat Popple-What- Fort."

"*Poppleford* Court!!" corrected Edwin loudly.

The proposed 'French lessons' with Suzy J-L.

Several days after encountering Suzy Johnson-Little again, Roddy entered the Common Room. He had just conducted an enjoyable afternoon training session and hoped to grab a cup of tea before having a shower. He noticed that there was an interesting looking white envelope in his pigeon hole on the wall behind the huge, ancient sofa. There was no stamp on the envelope but it was addressed, in large swirling writing, to 'Mr R. Amport, The Common Room'. Internal school mail was usually enclosed in brown envelopes. Roddy poured himself some tea and was pleasantly surprised that there were still some biscuits in the jar; obviously Drinkall had not yet arrived.

Inside the envelope was a smart personalised card, with the address printed formally across the top. In large, neat handwriting writing, it read:

Dear Roddy,

Gerald and I have discussed the idea of receiving French lessons from you. Gerald thinks it is an excellent idea and they will be of great use when we are in our little hideaway near the Loire.

Gerald thinks that it is unlikely that he will be present at many - or any (!) - of the lessons as he travels away from home so often.

However, he is delighted that I will be kept out of mischief by studying with you.

Please make contact so that we can discuss terms and get started as soon as possible.

With best wishes
Suzy (Johnson-Little)

Roddy felt a slight flush of excitement around the back of his neck. Suzy Johnson-Little had hardly been subtle in her overtures and the exclamation mark following the reference to Gerald's absence was surely a sign of adventures ahead. The dark features which appealed to so many women meant that Roddy had been propositioned before. Recent experiences with Angela and the delightful girl by the swimming pool during the Cricket Week - Rosie - were obvious examples. He still wondered why she, Rosie, had never left him her address. However, Roddy had never tangled with a married woman and he was not sure whether this would be advisable. Suzy J-L was very attractive, almost certainly 'available' and was even offering a financial reward. Rejecting her offer, without at least exploring the idea a little further, seemed an unlikely option.

The idea rattled around in Roddy's mind over the next day or so but life in the school was busy. The classroom and the games field were not his only areas of activity: supervising supper, reading to the younger boarders, being challenged on the table tennis table and searching for lost possessions were just some of his varied activities. He particularly enjoyed teaching his two French lessons. Perhaps he could justify accepting Suzy J-L's invitation simply because it was an opportunity to teach more French. Yes, he decided, that was the *real* reason he would contact Suzy Johnson-Little....wasn't it??

After school, when the day boys had gone home, Roddy was walking out of the main door to find a phone box. He did not wish to use the one phone available to residents as it was in a corner of the Common Room where eager ears might hear him. However, as luck would have it, Angela was just entering the school, carrying a shopping bag, after visiting the village shop. She smiled at Roddy.

"Not going for a quick trip to the pub without me, I trust. I'd be most upset if you were," she teased.

"No. I just want to make a phone call."

"Oooh! Secrets? What's wrong with the Common Room phone?"

"Leslie is in there - marking. I gather that he hates being disturbed," explained Roddy who appeared to have a genuine excuse.

Angela nodded sympathetically and moved past Roddy but then turned.

"By the way," she said with affected indifference, "did you find the note I put in your pigeon hole? Taylor Johnson-Little's mother asked me to put it there for you." Angela gave Roddy a powerful look, full of unspoken meaning.

"Oh yes." Roddy's face reddened. "I read it. Thanks."

"And??" Clearly Angela expected a more detailed reply but Roddy had no intention of providing one.

"And...I will answer it," he continued. He paused, then headed outside. "See you later."

As the Austin rattled down the school drive, Roddy ruminated on the rum luck of Angela catching him as he went to phone Suzy J-L. It was also galling that it was Angela who had hand delivered the very letter which might instigate an assignation. Roddy had often wondered if any other teachers had been ensnared by her and had shared vast quantities of whisky with her.

When he located the nearest phone box, not far from the village shop, Roddy was relieved that it was Suzy who answered his call. He had feared an awkward exchange of pleasantries with her husband. Suzy spoke with engaging and purposeful warmth. She asked which evenings Roddy was on duty and discovered that Thursdays were mutually convenient. Gerald, it seemed was in the Far East for ten days but, as it happened, he often worked late and stayed at his club in London on Thursdays.

"Actually, I think he may have a little floozy up there. Isn't that dreadful?" Suzy giggled mischievously. She made it seem great fun.

She told Roddy how to find her house and, before he had time to hesitate, gave him a date - the following Thursday - and a time to arrive

"And I'll cook us a little supper," she added.

It was on this point that Roddy stood his ground and declined this culinary invitation. He knew that if he did not appear for the 7.00pm Common Room Supper, questions would be asked and Angela would certainly interrogate him. Roddy intended to slip out of the school after supper, unnoticed. He just wished his car wasn't so noisy.

When he returned to the school after making the phone call, he fully expected to bump into Angela. He drove up the school drive as slowly and as quietly as his old Austin would permit. Fortunately, and rather surprisingly, there was no sign of her.

Wesley: The new rugby star remains loyal to Roddy.

The unexpected metamorphosis of Edwin Stevenson on the rugby pitch - from no-hoper to the now-respected 'Press-up' - was noted by many. On the pitch he had become a demon tackler and had now learnt the importance of tackling his opponents and not just the nearest person wearing rugby shorts. The Damascene conversion of Wesley into a rugby powerhouse, and Roddy's infectious involvement, meant that the 'Also Ran' boys of Game 2 were buzzing. They could not wait to get to grips with Poppleford Court.

This excited buzz did not go unnoticed. The boys in Game 1, which provided the 1st and 2nd XVs, soon became aware of it and they were particularly keen for Wesley to be given another trial for their game; if Wesley had become a star, they wanted him in their team.

When Michael Briton, the master in charge of Game One, approached Roddy on the matter of Wesley's recent improvement, Roddy was as economical with the truth as he dared to be.

"Yes, Wesley has his moments," Roddy reported blandly.

"Well, I'd better have another look at him during games this afternoon, although he was pretty useless when I saw him before," said Briton.

On the way to the games' field later, Roddy passed Wes.

"Good luck on Game 1," said Roddy with mixed feelings.

"Don't worry, Sir," replied Wes with a wink, "I won't let you down." Roddy was uncertain about how to interpret the Wesley wink.

That afternoon's rugby session for the Game 2 'also-rans' was uncharacteristically flat. There was a lack of urgency and effort. In spite of Edwin's continued enthusiasm, Wesley's absence was significant. There was an indefinable aura about Wesley. It was, therefore, the firm view of most of the boys that Wes would undoubtedly be re-claimed by Mr Briton to play for a senior team. The possibility of an unexpected 3rd XV success against Poppleford Court now seemed remote.

After the practice, Roddy changed quickly and entered the Common Room earlier than usual for a cup of tea before the late afternoon's teaching. He was the first there and even had a choice of chocolate biscuits. He grabbed a newspaper and waited.

"Well, I had a look at your Master Wesley Berkshire," boomed Michael Briton when he arrived. He then said nothing more.

Roddy was puzzled. He turned to look at Briton, a man in his late forties, still wearing his rugby kit and stirring a mug of tea.

"And..???" asked Roddy, fearing bad news.

"A complete…..waste…of….. space." Briton paused. "Useless!!"

Roddy couldn't believe what he was hearing.

"Really?" Roddy replied without disclosing his inner, uplifting thoughts.

Briton moved past the large, cluttered table in the centre of the Common Room and sat in the old armchair opposite Roddy.

"Your friend Wesley arrived late, gave no apology and then spent over five minutes fiddling with the laces on his boots.

" 'Knotted badly, Sir,'" mimicked Briton with heavy sarcasm. He now appeared angry as well as frustrated.

Roddy fought to keep a straight face.

"By the time he had fixed his bloody laces, we were involved in a practice drill. Wesley didn't have a clue what to do. He just kept dropping the ball and messing it up for all the others. Eventually, we played a game and he just wandered about, a lost soul, contributing absolutely nothing."

Briton was really fired up now.

"No! I tell a lie," he continued. "He *did* manage to drop one simple pass and on one other occasion one of the opposition who was holding the ball ran towards him. It was James Norton, probably the smallest boys on the game and about half Wesley's weight. Wesley could have just opened his mouth and swallowed him. But what does Wesley do?"

Roddy was enjoying this and was desperately trying not

to show it.

"Wesley opens his big wide arms as if he is going to tackle the little minnow and then just allows Master Norton to run straight into him. Result? Wesley is knocked flat. Norton blasts past him. Path-et-ic!! You can keep him. I never want to see him on a rugby field again."

Briton stood up, abandoned his untouched mug of tea on the table, and stormed out of the room.

Roddy's mood brightened as he headed for the classrooms. He passed several boys carrying their books to another class. One of them was Wesley. Roddy raised his eyebrows and was about to question him but Wesley spoke first.

"Afternoon, Sir," he said rather formally. "Don't worry. I didn't let you down."

He then checked that no one else was looking before he added a wink - of pantomime proportions. Roddy smiled. His respect for the enigmatic Wesley Berkshire had gone up another notch.

CHAPTER 8

Suzy J-L and the first 'French lesson'

Suzy Johnson-Little spent a busy morning preparing for her first French lesson with Roderick Amport, B.A. This involved a half hour drive to the new 'tanning studio' in Malmstone and a further three quarters of an hour lying under a special lamp which was supposed to make her skin 'glow' and look as though her body spent its life in the Barbados sun. Back home in the afternoon, Tina from Travelhair arrived to 'shampoo and set' her hair and add 'highlights'.

In a further attempt to impress Roddy, Suzy had purchased a 'French Dictionary for Beginners' and a couple of new classroom-style 'exercise books' which she placed on the smart coffee table in front of the enormous sofa. She smiled as she anticipated that any exercise taking place on the sofa, during her French lesson would not require the use of books.

At about a quarter to eight that evening, Roddy had finished eating his Common Room supper. He had been wondering how he could extricate himself from the table without it being too obvious that he was not staying to partake in the usual post supper coffee and banter session.

He could not help thinking that Angela had a direct and supernatural line to his thoughts; he could imagine her questioning looks if he left the table prematurely. But it was Philip Pipe who saved the day by summoning him to his study 'for a quiet word.'

"Amport, we won't keep you long," Philip began, leading Roddy to feel as though there was about to be a summary dismissal, "but Dottie and I would just like to congratulate you – and thank you – for making such a splendid start at Whitsborough."

Roddy looked at Dottie who was nodding and delivering a measured smile.

"You've fitted in well. The Common Room like you, we like what you have done and several parents have already commented on the reports they have received about your teaching. But most of all, the boys like you, and, I emphasise, *respect* you. They know they are being taught well. Boys are surprisingly smart when it comes to recognising good teaching," Philip paused, "even if some of your methods are a little, er, unusual!"

Roddy did not know how to respond. Fortunately, Dottie spoke.

"Yes, Roddy – and you will, no doubt, be embarrassed to know that I have spoken to your mother and informed her." Dottie gave a little chuckle and added, "Dear Patricia wondered if I was talking about the right person. She kept asking if I was really talking about Roddy *Amport*."

Roddy smiled and hesitated:

"Gosh. Well…thank you… and…um…"

"Now off you go. Enjoy the rest of the evening. What's it to be? Marking? Lesson preparation? Or perhaps a well-earned pint?"

Feelings of guilt and awkwardness immediately flooded through Roddy's thoughts...

"Well, something like that," Roddy replied with an awkward smile.

He returned to his flat, pleased to learn that the boys

liked him. This was more important to him than any popularity he may have earned in the Common Room. However, he remained a little uneasy – but also excited- at the prospect of the forthcoming French lesson. He was not quite sure what would happen Chez Suzy but he was pretty sure Suzy had already formed her own lesson plan.

After a quick wash and a complete change of clothing – nothing too smart but certainly clean - he hurriedly ran a comb through his hair. Any physical involvement with the feisty Suzy J-L might prove enjoyable but there would undoubtedly be complications. Never before had he dabbled in illicit relationships. He wondered briefly how Suzy's husband would react if he found out. However, Suzy, he recalled, had joked about him having 'a little floozy' in London and made extra-marital activities seem simply no worse than schoolboy naughtiness. For a few moments, Roddy examined his own conscience but was distracted by thoughts of Suzy's neat, slender figure.

He grabbed a French Grammar book and headed for his car. He drove off, as quietly as the old Austin would allow. Suzy had provided precise directions about how to find her house, using the petrol station where she had first encountered Roddy as a reference point. After turning, as instructed, into a narrow road with high grass banks on either side, he took a left turn into a residential road with handsome houses set well back amongst the mature trees. This was a housing estate for the middle and newly wealthy classes. Roddy's own home was much more rambling and shambling: full of clutter, his father's old medical textbooks and ancient family furniture.

He spotted Suzy's car, 'SJL 2,' parked on the wide expanse of tarmac in front of a well-lit double garage. He was not quite sure why but he chose to park his old Austin in the shadowy part of the drive. Was he already feeling guilty?

As he approached the porch, he had visions of Suzy opening the door in a flimsy dressing gown with only minimal underwear revealed beneath it. This was not what he wanted – but it was what he feared. He really was not sure how to handle the lesson – or Suzy. Apart from the drunken episode with Angela, all his female conquests had been 'legit'. Married women, however, represented new territory. Perhaps, he was thinking, as the panelled front door swung open, that he should stick to terra firma – unmarried women of his own age.

"Ah! Monsieur the French Teacher. Welcome. Entrez. I am Gerald by the way." A gentleman of medium height and late middle-age stood back and held his hand out, offering a firm handshake.

Roddy was stunned. He felt a rush of blood to his head; he had not envisaged a *welcome* from Suzy's husband. He was invited into the large hall and he attempted to introduce himself - but Gerald took charge.

"Yes, you are Roddy – or *Mr* Amport to Taylor, my son, whom you may have met. Funny little bugger: lazy as hell but no fool when he wants something or something interests him."

Roddy had wisely made a point of observing the boy. Taylor was not in any of Roddy's classes but he had noted him around the school. He seemed a fairly typical if unremarkable chap.

"Well, he seems a pretty normal sort of boy to me. I look forward to teaching him some time," commented Roddy, a little uneasily.

"Now come in and have a drink. Suzy's upstairs powdering her nose. Wants to look smart for her French teacher," he added with a wink. The wink only served to unsettle Roddy. "Beer, wine, gin?"

"A glass of beer would be fine, thanks," replied Roddy as Gerald gestured to him to sit down on the sofa in the large drawing room. Suzy's new exercise book and French dictionary lay innocently on a low table in front of it.

"I'm afraid I won't be joining you for the lesson. I often stay in town on Thursdays but I've got a meeting with some of the local bigwigs. The golf club Mafia. All scoundrels and rogues, of course, but I like to stay in touch."

Suzy appeared at the door. Roddy was relieved to see that she was dressed respectably, in jeans and a sweater. The thought of her appearing in some sort of revealing attire had proved incorrect.

"Glass of wine, Darling?" suggested Gerald, unaware that Suzy had already drunk two large glasses in her bedroom.

"Don't worry. I'll get it myself. You'd better go. I'm sure Roddy wants to get down to work." She gave Roddy a look that could have been interpreted in a number of interesting ways.

Gerald glanced at the carriage clock on the mantelpiece.

"Yes, I'd better hurry. I stupidly put my car in the garage. Mind if I take yours?"

"Of course," said Suzy. She gave him a loving kiss on the cheek. "See you later. You probably won't understand me by then; I'll be speaking French!"

Gerald chuckled, bade Roddy goodbye and promised that he would do his best to attend one of his lessons in the future. Suzy poured herself another large glass of white wine as they heard Gerald start her car and drive off. Roddy – 'laid back' Roddy – found himself feeling unusually nervous. Where was the evening heading and where would it end? Was he *really* going to tangle with a married woman?

Suzy sat on the sofa and patted the cushion beside her where there was a space for Roddy. Her eyes sparkled and it was clear what she had in mind. Roddy felt that he had observed this very scene in a film somewhere: a notorious seduction sequence. Was Suzy really a…..what was it? A cougar? And was he her prey?

He guessed that Suzy may only have been in her early thirties, thirty-five at the most. Gerald may well have been twenty or more years older. He wondered if Suzy was his first wife – or whether he had abandoned a first wife in favour of this younger model: his office secretary or P.A. perhaps? Suzy might, therefore, be only about ten years older than Roddy. He had never grappled with an older woman before –or had he? Angela, of course! Angela was certainly older than he was but he had only a vague, blurred, intoxicated recollection of that occasion.

He took a large gulp from his glass of beer and decided to take charge. He sat down, close to Suzy and she immediately nestled towards him. However, Roddy meant business. He stretched forward, opened one of the French grammar books he had brought with him and pointed at the text: verb conjugations.

Suzy's eyes moved slowly from Roddy's pointing finger, along his arm, up to his shoulder and then fixed themselves on Roddy's eyes. Her message could not have been more obvious. Suzy wondered what "Take me" was in French.

Roddy fought to control his natural urges and was determined to deliver a French lesson….and then…perhaps…..he might let events follow a more physical path.

"I've come to teach you some French and I want you to be able to impress Gerald when he returns."

"Yes… Sir," replied Suzy with a grin. Her natural, cunning streak informed her that she must humour Roddy first. She would be a sensible, enthusiastic pupil, pay attention, make him feel good about himself….and *then* she would strike!

For nearly half an hour, she played the game and surprised herself by learning much more than she had anticipated. Roddy really was a natural teacher: clear, sympathetic and knowledgeable, combined with a pleasant sense of humour. Having become familiar with avoir, etre and aller, - verbs she distantly remembered from her school days - Suzy was then taught a few useful words for her vocabulary: the names of the rooms in the house and various bits of furniture. However, having patiently proved herself a conscientious pupil, she felt the time had come to move on to the main purpose of Roddy's visit. Her campaign represented a war of attrition. Roddy had not been duped by her demand to know the French for random nouns such as bedroom, leg and naked. Explaining to Suzy that 'naked' was an adjective and not a noun almost led to his submission: she had edged closer and closer and her subtle perfume very nearly led him to lower his guard. Submission seemed only moments away when the phone rang.

"Oh let it ring. I'll pretend I'm out for the evening," she murmured softly as she closed in.

Roddy's feelings of unease re-emerged.

"But it could be your husband. He knows we are here – and if you don't answer he may think we are......."

"Oh all right," said Suzy as she reluctantly slid away from Roddy and crossed the room to the phone. She gave Roddy a mock 'daggers' stare just before she picked up the receiver. It indicated that he appeared too grateful for the timing of the call.

"440-778," she answered. "Yes, it is. Oh, hello... Mrs Pipe." Suzy turned to Roddy with a heavy, puzzled frown. She listened as Dottie Pipe explained the reason for her call.

Roddy's mind was racing and, unusually, he could sense his heart beating fast. Did Dottie know where he was?

"Well, do you want to speak to him?"

Roddy pointed guiltily at his own chest. Why did Dottie want to speak to him? Had he been caught red-handed? He waved his hand and tried to attract Suzy's attention, which was something he had been attempting to avoid all evening.

"Well, he'll be back later – but I don't know what time."

Roddy felt a moment of relief; Dottie must have been referring to Gerald, not Suzy's unnerved French teacher.

"Yes, of course. When can I come and see him?"

Dottie was obviously explaining something as Roddy prowled uncomfortably around the room. He paused by the mantelpiece to examine a silver-framed wedding photograph. The difference in Gerald's and Suzy's ages seemed marked. Suzy seemed to be barely out of her teens while Gerald appeared, then, to be in his mid-forties. It confirmed his earlier assessment that there might be a twenty year age gap. Roddy turned away and failed to notice a low coffee table which he caught painfully with his shin. He let out an oath which he prayed Dottie would not have heard.

"Thank you for phoning. Tomorrow morning, Mrs Pipe. Yes. Goodbye". Suzy replaced the phone and Roddy slumped into an armchair, avoiding a return to the perils of the sofa.

It transpired that Taylor J-L had been sick soon after going to bed and he seemed to have a slight temperature. Dottie did not feel that there was anything to worry about but felt it was her duty to alert his parents. There was a mild possibility that it might be advisable to take him to see a doctor in the morning. The school would normally arrange this but as Dottie pointed out – with just a hint of disapproval –Taylor was only a *local* boarder so one of the Johnson-Littles might like to collect him and take him to their own doctor. It sounded a justifiable suggestion but Dottie feared that she, herself, would probably end up in the waiting room with Taylor and she would much rather that Taylor wasted a parent's time than her own.

Roddy chose to view the phone call as an omen. He used it to interrupt Suzy's campaign of seduction. It was a sign to leave the battlefield before her heavy artillery was mobilized. He had survived her opening salvo but decided he was uncertain about the wisdom of further immediate engagement. He swiftly gathered his own books, delivered a perfunctory kiss to Suzy's cheek, noting its softness once more.

Grasping his arm, Suzy looked temptingly into Roddy's eyes.

"You will come again next week, *won't* you? We have a weekly arrangement – and I doubt whether Gerald will be here on another Thursday evening."

The message was clear and Roddy was pleased that Suzy remained *available*. He had a week to decide whether to succumb to her tempting proposal. As he exited the front door, Suzy glowingly reminded him that she might see him when she went to Whitsborough to see how Taylor was feeling. Roddy nodded enthusiastically but made a mental note to avoid seeing her at school next day.

Taylor's illness and more financial problems.

As Dottie replaced the phone in Philip's study, she noticed how tired her husband appeared. His eyes were closed and his head lay on the back of his favourite armchair. He was not asleep and Dottie knew that he would have listened to every word of her conversation with Suzy Johnson-Little.

"And how did she take the news?" asked Philip without opening his eyes.

"Didn't seem to be too concerned. It was almost as though I was interrupting her evening. Probably in the middle of a dinner party......or some tasteless programme on the television."

"You really don't like her, do you?" commented Philip. "You know, she is a very good-looking young woman."

This remark earned Philip a semi-playful poke in the stomach, a thrust which was not entirely unexpected.

"Yes, Philip. I know she's 'good–looking' and it's perfectly evident from her manner that she is very aware of it too. Anyway, you are an *old* has-been. She wouldn't give you a second look...and," she added, "she probably wouldn't even bother with a *first* one either!"

Philip chuckled. The verbal sparring in their long marriage remained alive and unwrinkled. Philip had another observation:

"But that husband of hers, George,..."

"Gerald," corrected Dottie.

"Gerald, then. He must be twenty or so years older than she is." Philip paused and thought for a moment. "So she obviously prefers older men. And I am an *older* man," argued Philip.

Dottie stood over Philip and poked him again, even though his eyes were wide open and he was expecting a riposte.

"No, dear, you are not an *older* man....you are an *old* one!"

Philip endeavoured to conceal a smile but there was one last shot which Dottie was determined to fire.

"But my feminine intuition tells me that Gerald Johnson-Little may possess one other highly significant attraction for dear little Suzy. One that you, my dearest, have never possessed."

Philip failed to guess what this might be.

"Money, Dear. The stuff that some fortunate people put in banks. The stuff that the Suzy Johnson-Little's of this world use to buy smart cars, new clothes and expensive holidays. Money, Dear. Ever heard of it?"

"Ah, yes." Philip pretended to be a slow learner. "Useful stuff for paying school fees which, you have to admit, the Johnson-Wotsits do – on time – every term. We don't have to squeeze it out of *them* with a loaded pistol. I wish we had more parents like that."

"What? Johnson-Littles? We should aim higher than that!" protested Dottie.

She said this with such force that Budget, who was curled up near Philip's feet, raised one ear and opened both eyes. Philip now feared that this good-natured banter might morph into a familiar area of disagreement.

"Dottie. We've been here before. We simply can't be selective about the type of parents who want to send their sons here. Our beloved Chairman of the Governors, 'Money-Bags' Stilton is constantly warning us of the importance of keeping the school numbers up. Money is money – and we need it badly. It's boys we need if Whitsborough is to survive: almost *any* boys; they don't have to be the sons of dukes and earls."

Philip stood up, edged past Budget, and placed his hand calmingly on Dottie's shoulder.

"I'm going up for an early night. Why don't you have one too?"

"I need to finish planning the grocery requirements for the next fortnight. Why is it that boys eat so much? We'd save a lot of money if we starved them."

"Excellent idea," agreed Philip as he left the room. "Will you inform the School Inspectors when they next come – or shall I?"

Angela's sixth sense?

As the Pipes headed for bed, Roddy was easing his car along the drive, coasting wherever possible, in order to keep the noise of the engine to a minimum. Most of the lights in the upper rooms appeared to be out although a light glowed behind the curtains in Angela's sitting room. He could not help watching her window. He felt that she had a sixth sense when it came to observing his activities. He was convinced that at any moment he would see the curtains twitch as Angela detected that he was returning from a nocturnal jaunt. He managed to park his car quietly and without noting any movement behind the Angelic curtains - but a sense of apprehension remained.

Next morning, he appeared at breakfast before the other resident masters. However, Angela was, inevitably, already seated and she offered to pour Roddy some coffee. Roddy smiled and thanked her.

"Well, did you have a productive evening?" she asked as she passed him the milk jug.

How was he to play this? Roddy wondered. Could Angela possibly know where he had been? Had she seen him leaving the school or, perhaps, returning up the drive?

Or was it simply an example of innocent breakfast chat. She may, of course, have just been asking if he had been busy marking or preparing his lessons. This might have been interpreted as a gentle hint to be more conscientious.

"Yes, I think I made some progress, thanks," he answered and realized that this was a suitably clever and non-committal reply. He then added that "It's always good to get on top of things," and immediately regretted such an ill-advised comment.

Angela looked him in the eye for a second or two longer than was necessary. Why did she always have to do this? Roddy sensed a reddening of his face and was relieved that at that moment a boy appeared at the door to speak to Angela.

"Excuse me, but I've just passed the Sick Room and Taylor Johnson-Little is awake now. I said I'd come and ask you if he should try to eat something. He looks better than he did last night when he puked all over the ….."

"Yes, thank you, Hugh. We don't need all the details now. Please tell him I'll be up to see him in a few minutes time," said Angela.

Hugh mumbled some sort of indistinguishable thanks, turned and disappeared.

"I think Dottie said she would phone the Johnson-Little mother last night," said Angela. "I do hope the woman's not going to come prancing about the school this morning. The corridors reek of her perfume when she's around." Angela then stood up. "Well I had better go and tend the sick."

Roddy kept his head down and concentrated on eating his cereal; he was convinced that Angela would only give him one of her knowing looks as she left the room. He also reminded himself to keep well out of the way of the S.J-L huntress during the next few hours.

Suzy J-L and Gerald's financial secrets

Suzy was in bed by the time Gerald had arrived home. She

had left a note for him, telling of Dottie's phone call and saying that Taylor had been mildly sick and that she would visit him next morning. She was half aware of Gerald as he undressed in the bedroom. She had not yet decided whether or not her evening had been a success. Certainly – and rather unexpectedly – she learnt quite a bit of French and that would impress Gerald if he bothered to ask. However, the planned seduction of the handsome Roddy had been frustratingly terminated by Dottie's phone call.

Suzy felt that she might have achieved her goal, given a little more time, even though she sensed that Roddy was unsure whether he wanted to join her in the pleasurable activity she had planned. All was not lost, however, because she intended to see him when she visited Taylor and she had arranged another 'date' with him in a week's time.

During breakfast the following morning, Gerald, of course, was concerned about Taylor but only made brief enquiries about Suzy's French lesson.

"Seemed a decent young chap" was his only significant comment. When Suzy ventured a couple of words in French, Gerald did not appear to notice. His concentration remained buried in his newspaper's financial pages. Only when Suzy asked him about his meeting the previous evening did Gerald respond with any enthusiasm.

"Well it was just the usual gang at the golf club – Doug, Nigel, Chester….."

"The usual Golf Club Mafia," interrupted Suzy.

Gerald acknowledged this customary dig at his friends.

"Yes, yes. The usual mob and a couple of others I hadn't met before. Not sure if they're actually club members. Anyway, it seems that there could be a large chunk of land coming on the market soon and it's pretty likely that it could acquire 'development' status."

"Which means?" asked Suzy.

"It could be built on. Loads of houses. The land could be worth a fortune once it had building permission."

"So?" continued Suzy as she squeezed an orange.

"Well, if we – or *someone* - bought the land now, or when it comes on the market, it could be sold – later - at a huge profit. Building developers would fight to purchase it once we –or *someone* - gained planning permission."

Gerald sat back and took a large gulp of coffee.

"Where is the land exactly?" asked Suzy.

"Ah. The 64,000 dollar question! I don't know. It remains a well-guarded secret. But I think it's somewhere in the area, possibly not all that far away. There are plenty of rural areas all around us – and many of the farms seem to have fields lying fallow."

"Well most people round here like that. It's one of the attractions of living here – space, quiet, Nature."

Gerald seemed surprised to hear this.

"I thought you were a city girl at heart. Shops, bars, smart restaurants..." said Gerald.

"I certainly *was*. But I am not quite sure whether I still am. I am older now, more…mature?"

They both laughed. Gerald was firmly of the opinion that Suzy was still only eighteen at heart. It was one of the reasons he married her after divorcing his first wife, Daphne. Daphne was, to his great frustration, only excited by books, concerts and the opera. He still could not understand why he had ever married her or indeed how the childless marriage had lasted for over ten years. But there was a very straightforward reason that they had had no children: Gerald satisfied his masculine urges elsewhere whilst Daphne was content to turn a blind eye and attend concerts and plays with her unmarried sister.

Suzy's secret note.

It was 9.30 am as Roddy ushered Form 3C into his classroom for an English lesson which would then be followed by a History lesson with the same boys. He was distracted by the thought that Suzy would appear at the school around this time: if she appeared much later in the morning, she might be deemed uncaring and unconcerned about Taylor.

Before closing the door and starting the lesson, Roddy crossed the corridor outside the classroom where there was a clear view of the front drive. He checked to see if Suzy's Volvo had appeared yet. As there was no sign of it, he felt that he was 'safe' until Break at 11.00 am. Surely a caring mother of a local boarder would have appeared – and hopefully *dis*appeared – before then. Roddy prayed that he was right and that he was safe from her while he was teaching.

After twenty minutes of 'chalk and talk' about different ways of beginning sentences, Roddy wrote several examples on the blackboard. The boys were then asked to write them in their exercise books and alter or 'introduce' them in alternative ways. He timed an unfortunate coughing fit to strike him at this point and he left the room briefly – and apologetically – so that he could check the front drive.

Suzy's Volvo was parked right outside the front entrance. Roddy checked his watch; there was another hour and ten minutes before the morning break. He felt sure that Suzy would not spend over an hour with Taylor as Dottie would certainly encourage her to leave. She would, therefore, certainly have left before Break began and he would be safe from embarrassment - or so he thought.

However, about half way through Roddy's History lesson, just as Nelson was signalling 'England Expects...' at the Battle of Trafalgar, there was some unexpected movement from one of the boys seated near the door. A folded sheet of paper had appeared beneath it and, while Roddy was writing on the blackboard, Toby Batchelor, seated close to the door, was encouraged by his neighbouring classmates to pick it up. There was no addressee written on it so, urged on by his nudging neighbour, Toby unfolded the sheet and read the note:

"R.
It was a lovely evening. Can't wait for next week!
S."

By the end of the lesson, the note had been read by all the boys seated in the two rows at the back, nearest the door. When the bell rang, Roddy dismissed the class and stationed himself by the door so that he could see the front entrance.

The Volvo had gone and Roddy relaxed. Toby Batchelor was the last to leave the classroom. As he did so, he handed the folded note to Roddy.

"I found this under the door. I think it may be for you, Sir. Bye."

Toby scurried away before Roddy opened the note. As he read it, Roddy felt his face redden. He wondered if Toby or any of the other boys had read it. He thought back to his own schooldays and wondered what would have happened if there had been a similar occurrence during one of his own lessons. The answer was all too obvious: most of the class would, indeed, have read it!

When he entered the Common Room at Break, Roddy felt embarrassed even though there was no reason to think anyone there would suspect anything. He hadn't done anything to make him feel guilty – yet. He overheard Angela complaining to Drinkall about the appearance of Suzy Johnson-Little:

"The boy's perfectly ok now. The little toad just wanted to see his mother and have a morning in bed."

Somehow, Angela made it sound as though the boy had committed a major war crime.

Drinkall, knowing exactly how to rile Angela, commented:

"Ah, so now I know who was wearing that delicious perfume wafting through the corridors."

Angela turned away in disgust. Her eye caught Roddy's

who was pouring himself some coffee.

"Have you come across the Johnson-Little woman yet, Roddy?" she asked him, making *Johnson- Little* sound like the name of a contagious disease.

"Well, I gather that her son is sick," replied Roddy, stirring his coffee.

"Sick? He's nothing of the sort," returned Angela just as Dottie entered the Common Room.

"You're talking about Taylor, I take it," intervened Dottie. "Do you know, that boy's mother only spoke to her son for about five minutes – the boy's perfectly all right now but she just hung around for no apparent reason. *Dear* Taylor had little to say to her and she had little to say to him. I don't know why on Earth she bothered to come."

Roddy avoided any eye contact with either Angela or Dottie and was grateful when Drinkall could be heard complaining – loud enough for Dottie to hear – that the coffee was lukewarm and there were no more biscuits - AGAIN!

CHAPTER 9

A practice match against the 2nd XV

Roddy found that the zest with which the 'Also Rans' now approached each rugby session was a reward in itself. The boys had been delighted and relieved that Wesley had re-joined the game. They now could not wait for the Poppleford match.

The issue of the captaincy remained unresolved when Michael Briton suggested to Roddy that the 3rd XV might like to have a brief practice game against the 2nd XV. In his practice games, Roddy only had enough boys to play in teams of seven or eight so the opportunity to field a team of fifteen boys – in proper positions – would be invaluable preparation.

His boys were excited at the prospect of playing against the 2ndXV and much of the excitement focused around who would be captain. Many of the boys assumed that Wesley was the obvious choice. Although Wes was now the star player, Roddy had a feeling that this rather unusual boy might prove unpredictable. He felt that Edwin – of 'Press-up,' fame - might provide a more thoughtful and reliable choice. In the end, Roddy decided that each candidate would be captain for half of this match and the players seemed happy with this decision.

Before the match, there was some good-natured banter from the 2nd XV about just how many hundreds of points they would score. However, when the game started, they were soon aware of a shock. This was not to be a one-sided victory. After fifteen well-contested minutes, the 2nd XV finally scored, largely because the 3rd XV were unused to playing fifteen a-side games. Having been issued with corrective instructions by Roddy, the 3rd XV prevented any further scores before half time. Wes had played hard but had been almost silent.

After half time, Edwin, as agreed, took over the captaincy. This produced instant results. Edwin roared instructions and encouragement. Everyone on the team responded to his shouts and additional engine noises. Roddy found himself trying to control the game and his own laughter. Wes became like a man possessed. The 3rd XV's Titanic defensive efforts held out. In the final minute Wes picked up the ball near the half way line and accelerated towards the 2nd XV's try line. Several boys attempted to tackle him but bounced off his ample backside. He was on the point of scoring an equalising try when Roddy spotted that Michael Briton had just appeared to watch the game. He therefore blew the final whistle. There were groans and moans from Roddy's team:

"But Sir, we were just about to score!" complained Edwin. "Why did you have to blow the whistle? We only needed a few more seconds."

Roddy mumbled a few excuses.

"Time is time," he claimed apologetically.

The match, however, represented a moral victory for the 3rd XV. Everyone knew that the result should have been a draw and this, itself, represented almost a triumph for the 'Also Rans'.

Michael Briton apologised:

"I'm so sorry, Roddy. I meant to end my practice with Game One early and come and watch but we started late and ….somehow…..".

"No need to apologise, Michael. It was a really useful experience for my boys. Thanks for suggesting it."

Michael nodded:

"Well that's the main thing." He then left Roddy to speak to his team before they returned to the changing rooms.

Full of genuine enthusiasm, encouragement and congratulations, Roddy told them truthfully how well they had played. Poppleford Court, he promised, were in for a shock.

As the boys made their way cheerfully back to the showers, a beaming Edwin made a point of thanking Roddy before trotting ahead to join the others.

Behind Roddy, Wes was shadowing him, padding along quietly like a giant cat in stalking mode. He was waiting for a quiet moment before he caught up and walked beside Roddy.

"I know why you stopped the game early," Wes commented. "You didn't want Mr Briton to see how hard I play for your team, did you? – especially as I was just about to score."

Roddy stopped and so did Wes. Roddy stared into Wes's eyes. Wes stared back knowingly.

"You, Lord Berkshire, are too old for your years!" said Roddy with the hint of a smile. Wes paused and then grinned.

"Thought so!" he replied before striding contentedly away to the changing rooms.

Edwin becomes an 'Honorary Motorist.'

Edwin Stevenson was having the term of his life. His father's holiday training regime had proved unexpectedly successful and his remarkable success on the rugby field opened a new world to him. His resultant infectious enthusiasm caused him to 'motor' his way around the school like a racing car on high octane fuel.

The engine noises emanating from the Stevenson persona were becoming louder and more frequent. This began to irritate some of the teachers. He could be heard moving along the school corridors from an ever increasing distance. Edwin motored around the school, making revving and braking noises. Derek Drinkall even complained to Philip Pipe after he had collided with Edwin when he had unexpectedly effected a three-point turn outside the Library, without signalling first. The books Drinkall was carrying had been spilled everywhere.

Concern, though, was raised because Edwin had developed considerable influence over his team mates. Several members of the team began to imitate Edwin. Gradually, more boys took up the noise. After a few days, passing through the narrow school corridors was like walking across Westminster Bridge in the rush hour.

Fortunately it was Philip himself who, after three days of enduring motoring mayhem outside his study, decided that it was time called a halt to the practice. Motoring would now cease inside the school. With a twinkle in his eye and a sharp understanding of schoolboy humour, he announced that he would, however, grant the 'Honorary Status' of 'Motorist' to Edwin Stevenson. Edwin, alone, would be allowed to continue driving – quietly – around the school. During Assembly, he invited Edwin onto the dais and awarded him, to popular applause, a small toy motor car. Edwin grinned proudly and the boys accepted that the joke was over. Philip had skilfully defused the situation. Humour, he had always maintained, was a powerful weapon in man (and boy) management.

Rosie Pitchworth's missing note

After lessons were over one evening and when the day boys had gone home, Roddy was heading slowly down the school drive in his car, conscious of the noise the rusty exhaust was now making. He had a pile of English books to mark that evening and he was driving to the village shop to purchase a jar of coffee, some milk and plenty of biscuits as it would be a long post-supper session.

As he passed the main entrance, he observed Dottie who was attempting to wave him down. Roddy braked and Dottie hurried towards the car. She opened the passenger's door.

"Roddy. You aren't heading for the village are you?"

"Yes, I am actually. I am heading for the shop," and added with a grin, "I need some 'tuck'".

"Well could you wait one moment, while I fetch my handbag, and then give me a lift? I've managed to get an evening appointment with the chiropodist but Philip is out with the car and is late back."

"Of course, Dot…er…*Mrs* Pipe. I'll wait."

"Thank you. I won't be a moment."

As Dottie closed the passenger door, Roddy glanced at the debris on the passenger's seat and on the floor of the passenger's foot well. It was ages since he had cleaned his car, either inside or outside. He realised that he couldn't possibly allow the headmaster's wife to sit in such squalor.

He jumped out of the car, hurried round to the passenger's side and grabbed the various bits and pieces lying there. Much of this rubbish had been there for months. He quickly scooped up various items of sports equipment, including a cricket sweater, a solitary batting glove, an apple and several old chocolate wrappers. As he shovelled this wreckage into the boot, a small, folded piece of paper, otherwise hidden amongst the debris, fluttered onto the gravel drive. Written clearly on it, in large, neat handwriting was the London address of Rosie Pitchworth. Underneath, Rosie had added:

"I can't wait for our next swim!!"

Roddy felt a sudden wave of guilt, partly because he sensed that Dottie was looking over his shoulder but mainly because he realised that he had not made contact with Rosie since the Cricket Week.

"It's all right after all, Roddy," called Dottie, "I can see

Philip's car coming along in the lane. I shan't need a lift but thank you, anyway."

Roddy acknowledged her thanks and returned to the driver's seat. He folded Rosie's note and placed it in his pocket. Although he rarely 'chased' the fairer sex - because they usually chased him – he considered himself a man of his word. He recalled very pleasant memories of the brief time he spent with Rosie; her feisty conversation, her kindness to the little girl who fell off her bike by the cricket pitch, her spirited performance in the swimming pool - and afterwards! He also rather guiltily remembered that he had promised to contact her. Roddy knew that he had his faults but he always endeavoured to keep his word. Because he had not received Rosie's promised address, he had assumed – with a certain degree of disappointment - that Rosie did not wish to further the relationship. Now, belatedly, he discovered that this was not correct and – furthermore – Rosie would be under the impression that it was Roddy who had not kept his promise.

As he drove to the village, he decided that he must immediately write to Rosie, explaining the situation and the 'lost' note. She had not provided a telephone number and Roddy guessed that she did not know it at the time of writing.

When he returned from the village, he wrote a brief, apologetic and explanatory letter to her. While he was writing, he dwelt upon their fleeting relationship. The more he recalled it, the more he realised how much he had enjoyed being with her. He wrote that he would certainly like to meet her again and he ended the letter with a tennis reference which he thought she might appreciate:
"The ball is now in your court."

He finished the letter just before it was time to go to the dining room for supper but he was annoyed that he had forgotten to buy a stamp in the village. When he asked Angela if it was possible to buy a stamp from Fiona, Angela advised him simply to place the unstamped envelope in the little tray on Fiona's desk in the school office. He should write his initials where the stamp would be placed. Fiona would then provide a stamp and deduct the cost from his monthly salary. She would later post it along with any official school letters.

"Ah, a very useful system. Thanks, Angela. I'll do that straight after supper," said Roddy.

About half an hour later, Roddy returned to his flat. He collected the letter and walked through the noisy corridors and past the dormitories where the younger boys were preparing for bed. Fiona's office door was open but the light was not on. Roddy clicked the light switch and saw the silver tray with several letters waiting to be posted next morning. He placed the letter on the tray and then almost forgot to write his initials where the stamp was required.

While returning to his flat, he glanced at a framed school photograph on a corridor wall, noting how young Philip and Dottie appeared. He recognised several Common Room faces but wondered who the young woman teacher was, seated near the end of a row. She was slim, had long, dark hair and looked vaguely familiar. Could it really be Angela? he wondered.

"Evening, Sir," said a boy wearing a red dressing gown and heading for the wash rooms. Roddy paused.

"It's Hugo, isn't it? I think I have mastered most of the names now."

Hugo smiled and nodded, pleased to have been recognised.

"I had a thick dressing gown like that when I was at school but it was blue not red. I used to sleep wearing it on cold nights. Wearing rugby socks as well!"

Hugo's eyes brightened but he was a little surprised.

"I might try that, Sir. I already use my duffel coat as an extra blanket - but I am not really supposed to."

"Well, good night and don't tell anyone what I suggested," said Roddy.

Roddy boiled his kettle when he returned to his room,

relieved that he was now armed with coffee for the next few hours. At about the same time, the door of Fiona's office was being quietly opened. The light was clicked on and Angela cast her sharp, inquisitive eyes over the little stack of letters awaiting stamps. She wanted to see the name and address on the envelope that had just been added to the pile.

Norman Stevenson – rugby spy!

Edwin had become uncharacteristically communicative this term and Norman Stevenson was thrilled to learn that his exacting fitness regime had paid dividends. He now knew of Edwin's nickname and of Roddy's enthusiasm. With Edwin's selection for the team assured, Norman was no longer having sleepless nights about whether or not Edwin would be in the team. Instead, Norman was now having sleepless nights about the possible result of the Poppleford match; he was so excited that it took all of Edwin's persuasion to stop him from appearing by the pitch to watch the Also Rans practising in the afternoons. Such an embarrassment (a father watching a team practice!!) would have resulted in Edwin being teased mercilessly. Fortunately, Edwin remained unaware of a most embarrassing incident near the front of the school. It involved his father, a small step ladder, a pair of high powered binoculars, and the school's part-time groundsman.

Unable to control his excitement about the Poppleford match, Norman simply could not resist the desire to watch Edwin's team in training. He believed that if he could hide amongst the hedges and rhododendrons, which grew parallel to the school drive, he would have a distant view of the games' fields. He therefore planned to hide in the hedge, peer over it and spy on one of Edwin's practice sessions.

Thus, one afternoon, Norman parked his Vauxhall in the quiet lane about a quarter of a mile beyond the main school entrance. With an old flat cap pulled down over his forehead, he walked back along the quiet country lane which led to the school. Endeavouring to conceal a small step ladder, he paused at the school gates and looked around furtively. The only evidence of human activity came from the distant shouting of boys on the games' fields. An ancient, unattended tractor and trailer were parked at the top of the drive. Norman scampered a few paces up the drive before heading sideways, across the adjacent grass towards the hedge and the cover provided by the rhododendron bushes.

During this short dash, he managed to whack the shin of his right leg painfully on the bottom rung of the step ladder. His mission was therefore delayed for several minutes while he rubbed his shin firmly. Eventually the pain eased. He now manoeuvred the ladder into a position behind a bush, close to the hedge and yet hidden from the school. He opened the ladder's legs, secured the base after some disquieting wobbles and then realised that, in the adrenalin-fuelled process of acting like James Bond, he had left his binoculars in his car..

Using language forbidden at Whitsborough and indeed at any other school, Norman descended the ladder and re-traced his steps, to fetch the binoculars. This unforeseen activity now increased his feeling of embarrassment and guilt. Nevertheless, he returned to the drive with the binoculars but soon became aware of the noise of an engine of some sort. When he reached the school gates, he crouched behind one of the brick pillars to observe the previously unattended tractor, now trundling down the drive and being driven, he assumed, by the school's groundsman.

Norman pinned himself behind the gate pillar as the driver slowed, peered and then stopped a little way along the drive. Dismounting, the driver wondered over to an object he had spotted partly hidden behind a rhododendron bush: the step ladders. Shaking his head and looking puzzled, the man walked over to them and carried them back to the tractor, depositing them in the trailer on top of a mound of fertilizer. He then re-started the tractor and headed down the drive and out onto the lane, in the direction of the village.

He failed to notice an embarrassed and nervous 'birdwatcher' leaning beside one of the pillars, gripping some high-powered binoculars and apparently gazing at an imaginary buzzard circling at high altitude.

CHAPTER 10

Roddy conducts a school tour

On the Thursday morning of Roddy's second scheduled French Lesson with Suzy J-L, Roddy was called into Philip's study unexpectedly. Philip's important six-monthly check-up with his heart specialist in London had been moved forward at short notice. Unfortunately, it was the morning when Kate McNally, a film actress with a growing reputation, had arranged to view the school with her son.

Philip knew little of the film world but he knew enough about it to have heard of Kate McNally. Her appearance in her latest film, an historical drama which received wide publicity, had demanded that she exposed rather more of herself than Dottie would have permitted. Retaining an appreciative eye for the female form, Philip much regretted his call to London. Furthermore, he feared that if Dottie showed Kate McNally round the school it might not prove to be an harmonious experience.

Philip believed that, if he had correctly interpreted a couple of comments Angela had made about Roddy's appearance, Kate McNally might enjoy being shown round the school by Roddy, rather than Dottie. Somebody – he thought it was Angela – had described Roddy as 'Box Office'. Philip could only guess what this meant but he imagined that Kate McNally would certainly know. Thus, it was Roddy who was delegated to greet the attractive film actress at the main entrance.

Roddy's lessons were to be taken by Philip's old friend, Commander Dunsford. This capable retired naval commander was always willing to help out at short notice. He was an amiable widower in his late seventies, who was always delighted to don his blazer, chat to the boys, earn a few quid and receive a decent school lunch. His placid black labrador, Hood, seemed to enjoy the day out, too.

Dottie had not been consulted about these arrangements and was rather cross when she learnt that Roddy would take her place. However, she was secretly relieved that she would not have to spend her morning fawning over an actress of whom she did not approve.

"But why Roddy, Philip?" she asked.

Philip paused and attempted to avoid smiling.

"Well, Angela speaks highly of him and," Philip was not allowed to finish.

"Ah! Angela. Of course," interrupted Dottie. "So she's an expert in this area is she?" Dottie's sarcasm was evident.

"Well, I think Roddy might produce a youthful, dynamic image. He seems to be popular with almost everybody." Dottie listened with a degree of doubt. Roddy was certainly popular but could he 'sell' the school, she wondered.

"My taxi will be here soon," continued Philip, "and Dunsford's coming to cover Roddy's lessons. Perhaps you could give him 'coffee and chat' when he arrives, dear." He patted Dottie on the shoulder as he left the room.

"Well I do hope that damned animal of his is not on heat again. Do you remember how excited Budget became last time she was in the school," said Dottie as he disappeared. She then mumbled,

"Let's just hope the McNally woman doesn't have a similar effect on Roddy!"

At 10.30 am, Roddy stationed himself near the Front

Entrance, waiting for the celebrated actress. He had not seen any of her films but had seen photographs of her. He felt that 'glamour' would not impress him. He recalled Rosie Pitchworth's simple, natural attraction and Budget settled down beside him as he waited.

At 10.45 am, Fiona came out of the School Office to speak to Roddy.

"Typical! Late, of course. One of the privileges of fame," she said disapprovingly.

Roddy raised his eyebrows; Fiona was probably right.

"Why don't you go and grab a cup of coffee, Roddy. You will miss Break if she does eventually appear. I'll come and get you when …and if… she comes."

Roddy smiled and thanked her. He walked into the empty Common Room and was about to pour some milk into a mug when Fiona poked her head round the door.

"Action stations! She's just getting out of her car."

Roddy hurried to the Front Entrance where Fiona had already intercepted a casually dressed and most apologetic Kate McNally. She was holding hands with an eleven year old boy who was looking rather uncomfortable.

"I'm terribly sorry I'm late. Miles was feeling a bit sick and I had to stop the car. Just in time, as it happened. I'll spare you the details."

This seemed like a 'normal' mother speaking, not an overconfident actress. Fiona offered to take Miles to the Sick Room but Kate thanked her, explaining that she always carried 'emergency' equipment in the car. She had already cleaned Miles up and all was now well.

"Just a spot of car sickness and nervousness at visiting a new school," she explained. "I'm a bit nervous too, actually. School was never really my thing."

Having explained and apologised for the Headmaster's absence, Fiona introduced Roddy, as Kate's 'tour guide.' Roddy and Kate shook hands. Kate's shoulder-length dark hair framed her smiling, photogenic face and there was a brief exchange of eye contact, perhaps lasting no longer than a second or so. Neither Kate nor Roddy was sure of the other's interpretation of this but both parties were aware of this moment.

With his usual relaxed and unaffected charm, Roddy led Kate through the various corridors, stopping at noticeboards to explain activities, pointing to the Dining Room and pausing to peer inside classrooms through the small, shoulder height windows. Miles had to stand on tiptoe so that he could see for himself. Dottie would have thrown open these doors and marched inside, disturbing the lessons and expecting every boy to jump to attention. Roddy knew that other teachers hated these bombastic intrusions and certainly did not presume to emulate her.

The bell for Break sounded a minute or so earlier than Roddy would have wished. He hoped to have been outside, showing the visitors the playing fields by this time. However, as a number of boys passed him in the corridors there were some friendly greetings.

Several boys issued a "Morning, Sir" and there was a "Hello, Sir. I'm looking forward to this afternoon. Broom, broom," when Edwin passed, manoeuvring his way towards his 'milk and buns'.

"You seem to be a popular figure, Mr Amport," commented Kate, obviously impressed.

"Oh, it's Roddy, please," smiled Roddy at which point Wesley appeared round a corner. Wes carried his books in a brief case.

"Good morning, Sir," boomed Wes, adding, before continuing his journey, "A most pleasant one, I think."

Kate endeavoured to contain her amusement.

"Was that a boy - or a member of your Common Room," she asked.

"Good question! That was Wesley Berkshire, aged twelve – but he behaves as if he is about fifty-five. Great chap and an unlikely star of my rugby team."

Roddy recounted the unexpected discovery of Wes's talents and the significance of the engine noises made by

Edwin, the school's 'Honorary Motorist'.

Kate was delighted and intrigued by these unconventional pupils and practices. Having hated the rigid, humourless structure of her own schooling, she was finding Whitsborough – and Roddy – a breath of fresh air. She felt that Miles might enjoy just such an environment.

When Roddy led Kate out to the games' field and he walked her towards the lake, he spotted Angela and Drinkall having a break-time 'stroll'. They would, of course, claim that they were keeping a dutiful eye on the boys playing outside but really they had come out to be introduced to Kate. Roddy could only see three boys on the fields and they were just gently kicking an old football round. The two spies approached.

"I do hope Mr Amport is looking after you. I am Angela Bailey. I teach French." ("I've come to have a good look at you," was what she really meant.)

"And I'm Derek Drinkall – Science and Soccer," said D.D holding out his hand.

Kate gave him a routine smile and shook Drinkall's chalky paw.

"Yes, Roddy is being the perfect guide, thanks. You're lucky to have him here," Kate added, looking innocently at Angela. Angela took the use of the name 'Roddy' to be the sign of incipient bonding and she experienced a dart of jealousy.

"I enjoyed seeing your last film," (The one in which she exposed some exciting parts of her body) said D.D. "I didn't know you lived in the area."

"Well, we've only just moved in, haven't we, Miles? Whitsborough is close enough for Miles to be a day boy and yet he could board if I am away filming."

Further conversation was precluded as the bell for the end of Break could be heard across the grass. Kate seized this as an opportunity.

"Thank you so much for introducing yourselves. I expect you'll have to go back to your classrooms now."

There was a faint note of dismissal in Kate's voice. Angela and D.D. said goodbye and walked back across the pitch feeling a little crestfallen, as though they had been outstaying their welcome.

"Would those teachers normally have been outside during your break time?" asked Kate.

"Er, no. I don't suppose so," answered Roddy, puzzled. What did she mean?

"Oh, don't worry. It's just one of the downsides of being recognized. Never mind. Do lead on!"

The tour ended twenty minutes later as Roddy led Kate back to the Front Entrance, via the Changing Rooms which were, mercifully, tidy at this time of the day and there was no question of her discovering the temperamental boiler's reluctant efforts to deliver hot water. Kate noticed a car, tucked away under the large horse chestnut tree nearby.

"Gosh! An old 1100. I used to have one of those. Daddy bought me one when I was learning to drive. Great car!"

"Well, actually that's mine. Not in exactly sparkling condition, I'm afraid," said Roddy.

Kate walked over and looked inside.

"Yes, I see what you mean. Needs a bit of a tidy up. I kept mine spotless. The woman's touch!" commented Kate, giving Roddy a long look.

"Well, one day I'll clean it out. I have a feeling I've lost some of my cricket kit inside somewhere so I'll certainly tidy it…. before next season!"

Kate laughed. Miles wondered off to search amongst the leaves where there was the promise of some conkers.

"Look, I'm having a house warming party at the weekend. There won't be too many people there. My husband (as you may have read in the bloody papers) buggered off some months ago, which is why I moved down here: to get away from London. Do come. All very casual. Old friends, no actors, so don't worry. I do have some normal friends!"

Roddy was a little surprised and rather flattered. He was about to question her further but spotted Dottie coming towards them. She must have come from the Front Entrance and Roddy had been expecting her to appear at some point.

He coughed pointedly and looked in Dottie's direction. Kate was quick to understand the significance of the look. She smiled and gave Roddy a penetrating glance, loaded with possibilities.

"The Old Coach House, Loxyard. Saturday. About 8.00pm," she said quietly.

Roddy felt a rush of excitement.

"And dress," she paused...and then grinned. "Is optional!"

She then took a pace backwards, as Dottie was now in hearing distance, and she smoothly moved into parental mode:

"And what sort of English do you teach them, Mr Amport? Is it nouns and verbs or Dickens and Shakespeare?"

Roddy, too, became more formal as Dottie joined them. He supplied the introductions. Kate was a little embarrassed because Miles was more interested in searching for conkers than saying hello to Dottie.

"Mr Amport," (Roddy was grateful for this apparent formality) "has been doing an excellent job, Mrs Pipe. And the boys I have met seemed very polite and several were rather amusing."

"Edwin and Wesley," explained Roddy. Dottie acknowledged this information with a nod.

"Well, they are not *all* mad here," said Dottie apologetically.

"No. I meant that as a compliment. The boys were charming. There is a definite sense of fun. I hated my school. All very serious. Probably why I ended up as an actress."

Dottie had not expected such pleasant modesty. She had

expected that she would have to adopt a 'your fame does not impress me' tone but she found Kate to be genuine and engaging. Dottie therefore switched into her own 'charm' mode. Roddy saw this as the moment to take his leave and said that he hoped that Kate had enjoyed her visit.

"Yes, thank you so much, I look forward to meeting you again sometime." She shook hands with him but Roddy ensured there was no lingering eye contact; Dottie was a sharp old bird and would surely have noticed.

The afternoon's rugby practice went well. Roddy could not help feeling a glow of satisfaction as most of the boys now passed the ball with a degree of competence. His chief worry, however, was that the boys enthusiasm would dwindle in the weeks before the Poppleford match. Fortunately, Edwin remained focused but Roddy had doubts about some of the others. Wesley operated with bursts of energy but he was not consistent. Roddy decided that he would try and locate a football before the next day and organise a soccer match. He felt that a temporary change of sport might prove refreshing and beneficial.

CHAPTER 11

Suzy's second French lesson

When Roddy showered and changed before supper that evening, he was still in two minds about how to handle Suzy. He was well aware of her intentions but was not quite sure what his own feelings were. She was certainly very attractive and, having recognised the significant age difference between her and Gerald, he could understand that she might well enjoy a romp with a younger male.

He was relieved to find that Angela was having supper with the Pipes so he would not be subjected to her intuitive scrutiny. Several other residents were engaged in a discussion on the relative importance of their own subject areas: Geography v. Science v. Scripture. Roddy was happy to avoid involvement and was therefore able to ease away from the dining table. He returned to his flat, vigorously brushed his teeth and rather surprised himself by applying a touch of after shave to his face. He noted the feel of the day's growth of dark stubble on his cheeks. Should he shave quickly, before leaving? No, he decided, the stubble might deter Suzy…but did he want that? Avoiding further dilemmas, he hurried to his car. The engine turned over slowly before finally starting, reminding him that the battery was nearing the end of its life.

As he drove, the thought of Kate McNally's party on Saturday crossed his mind. It was certainly an intriguing proposition. Kate seemed gorgeous, warm and genuine. The next few days could be rather interesting! As he braked at a road junction, he heard a hidden cricket ball fall off the back seat and roll onto the car's floor; and then he remembered Rosie and the Cricket Week. Another pleasant experience.

When he reached Suzy's house, Roddy was relieved to observe that although the doors of the double garage were open, only Suzy's car was inside. Gerald was, as he had been told, obviously out. Having rung the bell and later used the large knocker on the imposing door, there was a delay before the door opened. An apologetic and scantily clad Suzy opened the door. She explained that Gerald was in London for the night, she had lost track of time and she was in the shower when the doorbell rang.

She hauled Roddy inside and gave him a huge kiss. She then stood back and admired her prey. One hand gently rubbed the side of his face.

"Hmm," she said with mock disapproval, "you might have shaved for me." She then closed her arms around him. "But 'mmm,' you smell delicious."

Roddy was unable to resist her embrace. The soft skin on Suzy's face only served to trigger the thoughts and temptations which he had been trying to overcome. Furthermore, on placing his hands round her exhilarating body, it was evident that she was wearing nothing at all beneath her flimsy dressing gown.

Roddy forced himself to escape from this embrace.

"You're looking lovely, Suzy. And by the way, Taylor seemed in good form today."

"Well that's good. I'll be seeing him at the weekend. I do miss him but Gerald insists that boarding will be good for him, being an only child."

Her eyes narrowed. The cat was about to spring on the mouse but Roddy stood back deliberately.

"The French call that a peignoir," he informed her.

"Really!" said Suzy. "Good. That's my French lesson over for this evening." Clearly, she was intending to get down to business straightaway.

Roddy was still trying to avoid the moment of decision. Should he or shouldn't he? This was a new dilemma. In the past, when dealing with women, there had never been such a question; the traffic lights were always green. But at the moment, he was on 'hold'. The lights remained on red and amber.

He moved out of the large hall and into the drawing room. He spotted the French books he had left with her the previous week but they were on a window sill, exactly where he had left them. He moved smartly over to collect them, sat on the sofa and patted the seat beside him.

Suzy, though having had her initial plans thwarted, decided to play a waiting game. She would have to give Roddy the satisfaction of teaching her some French. Then she would pounce.

"Very well, Mr Teacher. But first, I am going to pour us both a drink."

Seated dutifully beside Roddy, who ensured there was no knee or other physical contact, Suzy played the role of semi-interested pupil. Roddy was not fooled by this but Suzy managed to convey just enough enthusiasm and competence to keep Roddy semi-satisfied. At one point, while attempting to formulate a simple French sentence, she lay back on the sofa allowing her peignoir to ride tantalizingly up her perfectly formed thighs. At this point Roddy nearly surrendered. He moved forward to place the French grammar book on the long coffee table in front of the sofa but one of Suzy's extended limbs touched a leg –

not Roddy's as she had intended – but a table leg. This caused her tall wine glass, half full of a respectable Merlot, to topple over and spill the contents onto the pale green carpet.

Suzy instantly went into panic mode. She jumped up and ran into the kitchen to find kitchen rolls, sponges and water.

"Gerald will kill me! We've only just replaced the last carpet. He expects everything to be so immaculate."

Suzy forgot about her (lack of) clothing and knelt down and scrubbed furiously. Roddy pointed out that trying to absorb the wine might prove more effective. He had seen his mother do this once during a New Year's Eve party. As he stood on the kitchen roll with his large shoes, gradually the wine was sucked into volumes of kitchen roll. After twenty minutes of absorbing, sponging and rinsing, Suzy realised that the cleansing and stain prevention action appeared to be working. Her tears began to subside and her feelings of panic dissipated. She turned to Roddy and gave him a huge hug.

"Thank you," she said warmly. "What would I have done without you?"

"That's all right," replied Roddy with a big smile.

Suzy reached for his hand.

"And now I know what I want to do *with* you." She pulled his arm and led him out of the drawing room, across the large open hall and up the stairs. Obediently, Roddy allowed himself to be steered towards what was obviously a large spare bedroom where there was a wide bed with the covers already pulled back. Roddy surmised that this had been prepared for this activity. The spider had spun its web earlier; the fly was now trapped.

Suzy closed in on Roddy. One arm went round his neck as she delivered a long meaningful kiss and her other hand began to stray. Roddy realised that further resistance would be impossible.

"Give me five minutes," said Suzy. "I want to wash off

the wine and the smell of damp carpet. The television works. Do turn it on if you like."

She blew him a kiss and Roddy had the feeling that 'five' minutes might prove to be a considerable understatement. He fiddled with the television but nothing happened. As he played with the controls, he heard the shower running in Suzy's bathroom.

It was a minute or two before he discovered that the television was not connected at the mains. Just as he was kneeling to reach the plug, irritatingly positioned behind some full length curtains, he heard a knocking noise. He stood up and heard it again. Someone was knocking on the front door. He stood for a few moments, not knowing what to do. He ventured across the landing and peered into Suzy's bedroom. It was evident from the steam and noise coming from the bathroom room that Suzy was in no condition to open the front door.

For a moment or two, it seemed as though the knocking had stopped and that the person knocking had aborted his or her attempt to interrupt Suzy's plans. However, not to be thwarted, the knocker had evidently discovered the doorbell. It produced a loud, clerical sounding chime which had an element of urgency about it. Roddy decided that he had no option but to open the door. Visions of a car accident, a mugging, or the need for the emergency use of a telephone all crossed his mind. He hurried down the stairs dreading what he might find on the other side of the imposing front door.

As he opened the heavy door, he discovered a small lady, possibly in her late seventies, holding a lead on the end of which was a small dog. Roddy later learnt that it was a West Highland Terrier with a powerful personality. It was wearing a neat, canine, tartan waistcoat.

"And who are you?" demanded the septuagenarian party pooper firmly. There were elements of both surprise and disapproval in this question. There was no question of an apology for disturbing the evening's proceedings.

Roddy was about to reply in a matter-of-fact fashion. His normal, relaxed delivery had often proved invaluable in defusing situations but the diminutive human terrier in front of him wanted an answer, quickly.

"Where's Mrs Little? I don't suppose that husband of hers is in? Away as usual, no doubt!" she added with more disapproval.

Roddy found the woman rather irksome but endeavoured to retain his distinctive calm. The fact that she appeared to know Gerald and Suzy suggested that perhaps this woman lived nearby and was possibly a neighbour.

"May I ask who *you* are? *My* name is Amport, Mrs Johnson-Little's French tutor."

"My name is Allbury, with two 'L s'. I live in Green Briars, two houses further down the road. Perhaps I could have a word with Mrs Little?"

Her manner was now a little less demanding.

"Well, I think she is having a shower at the moment,"

Roddy immediately realised that this mid-evening ablution sounded a little strange. Suspicion returned to Mrs Allbury's voice.

"Really?? At nine o'clock in the evening?" Roddy wondered if this elderly lady was making accusatory suggestions.

A thought struck Roddy. The truth – or approximate truth – might end the woman's doubts.

"Well, she had an accident. She tripped." Roddy hesitated. "She wasn't hurt at all but she was carrying some glasses of red wine which spilled all over the carpet and over her clothing. We've just spent ages trying to clean the carpet and now she's gone upstairs to wash it off her dress, I think. She was rather upset."

Roddy hoped that this sounded convincing. Mrs Allbury was silent for a few moments. Was she assessing the truth of this account?

"Oh dear. How unfortunate." There was genuine

sympathy in her voice. "I know just how distressing these accidents can be."

Roddy decided that if he invited her inside, there would be an appearance of innocence in the gesture; suspicions would surely be allayed.

"Would you like to come in and wait for Mrs Johnson-Little?"

She gave Roddy a half smile and stepped inside. Roddy prayed that the little dog did not have muddy paws. He was about to show her into the drawing room. The door was open and there was, fortunately, evidence of the spillage: several chairs, the coffee table and the huge sofa were all out of place, leaving the carpet to dry. However, at this moment, there was the sound of a door opening, some movement from the landing above and the soft cooing of: "Roddy. Roddy? Where are you?" I'm re…"

"I'm about to show your visitor into the drawing room, Mrs Johnson-Little. It's Mrs All…?" responded Roddy hastily.

"Allbury. With two 'L's," interjected Mrs A. rather firmly and with a bewildered frown.

There was a delayed reply from the first floor:

"Oh!... Hello…Edna."

Roddy had been racking his brains which now had a sharpened response-time as a result of his daily dealings with the Edwins and Wesleys of the universe.

He called to the – fortunately – unseen figure above. Even her peignoir would have covered more of Suzy's body than what she was now (not) wearing.

"I've just been explaining about the accident… and the red wine which went all over the carpet and your clothing. I hope you feel better after your shower."

He wondered if any of this sounded convincing. Mrs Allbury's face betrayed no emotion.

Suzy was desperately gathering her thoughts.

"Roddy, I was calling down to see if you could locate one of my shoes. The one up here has a few splashes on it.

I think I must have taken the other one off when I was kneeling on the floor."

"Right. I'll have quick look." Roddy gave Mrs A. a nervous smile and moved into the drawing room. He was impressed by Suzy's quick thinking.

"I'll be down soon, Edna. What was it you wanted, by the way?"

Edna Allbury, who had just been confronted by a number of unexpected domestic circumstances in her own life, suddenly felt a little awkward.

"Well, while I was giving Bruce his evening walk, I noticed an old car in your drive. The lights are still on and they look rather dim. I was trying to save someone from having a flat battery. I had one once and …."

"Oh, Lord. That's my car. Thanks. Yes, I need to get the battery sorted out. I'll deal with that now."

Roddy emerged from the drawing room – having failed to locate Cinderella's slipper – and opened the front door.

Mrs A. had had enough. She was not sure now whether calling in mid-evening had been a wise move or not. And she was certainly not sure what was going on before she arrived. Whatever it was, she was anxious to leave.

"I must be on my way, er, Suzy. Bruce is asking for his evening biscuit."

"Oh, bye. And thanks," called Suzy, wincing as she spoke.

As Roddy politely held the door open for her, he bade her "Bon nuit" in a weak attempt to remind her of the reason he was present. "And thank you for saving my battery."

Mrs Allbury mumbled a reply as Bruce enthusiastically towed her out of the house and down the drive. Roddy wondered if she had been attempting to speak in French.

He opened the unlocked Austin, switched off the dim side lights to ease the strain on the battery and turned the ignition key while crossing his fingers. With a groan and extreme reluctance, the car condescended to start. He decided to leave the engine running as he did not want to risk trying to start it again that evening.

Suzy had come down stairs, having put on a large, blue, full-length dressing gown. It looked as though it probably belonged to Gerald. Suzy did not want to risk a return visit from Mrs A.

Roddy thought he spotted a tear in one of Suzy's eyes.

"I suppose you are going to tell me that you have got to go now, aren't you?

"Afraid so, now that I've got the engine going. It may not start a second time."

"Bloody woman!" moaned Suzy. "She's ruined the evening."

"Well it was my fault for leaving the lights on. Another hour or so and the battery would have been completely flat. I wouldn't have been able to drive back and…"

"And you'd have been stuck here all night…which would have been lovely!" replied Suzy who had moved close to Roddy and was looking up at his handsome face. Her arms wrapped themselves around his shoulders as she gave him a huge, tearful kiss. Roddy had to remove her arms and moved to leave.

As she closed the door, she pointed her hand, pistol-shaped, at him.

"Just you wait, Mr Amport, I'll get you next time!"

On his way home, Roddy promised himself that he would buy a new battery for the car at the first available opportunity. As the vehicle crunched on the gravel along the school drive, there was no movement from Angela's curtains but he noticed a light shining from a side door in the Pipe's wing. The door provided a private entrance to the school. It was just closing and he saw Budget's rear quarters disappearing inside. Knowing that Philip usually went to bed early, he wondered if Dottie might possibly have noted his late return.

The Berkshires - and more financial problems for the Pipes

Norman Stevenson was not the only Whitsborough parent who was aware of the forthcoming Poppleford match. At least half of the 'Also Rans' had kept their parents actively informed of the progress being made by the 3rd XV. Roddy's name was frequently mentioned and, though few parents had yet met him, many were now aware of his growing popularity. Most of these boys had never shown any interest or aptitude for rugby or, in the case of many of them, for any sport at all.

Although Wesley had given the impression that he was unaffected by his newly discovered rugby prowess, he had in fact written to his wealthy father in the Middle East expressing uninhibited enthusiasm. His father had always been a rather distant figure and their relationship had been a distinctly formal one. Although usually generous and willing to provide material help, his father rarely displayed any open affection towards his children. Wesley, however, recalled that his father had once mentioned that he had enjoyed rugby as a boy when he had spent some years at a famous English boarding school.

Dottie Pipe and Angela, who often shared gossip about the parents, remained mystified by the Berkshires. Chuselle had kept a low profile once she had secured places for her sons at Whitsborough. She had, though, smiled at Dottie on the few occasions they had passed each other.

"I'd love to know what Mr Berkshire gets up to in Abu Dookah or wherever it is he is," commented Dottie one day at tea time."

"Well, all I can say is that it must be pretty lucrative," replied Angela moving closer to Dottie whilst lowering her voice. "I took a detour the other day on the way back from town. I found out that they lived near the end of the lane leading to Spring Hill. Chuselle's house is one of several large Victorian houses - or should I say mansions - on the slopes. I didn't go up their drive but it looked pretty big to me. Masses of land. Some rather new looking swings and climbing frame things but there were high wire fences and huge gates. "

"He must be in oil," said Dottie. "There's only oil and desert in Abu Whatsit."

"Well as long as he keeps paying the fees for his three sons, I don't think it is really of much interest to us," commented Philip from behind the Times crossword. Dottie and Angela often gossiped more than he liked and this was his way of telling them to be quiet.

"Oh Philip, dear, don't be such an old bore! Can't you think of anything except school fees?" said Dottie, raising her eyebrows at Angela.

Philip looked up at the two women. They were standing close together, almost conspiratorially. He was determined to justify his remark.

"It is not the fees *per se* which matter. It is the *numbers* I am concerned about. We need a constant supply of new pupils. This then brings in the fees to pay for our upkeep, salaries, the pupils' food, the maintenance of the buildings and – one hopes – funds for future building projects."

Dottie stepped forward, anxious to calm him; she imagined his heart pounding feverishly. Placing a comforting hand on his shoulder, she signalled to Angela to move away. But it was Philip who apologised, not Dottie. He placed a hand over Dottie's while she attempted to calm the waters.

"I'm sorry, dear. It is just that I have had another Governor's letter from Ashley Stilton, emphasising the serious nature of our finances. He has always been so helpful in the past but recently his tone seems to have changed."

Football for a change?

Roddy's idea of playing a game of football one afternoon proved successful in many respects. There was a lot of laughter and it took the boys some time before they remembered that several significant rules had to be observed. Tackling an opponent by flinging oneself head first at the opponent's knees, and wrapping arms around his legs, was to be discouraged. Roddy had to remind the boys that the rules of soccer did not permit this.

Edwin had already floored two members of the opposition while implementing scything assaults on their legs. Giles Harmsworth, the second boy to be tackled thus, was already limping his way slowly towards the school building to seek Matron's aid. However, once the violence had subsided, Roddy's experiment proved an enjoyable diversion.

Wesley was one of the goalkeepers and he seemed to think that he was forbidden to handle the ball. This misunderstanding induced him to stop all shots at his goal with his feet, legs, stomach, upper body and head - but never his hands. When Budget wandered on to the pitch in the vicinity of the goal area. Jonathan Clesham, who was acting as a goalkeeper at one end, pursued the dog instead of the ball. While leading Budget off the pitch, leaving his goal untended, a random shot ricocheted off Roddy (the referee) and penetrated the defences of Jonathan's team. The sight of Roddy, lying spread-eagled by the blow (and over-acting madly), caused huge hilarity. Meanwhile, the deflected ball rolled slowly through the mud and into the vacant goal. It proved to be the only goal of the game.

CHAPTER 12

Kate McNally's party

It was an Exeat Saturday when the boarders were allowed to go home after their morning lessons. Roddy was unsure whether he should go to Kate's party that evening: he had a pile of exercise books waiting to be marked. Drinkall had already made noises about 'having a session' at the Huxton Arms although Roddy feared that might move him into choppy waters again as Angela would be there. At the back of his mind was the Suzy Johnson-Little issue – and whether it would or should develop any further. He then recalled the lingering look in Kate's eyes when she invited him to her party, adding, ambiguously, that 'Dress' was only 'optional'. That moment alone made the decision for him; now it was just a question of what he should wear – for the first part of the party at least.

Selecting a fairly respectable pair of blue jeans, together with an open necked, striped shirt, Roddy headed for Loxyard in his ancient Austin, which was now equipped with a new battery.

Not wishing to arouse suspicion in the Common Room, Roddy made discreet enquiries amongst the boys about how to get to Loxyard. The village was only about six miles away and, although he had no idea where the Old Coach House was located, he discovered it by accident when he had to brake a little harder than should have been necessary. A small red, convertible MG sports car, with its roof down, pulled out of a drive in front of him rather unexpectedly, driven by a young woman who waved her hand cheerfully and apologetically, acknowledging her error. However, Roddy, who had virtually come to a halt, noticed a newly written - and obviously temporary – house sign reading: 'The Old Coach House.'

He turned onto a narrow track with overgrown hedges on each side. Soon, after coming to a sharp bend, the track emerged into an open area, where there were several grassy fields marked with wooden fences. The Old Coach House was really just an attractive old cottage. There was a slightly more modern barn nearby, outside which a car was parked. It was not quite the 'chocolate box' scene that he had had imagined but it was a pleasant location and there appeared to be a small stream running nearby. A lone heron could be seen beside the stream in the distance plotting his next move, and an unsuspecting minnow's last.

Having parked his car near the barn, Roddy walked towards the cottage. There was no obvious path but he eventually found the front door and heard some pleasant music emanating from within. There was no bell so he knocked several times, using the rather underpowered and light-weight knocker which delivered high-pitched 'taps.' The door finally opened and a smiling, rather jolly looking young woman appeared. She immediately pointed at Roddy – as if engaged in a police identity parade.

"Roddy! – ah – ha," she chortled. "I'm Fee. I'm Kate's oldest and closest friend." She announced this so loudly that it was clearly for the benefit of someone else several rooms away.

"And an absolute pain in the ar..." called a distant voice from the kitchen which was drowned as Fee summoned Roddy to enter.

"Do come in!" continued the exuberant Fee, grabbing Roddy by the hand and dragging him inside as though he was a reluctant four year old being left at a children's party. "And mind your head. Some of the beams are pretty low."

By this time Kate appeared wearing a large green apron. She gave Roddy a kiss on each cheek and he noted her delicious perfume as she did so.

Roddy handed her the bottle of red wine he had bought earlier.

"I'll take that," said Fee.

She held it up and examined the label.

"Yes. I thought so. Chateau Corner Shop." She sniffed it dismissively. "It needs opening."

"Well that's about the one thing you *are* able to do," countered Kate, grabbing Roddy's hand and leading him away from Fee into the low-ceilinged drawing room which seemed full of furniture and large boxes waiting to be unpacked. Roddy was a little disorientated. What exactly was going on? Unpacking? A party?

"Are you sure I am not intruding? I feel a little out of place here?" He gestured towards the kitchen or wherever it was Fee had gone. "And I passed someone in a red MG who was coming out of your drive – rather fast."

Kate sat Roddy down on the one available chair.

"Don't worry, Mr Amport," she said with a twinkle. "Fee is a gem. My very best friend. We shared a bottle of vodka together one Sunday afternoon, at school. After a night of retching in the school sanatorium, we were both rusticated for a week."

"Blood brothers?"

"Yes. Kind of. She's determined to make sure that my so-called fame (short lived no doubt!) will not change me."

"Well you seem pretty grounded to me. You asked some pretty sensible questions when I showed you round – and you made some sharp observations."

Kate gave one of her endearing smiles.

"Why, thank you, Mr Amport."

Roddy wondered if he was being patronised but continued, "And so who was the racing driver in the MG?"

"That was Deidre. Deidre Lampton-Willis. Now she is another school friend, but she seems to have been much friendlier with me since I've become…."

"Er…Well known? Famous, perhaps?" suggested Roddy.

"I may be a little unkind but…"

"But I'm probably right, yes?" said Roddy.

Kate smiled again. She did not seem to want to be too critical of others. He wondered if she, an actress, was untypical in this respect.

"Anyway, she's gone off to the local pub to rendezvous with a couple of other London chums who have been invited. You can make your own judgement about her later."

Fee returned with some large glasses of wine.

"Here we are," she said, handing out the drinks. "This is 'Roddy's Red'. Cheers."

They raised their glasses.

"Hmm! Not bad for Corner Shop," said Fee with mild approval.

"Fee! Don't be so rude," replied Kate who felt obliged to defend Roddy. But Fee was clearly a *very* old friend who could get way with outrageous comments. She ignored Kate's apology.

"And I'd certainly send any children I had to be taught by you," continued Fee, moving close to Roddy and suggestively running her fingers along one of his shoulders.

"I can see exactly why Kate has invited you."

"Fee! Really!"

Kate grabbed Fee's hand and removed it. She looked at Roddy, raised her eyebrows and shook her head.

"Roddy. I'm so sorry. She really doesn't know how to behave."

Kate pointed to the kitchen and stared at Fee.

"To the kitchen with you" she pointed. "Get back where you belong."

Fee bowed her head in mock subservience, walked towards the kitchen and then turned, before entering it, and called to Roddy, as flirtatiously as she could:

"See you later."

Kate now looked at Roddy, shaking her head. She was about to apologise but Roddy spoke first.

"I enjoyed the play-acting. You're obviously *extremely* old friends."

Kate smiled, relieved to learn that Roddy was aware that it had all been fun and banter.

"Is she a little…" Roddy searched for the right words as he did not wish to appear conceited. "..er… jealous?

"Of me, for inviting you here?" said Kate.

Roddy had not intended to suggest this and was about to explain what he really meant. However, Kate continued.

"I expect there's a bit of that", Kate moved close. "But the real problem is that Fee is a far better actress than I am. At school, she usually had the major parts in all the school productions and got all the rave reviews. I'm not in her league. I was just lucky in London, happened to be in the right place at the right time and.."

Roddy interrupted,

"And look stunning."

Kate looked embarrassed but Roddy continued:

"And I suspect you are a much better actress than you are prepared to admit. However, I think it would be quite natural that she would be pleased for you – but jealous at the same time."

Kate drew away from Roddy and stood back to have an admiring look at him.

"You know, Mr Amport, there's more to you...or should I say *even* more to you than..." she moved close again, "meets the eye".

She placed both arms behind Roddy's neck and pulled his head towards her. Her hand stroked his cheek.

"Hmm. A bit stubbly. You might have shaved properly," she grinned.

Roddy recalled someone else making a similar comment only a few days earlier.

"Well, I certainly shaved this morning," said Roddy.

As their mouths touched, the engine of a small sports car could be heard outside. When the engine was switched off, the noise was replaced by the sound of laughter and shouting. Kate's friend Deidre had returned from the pub and now had brought three others with her, all joyfully crammed into the little two seater car.

"Damn," whispered Kate as she moved away from Roddy and went to the window.

"I'm afraid some of these will be rather noisy and....Oh no! Peter Valentine and goodness knows who else! I didn't invite them."

A second car had drawn up as well. It was a VW Beetle containing at least three more people.

"Roddy. I'm so sorry. I didn't invite all these people but you know what it's like in London; everyone likes to drive off to the country at the weekend to let off steam."

Fee emerged from the kitchen to see who had arrived. She went to the window but Deirdre was already coming through the front door with the first wave of invaders.

"Kate. I'm sorry. This is nothing to do with me. Somehow, Peter Valentine heard that you were having a party and..."

"Yes. A quiet dinner party," replied Kate, looking rather disappointed.

Deidre continued:

"...and Peter Valentine thought he'd like to visit you, Kate......as a former, er....friend?"

Roddy wondered what the term 'friend' actually meant but the boisterous arrival of the aforesaid Londoner drowned these thoughts. Peter Valentine immediately reminded Roddy of an archetypal, thick-skinned, school bully. In an earlier era he would have been called

Flashman. Easy-going Roddy Amport, for once, took an instant dislike to someone. However, school bully Peter Valentine's immediate aim seemed to be the renewal of his acquaintance with film star Kate. Meanwhile, one of the girls who had just arrived made a beeline for Roddy. She was about to introduce herself but was intercepted by Fee.

"Hi, Trix. I didn't know you had been invited. Long time – no see!"

"And long-time – no Fee!" retorted Trix with just a hint of sulphuric acid.

There followed a showy display of hugs and kisses, signifying their mutual dislike.

Fee generously allowed Trix to shake hands with Roddy, who was then suddenly tugged away from the two piranhas by Kate.

Kate snuggled close to him as she drew him across the room.

"God, I'm sorry about all this. It's not what I intended," she whispered. "Come and meet Mike. He's my brother's oldest friend. We practically grew up together and there's no need to be worried. He's engaged to a gorgeous nurse who's now working a weekend shift. He's a great sportsman. You'll like him."

Kate was right. Mike was a pleasant, friendly young lawyer. Exploratory questioning by both parties quickly revealed a mutual interest in a number of sports and that they may even have played cricket against each other. Time passed quickly until Fee eventually announced that supper was ready.

The guests were led through a narrow passage to a dining room at the far end of the house. It was a large room for a cottage of modest size and unpacked items lay beside the walls. Everyone expressed surprised admiration at the impressively large table. The dining chairs were a mismatched collection but Fee had performed miracles – as Kate pointed out – and produced enough food 'for the 5000' even though she had not expected so many guests.

. It was a noisy supper. Peter Valentine attempted to dominate the conversation with details of a recent motor biking tour of Argentina but Kate seemed acutely aware of the needs of the occasion. She asked other guests questions which enabled them to talk about themselves. It was Peter Valentine who filled a brief silence with:

"And what about you, Mr Teacher? Sharpened any interesting pencils recently? Beaten any of the little buggers yet?"

It was Valentine's 'Flashman' gene at work. It was a direct attack on Roddy: an attempt to bully and belittle him.

Kate immediately sensed the challenge. She hadn't invited Roddy to the party for him to be humiliated by an urbane and swaggering Chelsea bully. And Valentine was a gate crasher anyway.

Roddy paused. For a moment it seemed as though he was not able to formulate a reply. Even Trix and Fee exchanged glances indicating shared embarrassment. But Roddy held his ground.

He began his reply by acknowledging the odd situation that most young teachers experience: that of initially standing 'on the other side of the desk'; delivering a lesson rather than receiving one. Did this cause a sense of panic – or one of excitement? He then outlined how he had conducted – if that was the correct word - his first lesson. He told them about asking a boy (Edwin) to run across the games field and how he had learnt of Edwin's father's ambition for his son and all about his holiday training regime. There were chuckles when they heard how 'Press–up' had earned his nickname. Roddy briefly spoke of Edwin's motoring mania and the enigmatic Wesley. The audience were captivated but it was Kate who intervened:

"Roddy, you are going to make us all want to be teachers."

"Makes the legal world seem pretty dull," added Mike.

"You can teach me, any time." swooned Trix.

Flashman asked if there was any more wine.

"Now who's for pudding?" asked Fee. "There's fresh fruit salad or…fresh fruit salad," she giggled.

"Let me take your plates," said Kate.

Roddy eased out of his chair and stood up. He had survived his interrogation.

"I'll give you a hand with them," he said.

He and Kate carried the plates into the kitchen while Fee navigated a huge bowl of fruit salad from the sideboard and on to the table. In the kitchen, as Roddy stood by Kate unloading the dishes into a sink, Kate rubbed her shoulder against Roddy's. She turned her head and smiled warmly.

"That was such a good reply to that prig, Valentine. Not only did you put him in his place but you made most of us envious. Teaching must be such fun."

"It's not always like that, I can assure you," Roddy replied.

"Well I liked the atmosphere in the school – so did Miles."

"Heavens, I had forgotten about Miles. Where is he now?"

"Tucked up in bed….upstairs….in his grandparents' house. My parents live about forty minutes from here. Not too close, not too far. It's one of the reasons I chose to live in this part of the world."

She gave Roddy a brief kiss. It lasted just long enough to be one of expectation rather than mere formality.

"Come on. Back to battle," said Kate as she returned to the dining room.

When the supper finally drew to a close, it was Mike, the lawyer, who made the first move to leave. His fiancé was due to finish her long shift at around 7.30 am and he hoped to return to his flat in order to get some sleep, before collecting her from the hospital. Kate stood up, indicating that perhaps the others would like to follow. As they gave their thanks, Kate whispered instructions to

Roddy, making it clear that he was expected – or was it invited - to stay behind and 'help wash up.'

Fee had stacked most of the plates and dishes in the kitchen, ready for washing in the morning. She had also tactfully gone to bed in the tiny bedroom at the far end of the upstairs passage.

The previous owners had ensured that the master bedroom was of a comfortable size and was served by its own modernised bathroom. Kate led Roddy up to her bedroom, sat him down on the large bedroom chair and tossed him an old film magazine.

"There's a brief review of my first film which might amuse you but you probably won't recognise my photo. I'm wearing a short blonde wig!"

By the time Roddy had found the article, Kate was ready for her shower, wrapped in a very ordinary blue flannel dressing gown. It was partly Kate's very ordinariness that Roddy found so appealing. All that was exposed was the sight of two exquisite legs, from the knees down. Were they naturally brown, he wondered. She paused before entering the bathroom.

"I *would* suggest that you join me in the shower but it's a little cramped," she said with an air of real disappointment. Roddy looked up and smiled.

"Ok. I can wait. Just!" He watched her negotiate two awkward steps down and through the little door. She tossed her dressing gown carelessly on to the floor as she disappeared round the corner.

"You know," she called, "when I was about twelve I wanted desperately to be one of those beautiful models who appeared on the television adverts... for some sort of soft and sensuous soap – where the woman lay in the bath, toes pointed, slowly massaging the magic lather into her gorgeous legs."

"Well I'd be inclined to say that you have, therefore, exceeded your own ambitions," called Roddy.

Kate roared with laughter.

"Mr Roddy Amport. The Man with the Golden Tongue!"

She showered quickly and lent Roddy a towel when it was his turn.

"Now don't keep me waiting," she said as Roddy passed her on his way to the bathroom. "It's been a long hunt this evening and now I've cornered my prey, I don't wish to wait around for the feast!"

Roddy duly obliged. He was used to showering quickly. He dried himself and furtively made use of Kate's toothbrush and toothpaste. He tried to smooth his hair into place but the mirror behind the basin was steamed up.

As he turned off the taps and rounded the corner to return to the bedroom, he caught sight of rather more of Kate's delicious legs than he had seen before. She remained partially covered by the dressing gown but as she reclined on the bed, the dressing gown had folded itself around one of her thighs, revealing most of her right leg, an area of stunning natural beauty. Roddy stopped dead in his tracks.

"Wow!" he commented, "If the other leg matches that one, I won't know what to do with myself."

"Well just come here and I'll sort out that little problem for you," giggled Kate.

This, thought Roddy, will be a rather special and memorable experience. He took a pace forward, mesmerized by the vision of one of the most beautiful legs he had ever encountered. But as he negotiated the two steps back into the bedroom, with his eyes fixed firmly on Kate's exposed leg, his head collided heavily with the lintel above the small bathroom door. Unfortunately, the resulting collision between the seventeenth century lintel and Roddy's head represented a triumph for the solid craftsmanship of the seventeenth century. .

Only once before had Roddy experienced such a loud internal bang. The explosion inside his head was like the time when he had mistimed a rugby tackle. Then, his head felt the full impact of a speeding 16 stone forward's knee. He had suffered several minutes of confusion and had believed that he was, literally, 'seeing stars'.

Kate gasped in horror as she witnessed the accident. The noise of the impact alone suggested acute pain. She jumped up, placed her arms beneath his shoulders and managed to hold him upright as she manoeuvred him onto her bed. Here he lay, like a wounded knight while she endeavoured to ease his pain. She found herself having to administer First Aid. She managed to locate some ice in the kitchen and applied it to Roddy's forehead where, surprisingly, there was no sign of blood. Dazed and disorientated, Roddy was in no condition for any activity other than a long night's sleep.

He eventually woke, midway through the following morning. His head throbbed unremittingly. By now, Kate and Fee had completed most of the clearing up. He carefully negotiated the bathroom door, splashed water on his face, dressed slowly and made his way groggily downstairs.

"Thanks to you, Mr Amport, I had a much longer sleep than I had anticipated," complained Kate with mock anger, which she followed with a gentle kiss.

Fee walked over to Roddy and stood in front of him.

"Now, Mr Teacher, what was the first thing I warned you about when you arrived?" she asked.

Roddy acknowledged the question but was clearly in considerable discomfort. He sat on the nearest chair, holding his forehead.

"I   know.   I   know.   Mind   your   head!"

CHAPTER 13

Roddy's injury. A surprise visitor
Driving slowly back to Whitsborough later that morning, Roddy nursed his aching head. The bruise and the resultant swelling remained painfully with him whilst the delightful vision of Kate's legs as she lay on her bed was indelibly engraved on his memory.

Even though Kate had provided loads of paracetamol and Fee had given his forehead a powerful 'magic kiss' when he left the cottage, driving back to school was not easy. He was not sure whether he had selected the correct option at a fork in the road by a church. He was, therefore, relieved when he caught sight of the school gates towering beside a hawthorn hedge.

Accompanied by Angela, the Pipes were having their usual Sunday pre-lunch stroll around the school. This was a private ritual which had developed over the years and preceded a generous glass of dry sherry before either Dottie or Angela produced the Sunday roast. They had already passed the changing rooms near the entrance to Roddy's flat when Angela and Dottie had exchanged glances: Roddy's car was not parked in its usual spot. Where was he? Nothing was mentioned as Philip's view on what Roddy got up to, outside the school, was different from theirs.

Dottie manoeuvred herself beside Angela.

"It wasn't there last night either," she whispered.

"Has his attractions, has our Roddy," replied Angela, without betraying her own feelings about him. "Bit of a ladies' man, I should think," she added.

Having known Roddy from early childhood, Dottie only really thought of him as an overgrown toddler. It had never seriously crossed her mind to think of him in terms of male attraction. She decided she would assess him in a different light when she next saw him.

It was only as he was about to turn into the drive that it occurred to Roddy that he might have difficulty explaining his present condition. He had trouble thinking clearly as his head continued to throb like the failing engine of a pre-war lawn mower. Easing the car up the school drive, Roddy spotted Budget in the middle of the front lawn. Budget seemed particularly interested in a smell under a towering horse chestnut tree. Philip and Dottie had already entered their private, side door but Angela remained outside, calling to Budget. Fortunately, Budget responded quickly so there was no question of Roddy colliding with him as he waddled across the drive. Angela, however, observed Roddy's return.

The unusually gentle speed of the Amport Austin was itself suspicious. Unable to avoid eye contact, Roddy gave a half-hearted wave to Angela who made no attempt to disguise her keen observation of the return of the wounded stop-out. Even from twenty metres away, Roddy felt her critical, omniscient stare. He endeavoured to keep his bruised forehead away from her glare but even these measures, he feared, may not have been enough. Was it a knowing half-smile he detected on her face as he passed by?

Angela led Budget inside and, while Philip was pouring the sherry in the drawing room, she took the opportunity to report to Dottie on the latest news: Roddy's car was travelling unusually slowly and its driver seemed to be hunched rather uncomfortably over the wheel.

"What are you two gossiping about now?" asked Philip as he entered the kitchen carrying two generous glasses of sherry.

"I was just telling Dottie that Roddy is back. So there's no need to worry," said Angela.

"Worry? Worry?" replied Philip, clearly a little irritated. "He's a healthy young man, developing into a really promising teacher and he's been out – perhaps overnight."

Dottie and Angela exchanged glances.

Philip continued: "As long as he does his job properly, he's entitled to do as he wishes out of school time. I am not impressed by your clandestine gossiping!"

Dottie sensed that Philip was becoming overwrought and she was worried about his heart.

"All right, dear." She took his arm and led him calmly back to the drawing room.

"Angela and I were just amusing ourselves. A little bit of innocent fun. Roddy's doing well, I realise that."

Philip calmed down as Dottie seated him in his armchair.

"Old fishwives, the pair of you!" said Philip with a twinkle in his eye. "Leave him alone."

Angela heard this and allowed herself a private smile. She was already working on a plan to find out what Roddy had been up to: she would pay Roddy a friendly visit that afternoon.

The Sunday lunch ritual was an agreeable occasion. On Philip's insistence it was usually a traditional roast with plenty of familiar vegetables. Following the sherry, only water was drunk except on special occasions when Philip produced a 'good red', which meant a French wine. The talk was usually and inevitably about school: difficult boys and awkward parents figured regularly. Criticism – Philip called it 'analysis' – of members of the Common Room was also on the list of topics. School numbers was a subject Dottie and Angela always tried to avoid for the sake of Philip's blood pressure.

After lunch, Angela was determined to try and find out where Roddy had been overnight. She calculated that the best time to visit Roddy, assuming he had not disappeared once more, would be around 5.30 pm. It was a time when she might be asked if she would like a cup of tea but it was also close enough to 6.00 pm and therefore there was the possibility of an early evening drink at the Huxton Arms. She could even suggest a drink in her own flat although such a suggestion might prove mutually embarrassing. She spent most of the afternoon marking French exercise books but took a mid-afternoon break from her red pen in order to wash her hair.

It was as she emerged from her bathroom, towelling her dark hair furiously, that she heard the sound of a car on the gravel outside. From her window overlooking the drive, she saw a red Mini. The driver, a young woman, appeared to be stretching and turning her head as if she were either lost or looking for something. The car passed by and eventually stopped in front of the main entrance. The doors, Angela knew, were firmly closed and locked during exeats. Pressing her head to the window pane, she saw the woman get out of the car and walk towards the door. She was now out of sight but Angela, as nosy as ever, guessed she was pressing the large bell. The Pipe's flat was out of hearing range so, forgetting her state of undress, Angela keenly hurried along the corridors and down the stairs to answer the doorbell. By the time she reached the door, the bell had been pressed three times and there was a sense of frustration in its tone.

While Angela undid the heavy bolts and turned the key, the caller was descending the steps, about to abandon her efforts.

"Hello. Can I help?" called Angela.

The caller turned. The young woman, in her early

twenties, was informally but tastefully dressed in black jeans and a pale blue, patterned shirt.

"Oh, I am awfully sorry to bother you but I'm looking for Roddy Amport?"

Angela was putting two and two together – and making five. Was this young lady the reason Roddy stayed out last night?

"Roddy. Roddy Amport?" repeated the woman as Angela took her time to reply.

"This is Whitsborough, isn't it? Whitsborough School?" the woman continued, anxious to fill what appeared to be a frosty silence.

Angela's whirring mind stopped whirring.

"Oh, yes. Yes. Of course. Mr Amport, er, Roddy has some rooms at the side of the school." Angela was about to point the way but then thought she would show her round to them. This would be much more polite and, more importantly, might give Angela the opportunity to engage in some subtle interrogation.

"Come with me. It's just along here…and then up some steps… at the side."

"Oh, thanks. That's very kind of you."

They crunched along the gravel together in an awkward silence. Angela was busy deciding how to start her questioning and the Mini driver was wondering who on Earth this strange woman was. Angela had overlooked the fact that, having washed her hair in the basin, her shoulders were bare and her bra was only partly covered by the towel wrapped around it. Her drying hair was a tightly tangled mess. The Mini driver assumed that Angela was a member of the domestic staff.

When they rounded the end of the main building, they walked towards the changing rooms and the adjacent steps leading up to Roddy's flat.

The Mini driver noted:

"Ah, Roddy's old car. Still unwashed."

This puzzled Angela slightly. When had this girl last seen

Roddy? Possibly not the previous night after all? Angela realised she had wasted the opportunity to ask questions. She desperately wanted to be present when Roddy appeared and the two encountered each other. She was now not sure whether they had, in fact, spent the previous night together.

"I'll show you up to his flat," said Angela.

"Oh, no. Don't worry. I'd like to give him a surprise," said the woman hastily. "It feels like *ages* since I saw him." Angela was further confused: for ardent lovers the word 'ages' might be simply a matter of hours. The woman, she surmised, must be smitten. Angela felt an uncomfortable pulse of jealousy. She was suddenly keen to leave the scene.

"Well, I'll leave you to it." She offered a hand, awkwardly, and then added: "I'm Angela, by the way. Angela Bailey," and then added, after briefly hesitating, "Deputy Head."

This impressive title represented a new - temporary - appointment, of which Philip Pipe, Dottie and the rest of the school were unaware.

"And you are…?" Angela enquired.

The woman was by now at the top of the steps and about to use the heavy, rusting knocker. She turned to look down at the Deputy Head. With perfect timing she rapped on the door and answered Angela's question at the same time. Her reply:

"Rosie……an old friend," was completely drowned by the timing of her firm knocking. Angela was unable to make any sense of the reply. Rosie gave a slight, dismissive wave and a smile.

Angela interpreted the wave as a condescending gesture and cursed herself for not questioning Roddy's visitor more thoroughly. It was only then that she realised that she was still improperly dressed and her upper body was only partly concealed by a towel. She instantly broke into an embarrassed dash for cover.

Rosie to the rescue

Having managed 'to lose' Angela, who had fled back to her flat, Rosie Pitchworth had to knock even more loudly a second time. While she waited, praying that Roddy was present, she spotted, on the flat roof nearby, the sodden remains of a paper aeroplane, a short, plastic arrow and what once may have been a cricketer's batting glove. Rotting leaves appeared to clog some of the gutters. The heavy door needed a coat of paint.

She knocked a third time, now with a feeling of desperation. There was something important that she wanted to talk about to Roddy but she was not sure how she would raise the subject. Perversely, she welcomed the delay before she heard his reply. A feeble voice called:

"Come in. It isn't locked."

Rosie turned the handle slowly. The door opened and led to a short, dark corridor with a worn blue carpet. There were doors on both sides of the corridor, several of them were open. Further along, there was an internal door leading from the flat into the main body of the school. As she tentatively moved past the closed first door, she called,

"Roddy? Roddy? Hello?"

She reached the first open door on the left and saw the figure which had been featuring so regularly in her thoughts. Roddy was lying on his back, on his bed. He was still wearing the clothes he had worn the previous night. They were now badly creased and there was a dark shadow of overnight beard on his face. He was holding an arm protectively across his forehead.

"Roddy! Are you all right?" The call was one of alarm. Roddy did not look well. He moved his arm and peered blearily towards the new arrival.

"Kate?" he mumbled.

"Rosie! Rosie Pitchworth!"

Roddy was not at his sharpest. Rosie moved closer.

"The Cricket Week. Remember? You wrote to me! We

played tennis together and…." She wondered if Roddy was teasing her but in his dishevelled and uncomfortable condition he did not look as though he would be joking.

"Oh, Rosie. Yes. Yes… of course. I'm sorry." Roddy raised his head to have a better view.

"You don't look too good. Are you ill – or is it a major hangover?" Rosie enquired as though Roddy had been a naughty boy.

Roddy attempted to sit up and, as he did so, he removed the arm which had been covering his injury.

"Oooh. Ow! That looks nasty!" winced Rosie as she saw the large bruised lump, the contours of which now bulged from his forehead.

"What happened? It looks horrible"

Roddy made a brave effort to smile.

"I sort of… had an argument – with a door. I was in an old cottage with low ceilings and I…"

"Banged my head. Nasty! I hope the house is still standing!" continued Rosie.

Roddy attempted to smile.

"Well I hope you have been putting ice on it and…" She realised that Roddy had probably just collapsed on his bed

Roddy's failure to reply confirmed her assessment. Rosie therefore switched smartly into control mode:

"Have you got a kitchen here? A fridge? With an ice box?"

Roddy lay back on the pillow again as his throbbing head reminded him of his predicament. He pointed vaguely.

"I do have a so-called kitchen next door. There's not much in the fridge but there may be some ice. I've never really looked."

The 'so-called' kitchen was exactly that, and not much more. It was equipped for a bachelor who rarely cooked: a cupboard, a kettle, a few pans hanging on the wall, a pre-historic gas oven and a small but relatively modern fridge. Clearly Roddy hardly ever used it. There was, fortunately, an ice tray although it was only half full of ice cubes.

Extracting these cubes and wrapping them inside the only tea towel available, Nurse Rosie returned to the casualty ward.

The grateful patient held the ice to his forehead.

"Thanks. I feel better already," said Roddy, managing a half smile.

"Hmm," responded Rosie doubtfully. Her nursing gene – hitherto undiscovered – took over once more.

"Now have you taken any pain relief? Aspirin? Paracetamol?"

"I think I may have taken some this morning. I can't remember."

"Well do you have any here? Or in the school somewhere. Surely the school must have some. Shall I go and ask that Angela woman?"

The pain in Roddy's head seemed to increase suddenly.

"You've met Angela? How come?" he asked nervously.

Rosie thought she detected a note of anxiety.

"Yes, she showed me where your flat was. She was quite helpful. I think she said she was the Deputy Head?"

"The Deputy Head?? We don't have one. I think she was trying to impress you."

This was the last news Roddy wanted; he did not want the Pipes, and certainly not Angela, to know what had happened. They – at least Angela and Dottie - would undoubtedly want to know all the embarrassing details.

"No. Thanks. I'd rather she - and the headmaster- didn't know what happened. They might think I was drunk and had been behaving irresponsibly."

Rosie gave Roddy a look which suggested that she believed that behaving irresponsibly is exactly what he had been doing.

"Well, look. I'll go and get some paracetamol. Surely you want to get rid of some of the pain. I came through a village. Is there a local shop somewhere?"

Rosie insisted on carrying out this mission of mercy. The idea of reducing the pain was simply too appealing and Roddy thanked her and directed her to the petrol station only five minutes' drive away.

Just as Rosie hurried back to the car and had effected a noisy three-point turn on the gravel, the recently appointed Deputy Head (now fully dressed) cast a puzzled eye out of her window. Had Roddy dismissed the woman already? Had he rejected her? How could she find out?

At this point, Philip knocked on the door of Angela's flat and entered unexpectedly. Angela moved quickly away from her window and reluctantly agreed to join Philip in his study in a few minutes time. Philip wanted her help with some paperwork concerning the school's budget. This aspect of being a headmaster was something Philip disliked almost as much as dealing with awkward parents.

Angela was, therefore, unaware of Rosie's later return to Roddy's flat because Rosie now parked her car at the side of the school, next to Roddy's. Once dosed with paracetamol, Roddy felt a little better: not because there was any immediate relief but because there was now the possibility that he would improve. He was very grateful to Rosie and began to question her while one arm remained clasped over his head. Inevitably, the ice began to melt and had to be hastily removed by Rosie when the melt-water began to drip onto his pillow. Roddy had now had time to focus his memory. Rosie? There was the pub, the game of tennis, the swim and – ah, yes - the grassy bank: delightful memories of his Cricket Week.

Rosie had decided to come and find him as she desperately wanted raise an important matter, face to face. However, with Roddy in his present condition, she did not feel that this was the right time. Nevertheless, she chatted at length about her exciting job with the television company, her new flat and her wicked flat mate's activities. She asked Roddy about his teaching. At first, his answers were brief but his pain gradually began to ease. He found that he was able to remove the arm which had been cradling his forehead and he was even able to sit up without too much discomfort.

When Rosie returned from the kitchen, having fetched a glass of water for him, she seated herself on the side of his bed while they chatted. Roddy's pain began to diminish and he gradually became aware, once more, of Rosie's powerful attraction. He had forgotten the warmth of her personality. Furthermore, sitting at an angle on his bed, Rosie's body was not far from Roddy's hands. It's perfect outline was tantalisingly close, a fact of which Rosie seemed unaware – or was she?

The thought passed through his mind that this must be precisely why so many wounded wartime soldiers fell in love with their nurses. This unusual thought sequence, Roddy decided, must have been something to do with the effects of the paracetamol. The thoughts vanished, however, when he began to feel the light touch of Rosie's hand on his knee. Rosie was attempting to gather the confidence she required to raise an awkward subject: the main reason for her visit.

Unfortunately, the sound of someone approaching along the corridor leading to Roddy's flat interrupted her. There was a perfunctory tap on the internal door which led from a first floor corridor. Rosie stood up and moved away from the bed.

"Roddy? Are you all right?" called Angela as she hesitated briefly at the front entrance. She called from a distance, warning him of her arrival in case he was improperly dressed.

Whilst Rosie had a perfectly legitimate reason for her visit, Roddy did not want the two females, with whom he had shared private moments, to meet in his bedroom. But it was too late.

Angela appeared at the door.

"Oh! I'm sorry." Angela was genuinely surprised. "I didn't realise that er... your lady friend was *still* here." Angela made Rosie's presence sound like a mortal sin. "I thought I saw her drive off some time ago."

Roddy made it obvious that Angela was not welcome. He told her how he had clumsily bumped his head at a party the evening before and that his 'lady friend' – using Angela's terminology - had *kindly* been out to buy some paracetamol for him.

"Surely she could have brought some paracetamol with her if she knew about your accident," said Angela, who was still uncertain of the status and identity of Roddy's visitor. Rosie and Roddy exchanged glances but did not give Angela any satisfaction by clarifying the situation. Angela attempted to fill the awkward silence for which she was responsible.

"Anyway I could have found you some in the Sick Room," she continued, before turning to Rosie. "You should have come to ask me, silly girl."

Rosie's face reddened. Being called a 'silly girl' was clearly offensive but Roddy stepped into the ring to defend Rosie with a master stroke.

"Actually, I stopped her from doing that because she did not want to disturb the *Deputy Head* again, Angela."

Rosie was not quite sure of the meaning of this hostility. However, Angela was now clearly embarrassed:

"Ah...well...perhaps I was rather jumping the gun...when I mentioned being Deputy Head. And I think that probably..."

Roddy interrupted her:

"… and you think that you had *probably* better not mention my 'headache' or my friend's visit again, *Deputy Head*?" Roddy now felt that as Angela did not seem to know Rosie's name, this was an advantage he intended to maintain.

Angela understood this not-so-subtle, threatening message.

"Yes. All right, all right." said Angela hurriedly. She gave a nervous half smile and nodded awkwardly to Rosie without managing to articulate a proper apology. She backed away and headed back along the corridor.

Rosie stepped towards Roddy and bent down to give him a huge hug.

"That's for sticking up for me," and before Roddy could reply she placed her index finger over his mouth. "And if you ever need any more ammunition against that woman, just ask her what she was wearing when she first showed me to your flat."

Roddy removed the finger.

"And she was wearing....?" he asked.

"Not very much! Just ask her!"

Roddy smiled. He thought he was beginning to feel much better now. He eased himself off his bed and stood up. For a moment all was well but then he soon began to feel dizzy again. Rosie saw his expression change and helped him lie down once more.

"Slowly. It's going to take time before you can go jumping about again. Lie still!"

Roddy acknowledged her advice.

"Sorry," he said as he closed his eyes. He was unaware of the affectionate pat he received on his chest.

Realising that she would have to wait until another time to talk to him, Rosie found some paper and wrote a note saying that she would be in touch again soon. While Roddy slept, she then descended the steps from his flat, glanced at the untidy mess inside the Amport Austin and drove back along the school drive. She wondered if the Deputy Head would be spying on her.

Kate's guilt after the party.

Only a few miles away, Kate McNally had spent much of the day worrying about Roddy. She felt responsible for his accident and would like to have looked after him. Roddy, however, had insisted on returning to the school. He had stressed that staying out overnight might be acceptable but returning much later in the day – and evidently injured – might lead to awkward questioning. Kate racked her brains to find a way of learning if Roddy was recovering. She understood that there was only one school telephone line and that it would be unwise to use it. She could not, of course, drive to the school on a Sunday in order to attempt to find him.

It was late in the afternoon. Fee had left and Kate's parents had brought Miles home, when she stumbled on an idea: she was tidying a pile of magazines, stacked in a far corner of the dining room, when she noticed the school prospectus that she had been sent by Fiona, the school secretary. She wondered if she could pretend that she had mislaid her copy and needed a replacement to show her parents. She could say that they were considering helping her pay the fees. Surely this did not sound too far-fetched?

If she drove to the school on a Sunday afternoon and asked apologetically for another prospectus, she could (subtly!) ask after that charming young man who showed her round the school: now what was his name?? It would be wiser to wait until Monday but what if Roddy was suffering concussion?

Miles was not at all keen on the prospect of visiting Whitsborough but Kate promised that they would not be there long. She changed her shirt, applied the minimum of make-up and instructed Miles to use a comb.

As her car splashed through the puddles left from the overnight rain, her feelings of guilt about Roddy re-surfaced.

"Look. There's the school," she said after about ten minutes, pointing across a field to some buildings in the distance. Several crows flew near the rugby posts which towered over the playing fields. .

"Mum, I don't think this is a good idea. It's so embarrassing – being seen by all the boys."

"Don't worry. There won't be any boys around. It's an exeat Sunday – that's when the boarders all go home," explained Kate.

"How do you know that the boys won't be there?" asked

Miles turning to look at his mother. Kate cursed herself for trying to be too clever. She could hardly tell her about Roddy and his visit to their cottage.

"Oh, I think the Headmaster's wife mentioned it," answered Kate, "when we visited."

Kate hoped that Miles would drop the subject.

"You mean Mrs Pipe?"

"Yes, that's her name. She seemed very nice," said Kate.

"Yeah, she was OK." There was a long pause and Kate braked at a narrow part of the road to allow an oncoming estate car to pass by.

Miles continued, however:

"I preferred the bloke who showed us round. He seemed *really* OK."

This was high praise in Miles-talk.

"Yes," agreed Kate, "he was really OK!". She smiled inwardly.

"Roddy. His name was Roddy," proclaimed Miles.

"Really? Roddy was it??" said Kate, affecting surprise.

She wondered just how she would have delivered that line if she had been on camera. They were now approaching the school drive.

Miles continued: "And his surname was Amport. Roddy Amport."

Kate was surprised that Miles had been listening so carefully. She believed that Miles had been completely uninterested when they were being shown round.

She turned briefly to look at Miles. They were nearing the school entrance and she briefly took her eyes off the road. She did not immediately see the car that had just emerged from the school drive. There was a sudden, strident blast from the other car's horn as Kate's car had driven across its path. She swerved abruptly to avoid a collision with a bright red Mini being driven by a young woman. There was a brief moment of eye contact as the two drivers passed each other. Miles protested loudly as he felt the car veer violently towards the verge.

"Hey, Mum! Careful!" he screeched.

Kate brought the car to a bumpy halt just beyond the entrance to the school drive. The near-accident was entirely her fault. The other driver did not stop but the blast from her horn had served to express her feelings. Kate's feelings of guilt were now further intensified: first, Roddy's accident in her cottage and now she had almost caused a collision. She thought for a moment and then spoke.

"I'm sorry, Darling. I wasn't concentrating. You're right. I'll call at the school on a weekday, when you aren't with me."

The driver of the red Mini had soon overlooked the near-miss and was hurrying back to London with a feeling of a mission only *partly* accomplished. Not only had she located Roddy but she had managed to tend the wounded beast and earn its gratitude. She had provided Roddy with full details of her address and, now, her phone number. He had promised to be in touch with her as soon as his busy life allowed. The important subject she had hoped to discuss would have to wait.

Roddy, himself, was surprised at how he had reacted to Rosie's unexpected visit. Her genuine warmth and kindness had soon become apparent. He had not realised that she possessed such endearing qualities. During his fitful sleep and gradual recovery, he thought seriously about the women with whom he seemed to be currently involved.

The Angela incident, never to be repeated, was the result of an alcoholic ambush; Suzy was chasing him and he felt that he would not really mind being caught – but of course she was married. Kate was delightful, famous and also a Whitsborough parent who was still, theoretically, married. Amorous involvement with a film star could possibly be the subject of publicity and its resulting complications. Rosie was kind, attractive and seemed genuinely affectionate. He realised now that he had been delighted to see her once more. Any future involvement with her would surely be more straightforward. He would certainly keep his promise and contact her again.

Edwin's Exeat and Norman's accident

Edwin was in fine form when he returned home for the short weekend break. This was a new Edwin: Edwin, the rugby player. This was a boy with a new, powerful string to his bow but he continued to switch into motoring mode at various times. Accelerating up the stairs could be a particularly noisy occasion and when he brushed his teeth there was usually the sound of an idling engine. It was Edwin who, on Sunday morning before going to Church, encouraged his father to join him in the garden. He wanted to play with the rugby ball which Norman had purchased several years earlier. Up until this point, the ball lay unused under the branches of the Cox's apple tree.

Norman at last felt the distinctive thrill of fatherhood as he was instructed to pump the ball up. Cecilia wanted to tell Edwin that his father had been so keen to observe him in action that he had even attempted to spy over a hedge to witness one of his rugby practice sessions. Norman managed to dissuade her from disclosing this particular piece of information and from mentioning the confiscation of his step ladders.

The rugby session in the garden proved to be an eye-opening affair. It was when they started passing the ball that Edwin began to feel uneasy. Mr Amport had shown the boys how to hold the ball, how to pass it and how to receive it. Even the previously termed 'Also rans' of the 3rd XV could now perform these skills with a fair degree of success. Norman, clearly, had never had the benefit of such instruction.

After the Church service, Norman, ignoring both Cecilia's and Edwin's scowls, for once accepted the vicar's invitation to join the other parishioners for coffee in the Church hall. Here, all parochial talk of Church flowers, brass cleaning and hassock mending was suppressed. This was because Norman regaled the assembled group with the news of the important forthcoming rugby fixture against Poppleford Court. Cecilia, aware of the raised eye movements of the attendant group, eventually managed to prise Norman away, hurriedly thanking the vicar and his wife.

After lunch, Edwin returned to his bedroom where he was constructing a rather strange six-wheeled vehicle out of Lego. However, Norman was keen to see if Edwin was using the correct technique when making a rugby tackle.

"But you must be careful. We don't want Edwin to be injured," insisted Cecilia.

Within minutes, Norman had instructed Edwin to hold the ball and to run at him at full speed. Edwin duly obliged and, when Norman was about to waylay him, Edwin pretended to accelerate past by on his father's right flank. As Norman lunged towards him, Edwin swiftly darted to his left, leaving his father to topple over and swallow a mouthful of daisies.

When instructed to have another attempt to evade his father, Edwin this time pretended to go to his father's left, and then to his right, before lowering his shoulder and driving it into the pit of his father's solar plexus. Such uncharacteristic aggression knocked his startled father backwards. Norman banged his head, twisting his knee as he fell and was severely winded.

As Norman struggled to his feet and limped towards the kitchen door, Edwin switched on his engine, shifted into first gear and headed upstairs, back to his Lego.

Cecilia had to drive Edwin back to school that evening as Norman's twisted knee was causing him a great deal of pain. Next morning, after a sleepless night, Norman was taken by Cecilia to the Accident and Emergency Department of the local hospital. An X-ray showed that he had not suffered from any broken bones. He had, however, suffered considerable damage to the ligaments surrounding his right knee. Ice, bandaging and walking with crutches for several weeks should, he was advised, help him to recover. The prospect of attending the all-important Poppleford match as a hobbling spectator did little for Norman's temper.

CHAPTER 14

Roddy's bruise: Next morning.
Roddy slept deeply throughout the night. He could not remember how many paracetamol he had swallowed before going to sleep but they seemed to have had the desired effect. Apart from a slightly muzzy feeling when he woke, the worst effects of the blow to his head had worn off. When he examined his forehead in the mirror, he could not detect any significant damage. Rubbing his fingers carefully over the area, he could feel a raised and slightly tender area.

When he appeared at breakfast, there were a couple of questioning looks but only Drinkall actually mentioned it.

"Had an argument with a doorpost, have you Roddy?"
From behind a Cornflakes packet, Roddy mumbled:

"Yes, something like that."

While he spoke, he caught Angela's eye. She was staring at him inscrutably as she sipped from a large mug of coffee. She did not, however, attempt to engage in conversation with him, fearing that the 'Deputy Head' issue might be raised in any forthcoming verbal skirmishing.

Of course it was in the classroom where the injury was,

indeed, addressed more directly. James Harrison, passed close to Roddy as he walked to his desk.

"Cor! Been in a fight, Sir? Hope you gave the other guy a good smack."

Roddy turned away and fumbled with some books on his desk. By the time he looked up again to start the lesson, all the boys were sitting politely and quietly at their desks. When they did eventually have a full view of the Amport injury, there was a sense of anti-climax. From their desks, only the boys in the front row could detect a mark on Roddy's forehead. A number of disappointed boys turned to Harrison, shaking their heads. Surely, he had been exaggerating.

Later in the morning, when Edwin's class appeared, Edwin stayed behind at the end of the lesson to inform Roddy that his father had been trying to teach him how to tackle at the weekend.

"…and frankly, Sir, I don't think he knows much about rugby."

It was then he noticed the mark on Roddy's forehead:

"Hmm? Did you have a game at the weekend? Bit of a swelling there, Sir."

"A swelling?" Roddy rarely used that word. "A swelling?" he mused. "Yes, that might just have been the cause of the problem," he commented with a wry smile. "Now off you go or you'll be late for your next lesson."

Dottie tours with more 'unsuitable' parents

At the start of the second lesson after Break, Angela appeared at Roddy's door. Roddy had forgotten that he had agreed to let her take the lesson and use it for a practice for the form's French dictation exam. At the time of the agreement, Roddy had appeared reluctant to surrender a lesson but on this occasion the opportunity for a brief rest seemed most agreeable: a time to take a couple of preventative paracetamol.

As he left his classroom, Roddy could hear voices

further along the corridor. Dottie was showing some prospective parents round the school. When he turned the corner near the noticeboards, he almost bumped into the little group. The couple were in their late thirties. The man was wearing a purple silk shirt, jeans and unpolished black shoes. His wife was wearing a revealing white mini skirt, white high-heeled shoes and a short multi-coloured fur coat. Dottie was obliged to introduce Roddy and he quickly sensed that Dottie disapproved of these people. The lack of enthusiasm was evidently mutual. The couple made no attempt to converse with Roddy, even though he politely asked if they had come far.

"London," said the man,

"Clapham Common," added the wife.

"And you have a son? Aged?" continued Roddy politely.

"Twins. Aged eight. We travel abroad a lot. We're in the Rag Trade," explained the woman curtly.

Dottie had no idea what the 'Rag Trade' was but thought it sounded most unseemly.

"So the little bug… boys will have to board," added the father.

Dottie had no wish to let the conversation develop. She did not want these people to become Whitsborough parents. The sooner their visit was over, the better. She wanted to complete the school tour charade as soon as possible.

"Well, we mustn't keep you, Mr Amport," said Dottie firmly and the group exchanged parting nods and mumbles.

Roddy had not previously been fully aware of Dottie's attitude to certain types of parents. It was fairly obvious that she had treated this couple as if they had evolved from an inferior species. Moving further along the corridor, Roddy spotted a figure hurrying in his direction.

"Ah, Roddy. Thank heavens I've found someone. There's no one in the Common Room." It was Fiona, the School Secretary.

"I've got an important overseas phone call coming through at 11.30. It's from Abu Dookah: Wesley's father. I think."

"Sounds interesting. The mysterious father. I'd like to meet him one day."

"But," continued Fiona hurriedly, "a prospective parent – who's already visited the school wants *another* copy of our prospectus – for *her* parents. She's in a hurry and will be dashing in at about 11.30 to collect one. Could you be at the entrance, ready to hand the prospectus over? I may well be on the phone and unable to answer any questions." Fiona raised her eyebrows, betraying her frustration. Roddy shook his head in sympathy.

"Life. Everything happens at the wrong time," he observed.

"Yes, well could you possibly be at the front entrance at 11.30 and hand over the prospectus for me. Philip is out and…"

Roddy interrupted.

"Yes. Of course." He looked at his watch. It was exactly 11.25.

A phone began to ring from the direction of Fiona's office.

"Oh hell! Why do people phone early?" she called as she ran to answer it.

Roddy followed her slowly towards the School Office. Fiona was already speaking in polite, parental mode. It was not the mode that Dottie had been displaying a few minutes earlier. Roddy listened briefly while trying to catch Fiona's attention. She was having to answer questions about dates and times and flights. Eventually, Roddy caught her eye. He mouthed the word 'pro-spec-tus'. Fiona signalled that she understood. She reached into a deep drawer in her desk and took out a large brown envelope containing the important literature. Roddy leaned across her typewriter and took it.

"Thank you," mouthed Roddy.

When he reached the main entrance, he noted a large, white Bentley parked beside the central lawn. Budget lay on the grass not far from the vehicle but appeared unimpressed. Roddy thought it was the latest model and was tempted to walk across the drive and look inside. It evidently belonged to the couple 'in the Rag Trade.' Judging by the disdainful manner in which Dottie was treating them, the Bentley was on its last visit to Whitsborough.

Not wishing to be seen examining the car too enthusiastically, Roddy wandered over to say hello to Budget, passing close to the car as he did so. He greeted Budget who then rolled gratefully on to his back to have his stomach patted. While Roddy stroked him affectionately, he told him about recent events. Budget appeared to understand, waggled his tail and moved his head in response. He sniffed the brown envelope and Roddy explained patiently what he was doing and why he was holding the envelope. During this conversational monologue, a car had driven slowly up the drive. The driver had stopped, had got out quietly and had walked quietly up behind Roddy, who was now gently rubbing his hand around Budget's neck. Budget's legs were pointing skywards and his bright pink tongue was hanging loosely from his mouth in pure enjoyment.

"I was rather hoping you would do that to me sometime," said a voice softly.

Roddy had only just that second mentioned Dottie's name to Budget and he had twitched slightly in recognition. But the voice from behind belonged to an attractive, bemused and gently smiling young woman.

Roddy was startled. What was going on? As he stood, he looked at the envelope properly for the first time.

On it Fiona had written: 'Miss Kate McNally.'

Roddy jumped to his feet, much to Budget's disappointment.

"Kate. What are you do…?" Roddy now understood the

157

situation. "Oh, I get it. It's *you* who wants another prospectus….for your parents???"

"Yes. Daddy thinks the school sounds perfect for Miles."

Roddy smiled, knowingly.

"And that's the *real* reason you came??"

"Yes," replied Kate. She paused and stared back at Roddy who remained silent. "Well, no. Of course that's not the main reason! I felt awful about what happened on Saturday – and wanted to check that you were all right."

Roddy ran his hand gently over the bruised area and Kate moved closer to inspect the damage. A subtle, delightful smell of soap or perfume caused Roddy to remember the unfulfilled excitements in Kate's bedroom.

"It doesn't look too bad now. I was going to come yesterday afternoon – to see how you were. But I lost my nerve at the last minute. Arriving on a Sunday afternoon might have been rather awkward."

Roddy cast his mind back over the events of yesterday afternoon and realised that Kate's appearance would indeed have been awkward. He turned his attention to more immediate matters. He was due to teach another lesson in about ten minutes and was keen to take some precautionary paracetamol. He could not be seen chatting with Kate for too long and she was, reportedly, in a hurry.

"Kate. Thanks for coming and..er…collecting the prospectus. I'm fine now, thanks."

Kate looked doubtful.

Roddy continued: "Well, I will be…very soon. I must go now. I have an English lesson in a few minutes."

Kate looked disappointed and spoke quickly.

"Roddy. I need to see you. We have unfinished business. I think there's the possibility that I may have to disappear filming for a while so I am trying to get the school to accept Miles as a boarder as soon as possible – midway through the term. I spoke to the School Secretary about it on the phone and she thought it should be possible but she would have to discuss it with Mr Pipe."

Roddy's reply was halted because there was the sound of voices at the main entrance. Dottie had completed the tour and was about to say goodbye to the Rag Trade pair in the firm hope of never seeing them again. However, Mrs Rag Trade, taking a final glance at the pleasant lawns in front of the school, noticed Roddy, whom she had met earlier, talking to a striking looking woman. She was instantly convinced that she recognised the woman. Several seconds later, she was able to name her.

"Isn't...isn't that Kate McNally, the actress?" she said excitedly.

Dottie cast her eyes towards the lawn. Had she seen the woman before? Kate McNally? The name seemed familiar. Mr Rag Trade, however, immediately confirmed the sighting.

"But what's she doing here? She's not filming surely?" bubbled Mrs Rag Trade.

By now, Dottie had remembered who she was and how she had found her to be charming – and not at all 'actressy'. Kate had even earned Dottie's approval. With a few more Kate McNally's, Philip could stop worrying about the school's future.

"Yes. That's right. She's sending her boy here. She's delightful," said Dottie nonchalantly. Mr and Mrs Rag Trade exchanged glances and a slight nod. Perhaps Whitsborough was the very place for their twins after all!

Having spotted Dottie, Kate realised that she should leave quickly. She shook hands with Roddy formally. As she did so, she spoke quietly.

"Visit me. Saturday. Supper. Just us." She gave him a deep, tempting stare then hurried to her car. She opened the car door and glanced towards Dottie who was now hoping to catch her eye. They gave each other a brief wave. This, somehow, made Kate feel a little less guilty. Dottie was also pleased to wave; she hoped this familiarity would humble the Rag Traders so that they might feel the school was out of their league.

The paracetamol proved effective and Roddy continued the day without thinking any more about his sore head. The rugby practice went well and Edwin was in particularly good and noisy form. Wesley, too, was developing well. He avoided using his power and speed too often and had learnt to pass the ball accurately. This enabled others to run with the ball and score..

Still in his track suit, Roddy was about to enter the Common Room after the game when Fiona appeared from her office.

"Ah, Roddy. I just wanted to thank you for your help this morning."

Roddy did not immediately realise what she was talking about.

"With the prospectus? Kate McNally?" she explained.

"Oh! That's ok. No need to thank me."

"Well, it's been a good day. Philip's delighted and looking a bit more relaxed."

Roddy awaited a further explanation. Fiona continued:

"Well, Kate McNally has been on the phone several times and she has persuaded Philip to accept her son almost immediately. Apparently she may have to go away filming soon. If so, her son will become a boarder almost immediately."

Roddy could not decide whether this was a good thing or an added complication as far as he was concerned.

"And the other news", said Fiona quietly, "is that we have twins arriving next term. The couple Dottie showed around this morning phoned as soon as they returned to London to confirm that they want to send their sons here. Two more boarders – that's three today! Philip's over the Moon!"

"That's good then," said Roddy who was now beginning to appreciate that money and marketing were just as important to the running of a school as cricket and exams. Fiona moved closer to Roddy and winked before opening the Common Room door.

"But," she confided, "I'm not sure Dottie will be so pleased... when she hears about the twins. I don't think she thought the parents were very...suitable. And, I nearly forgot, I briefly spoke to Wesley's father, Mr Berkshire, on the phone this morning. You may be interested to know that he is hoping to fly back to England from Abu Dookah, just to watch your big match!."

"Just for the Poppleford match? Wow! He must be worth a few bob," said Roddy.

"Yes," Fiona agreed, "but it is to remain a strict secret. Wesley mustn't be told! I am not even sure that his mother knows. Apparently *one* of his secretaries will keep me informed. It seems he is a very important gentleman." She made a gesture of surprise by dropping her jaw and looking upwards.

Roddy smiled: "Well let's hope he does come. Wes is our key man."

"Not Edwin Stevenson?" asked Fiona. "*His* father phones me about three times a week to check that dear Edwin is fit and well."

"Really? Well, Edwin's a great chap," said Roddy, "but I gather his old man is certainly a bit of an... 'enthusiast?' It'll be interesting to meet him as well."

CHAPTER 15

Suzy's plans and Roddy's dilemma

Two days later, Roddy's head felt much better. The Poppleford match was fast approaching and the boys were in fine spirits. Edwin was largely responsible for this as he set a fine example and introduced some more unusual engine impressions during the rugby practices. Roddy's mind was now occupied on the issue of Thursday evening's 'French Lesson'. He remembered clearly the words Suzy had used as he had left the previous week:

"I'll get you next time!"

Roddy's problem was that he was not sure whether or not he wanted to be 'got'. He most certainly enjoyed the physical side of his involvement with women. Previously, however, his relationships had been relatively uncomplicated. But both Suzy and Kate were older and married. He could not comprehend why Kate's husband had apparently 'left' her and could only assume that he must be what used to be termed, 'a bounder' – or worse. Suzy, though, had obviously married Gerald for his money and the lifestyle this provided. Roddy felt a little uneasy about his current predicament although the thought of sharing a bed with either of them would soon dispel this apprehension.

While Roddy was contemplating these forthcoming amorous engagements, Suzy Johnson-Little was in an assertive mood. On Thursday evening, she would strike, cobra-like. Roddy would be at her mercy. This time, there would no escape. With this long-awaited ambition in mind, Suzy entered her familiar, expensive hairdresser's salon on the Wednesday morning. It was more than twenty minutes' drive from her house but parking was easy and there was, importantly, an air of exclusivity about it. She had an idea about how she should look in order to ensnare Roddy; she thought that by having her hair lightened a little and perhaps moving her parting further to one side, she would look rather younger. Anyway, she decided that she would ask Maureen, her 'stylist', what she thought of the idea.

Maureen had been 'doing' Suzy's hair for nearly five years and had proved both an excellent hairstylist and a useful source of local gossip. Suzy rarely visited the salon without leaving enriched by some nuggets of information about people, events and activities in the area. However, Suzy was always extremely careful about what she herself divulged to Maureen.

After about fifteen minutes, Maureen had helped Suzy decide about her ideas for her hair. She had disclosed the 'ridiculous' amount that was being asked for the new, eight-bedroomed ranch being built near the river and mentioned that there were rumours of a big housing development 'somewhere' in the area. It was only near the end of the two hour session that Maureen supplied the most interesting piece of gossip.

"Oh, I know what I was going to tell you," she twittered. "Almost forgot! Your boy is at that boarding school isn't he? Whist...? Whitsbr..?"

"Whitsborough! Yes. Gerald insisted that Taylor went to a school where he could board because that's how he was educated," replied Suzy with a sigh.

"Well guess who was in here last week?" asked Maureen.

Suzy had no idea – how could she? She was tempted to be flippant: Florence Nightingale? Joan of Arc? Princess Margaret? However, she resisted and asked to be told.

"Kate McNally!! The actress! Just moved into the area," announced Maureen proudly, as though she had influenced Kate's decision.

Suzy had seen the film in which Kate McNally had appeared and which had made her famous.

"Oh, that's interesting," said Suzy flatly, not apparently impressed. Then realising that, rather unkindly, she had not appeared to appreciate Maureen's snippet of gossip, she added:

"Well, if she has bought a house nearby, Kate McNally must obviously have good taste."

"She seemed ever so nice," said Maureen, "and she promised to come here again whenever she's at home and not away doing her films, and," she added quietly, aware of a nearby customer's twitching ears, "it'll be good for business."

Suzy turned and noticed that one of the other customers was listening although she appeared to be reading a colourful magazine about kitchen furniture.

Maureen sensed that Mrs Johnson-Little was not particularly interested in the activities of Kate McNally. She did, however, add the relevant piece of gossip which she thought Mrs J-L would savour.

"She said she had been to look at that school of yours – Whits…"

"Whitsborough?" Suzy had suddenly switched to full alert.

"Yes, that's it. She wants to get her little boy in there as soon as possible. Got to go off filming apparently."

"Well, well." replied Suzy, gratefully. Kate McNally would certainly be good news for Whitsborough. Her mind raced ahead to her plans for tomorrow evening. She must certainly ask Roddy if he had, by any chance, come across her.

Ashley Stilton: Chairman of the School Governors

Philip Pipe had not had a meeting with Ashley Stilton for some considerable time. He had, however, received several letters from him indicating that the finances of the school were not at all healthy. Philip had always preferred to sweep financial problems under the carpet and ignore, or at least defer, them for as long as possible.

Ashley Stilton was the perfect example of 'a poacher turned gamekeeper.' A self-made man, he had begun his career selling second-hand cars. He combined the cheeky social skills which had so irritated his school teachers with a sharp business acumen. This brought him into contact with several legitimate car dealerships. He eventually became the sales manager of a German car franchise. Meeting people from the wealthier classes and learning to feel comfortable with them was reward in itself.

He married Jane North from a middle class family and they produced two sons. He joined a golf club where he met some local entrepreneurs who persuaded him to open his own dealership, selling increasingly popular Japanese cars. His privately educated wife persuaded him that the boys should be enrolled at the nearby private school, Whitsborough. The Stilton boys proved to be exemplary pupils. Ashley's own educational failure had taught him a great respect for schooling and he proved to be a remarkably supportive parent, too.

Dottie was always a little frosty towards him but he had managed to 'arrange' a very favourable deal on a car to replace the Pipes' ageing Morris Traveller. Philip persuaded Dottie that the school benefited from Ashley's financial acumen.

It was during his final year as a parent at Whitsborough that Philip Pipe asked Ashley to become one of the school governors, following the retirement of the local vicar. Dottie attempted to resist this move but using Ashley's local contacts, the re-roofing of the main school building was finally completed. Two years later, Ashley was appointed Chairman of the Governors.

However, Ashley's own finances came under pressure. The demand for his Japanese cars was declining. He sought new sources of income. Consequently, he became involved with a small group of local property developers. He was familiar with many of the darker practices of the second hand car trade but the tactics used by property developers to acquire land was, he discovered, in a different league of skullduggery. Ashley, somewhat reluctantly, found himself being drawn in to their murky world.

Philip Pipe's dreams

In the Headmaster's study, Philip was in a good mood. Dottie had now reluctantly become resigned to the acceptance of the 'Rag Traders' urchins' and 'the McNally boy' would also provide a boost to the school's finances. Furthermore, there had been another sign of an upturn in the school's fortunes that morning: a close friend of Kate McNally had phoned and spoken to Fiona. She had been recommended to visit the school for her boys who were unhappy at their London day school. The parents were planning to move out of London, quite possibly into McNally country.

Philip celebrated this positive turn of events by taking a walk around the school and its grounds. It was a bright, but chilly autumn morning. He heaved on his old duffel coat and Budget followed him. Wandering across the games' fields, Philip looked back towards the school. He stopped near the lake while Budget attempted to converse with the resident female mallard. The view Philip had was not at all unpleasant. The main Victorian school building was sound enough and was not entirely without architectural merit. Certainly another coat of paint on the windows would smarten it up but that would be another expense. The new roofing which Ashley Stilton had arranged had proved a worthwhile investment.

What the school really needed, apart from re-painting, was one outstanding new facility: squash courts, a sports hall or an indoor swimming pool. He turned to look away from the school. Hedges bordered the fields and there were distant views over the gentle hills, many of which were neatly ploughed and farmed. .

Philip was temporarily content to cast to one side his concerns about school numbers and the shadow of Ashley Stilton's letters. This morning, he was determined simply to remember why he had chosen to become a headmaster: the busy, fulfilling engagement with young minds and those who attempted to shape them. He wished that he was thirty years younger, busy in the classroom and coaching rugby in the afternoons, like young Amport.

Suzy's plans and Gerald's meeting

Suzy Johnson-Little woke early on the morning of her third French lesson. This was the day on which she would trap her prey, hit the bull's eye and finally score. She wasn't sure which of these metaphors was most applicable but as long as the evening resulted in some abandoned horizontal activity with her very own and very attractive French teacher, she was not too concerned about literary terminology.

The aforementioned French teacher, Roderick Amport, had now fully recovered from his accident. He was relieved that there was no longer any sign of bruising on his head which meant he would avoid any awkward questions from Suzy. Nevertheless, he viewed the day from a different perspective. He had a full morning's teaching ahead. There were two History lessons, two English lessons and a French lesson with some of the younger boys. It was a pleasant combination of subjects, offering scope for the fun and silly games which he and the pupils seemed to enjoy. There was talk of another short match with the 2nd XV which should also prove to be worthwhile as the Poppleford match was now so close. The only matter of concern involved the precise agenda for the evening's activities. He wondered whether he would even be given the opportunity to decide. Suzy's prophetic words spun through his brain:

"I'll get you next time!"

Would he be strong enough to resist? Should he willingly succumb?

Suzy was in a buoyant mood. The only matter that frustrated her was the speed —or lack of it - with which the hour hand on her watch moved. Why did time pass so slowly she wondered? She tidied the sitting room several times, even though her cleaner had been in the house only the day before. She knew that Roddy would not notice this but she wanted everything to be perfect. She even showered a second time in the afternoon, just in case. Just in case – what? Suzy recognized her own excitement but could not control it. By five o'clock, she was tempted to calm herself with a glass of sherry but felt that this would spoil the pleasure of the first drink of the evening with Roddy; the Sauvignon Blanc was already nestling in the fridge for that delicious moment.

It was as she was in her bedroom, brushing her hair for the fifth time that afternoon that her world fell apart. Gerald's car appeared in the drive. He was supposed to be in London, staying the night at his club. What was going on?

She rushed downstairs and met him in the large entrance hall where she had placed some fresh flowers.

"Gerald, Darling," she said giving him a dutiful hug. "It's Thursday. I thought you were staying in London."

Gerald gave her a hurried, perfunctory peck on the cheek.

"Yes, I know...but there's been a cock-up. You know this housing development scheme I've been slightly involved in…."

Suzy looked vague. She never took much notice of his

business activities. Had she heard anything about it? She thought not.

"You know. The meetings I've been to at the golf club. About some land that may be coming available."

Suzy feebly attempted to remember but was mainly wondering why Gerald was at home?

"Well I know you and your chums are up to something but I'm sure it's nothing I'd find interesting," she replied, wondering where this was leading.

"Well, Roger has gone and called another meeting at short notice. Apparently we've got to make some decisions – pronto."

Gerald headed into the kitchen to make himself some coffee. Suzy followed and asked him, nonchalantly, how long he would be out. How much time would she have with Roddy? Gerald turned to look at her and paused before replying. Suzy sensed an answer being formulated – one that she would not like.

"Well, because this is such a last minute arrangement, Roger couldn't book the committee room at the club. His house – and Peter's - are full of kids… There wasn't time to ask anyone else - so I said they could come here."

Suzy's face dropped. Blood rushed around her body in all sorts of strange directions. Gerald moved quickly over to her and placed a consoling arm around her.

"But don't worry. We are not going to upset what you may have planned for the evening."

A puzzled Suzy edged away from Gerald. She did not appreciate this unusual display of affection.

"No," continued Gerald. "Don't worry. I shan't expect you to provide supper for all of us."

He appeared to think that this most considerate act was worthy of Suzy's gratitude: gratitude which was not forthcoming.

"No, indeed. I have arranged for the Chinese restaurant in the town to deliver food for us."

Suzy turned away quickly and ran upstairs. Not only was

Operation Amport ruined but she could not allow Gerald to see how upset she was. Tears were flowing freely down her cheeks by the time she was halfway up the stairs.

Gerald, thoughtful as ever, called after her:

"Shall I phone the restaurant and order a dish for you, too, Darling?"

The bedroom door closed and Suzy's face was buried in one of the huge pink tissues from the box on her dressing table. She stared into the huge mirror, thinking:

"Dish? Dish! I had already bloody-well ordered one….. And he's due here, soon!"

She sat, looking at her miserable reflection, crying and wiping away her tears. She felt like throwing all her brushes, combs and make–up across the room. The mixture of frustration and pent up desire was a dangerous one. Although tempted to give full vent to these powerful emotions, she realised that even Gerald might wonder why she was reacting so vehemently. Suzy had her suspicions about what Gerald got up to when he stayed overnight in London but she did not want him to start having doubts about her own fidelity.

She decided to have a hot shower, her third of the day, while she regained her composure. By the time she was drying herself after a full ten minutes standing motionless under the shower and fighting back her remaining tears, she began to think clearly once more.

She looked at her watch. It was later than she thought. Roddy would arrive at the house in an hour or so. She certainly did not want him to run into Gerald's golf club cronies. She would have to stop him coming. They could not risk being spotted together in a pub or restaurant and, anyway, the activity that she had anticipated so intensely required rather more comfort and privacy.

How could she contact Roddy and tell him not to come? She did not dare phone the school in the evening as she might have to speak to the headmaster or his wife. She could hardly ask them to pass a message on to Roddy saying that their 'lesson' was cancelled. She would simply have to intercept him in her car and stop him reaching the house. Yes, that was it. It shouldn't be too difficult. After all, not many people in her tree-lined road drove a car like Roddy's.

Roddy prepares for the French lesson

In his flat, Roddy was changing out of his games kit before the Common Room supper. He was in two minds about how to approach the evening's liaison with Suzy J-L. Unfortunately, he was well aware that Suzy was firmly of only one mind: "I'll get you next time!" was clearly imprinted on her brain.

Roddy would have enjoyed using his excellent French and trying to convey some of his knowledge to Suzy. But there was another part of him which might readily respond to Suzy's feminine wiles. He decided he would play it by ear.

The Common Room supper proved noisier than usual. Drinkall, who often stayed for supper although he lived in a nearby village, was attempting to sell a car he had recently bought 'from a friend.' A possible purchaser was Miss Mia Lilliford, a peripatetic piano teacher who had stayed after lesson time for a free supper. Drinkall's immaculate 'low mileage' Ford was, it transpired, eleven years old and had rarely been driven by its elderly owner.

Drinkall seemed to think that this would be an easy sale because Miss Lilliford appeared very interested and suitably gullible. However, Drinkall had not observed the wink that Miss Lilliford had directed towards several other residents. She led Drinkall on with all sorts of deliberately naïve questions about whether the owner had been a vegetarian and if he had ever visited Egypt. Drinkall was becoming increasingly frustrated and Roddy slipped out at the same time as the Head of Science was trying to mask his tears of laughter by mopping his brow. Briefly, Roddy caught Angela's eye as he passed by but she said nothing.

She was busy enjoying seeing Drinkall, for once, being taken for a ride.

While Roddy was setting off, driving quietly away from Whitsborough, Suzy was trying to formulate her plan to intercept him. If she did not set off soon, she feared her car, nestling in the double garage, would be trapped in the drive by Gerald's guests' expensive saloons. Apparently unaware of the private tutoring his wife was due to receive, Gerald busied himself preparing the dining room table for 'a working supper.' It was only as Suzy announced that she was slipping out to buy some more milk from the late night shop that Gerald mentioned the French lessons.

"I forgot. Isn't it today when your French chappie comes? I've only just remembered," called Gerald.

"No. He couldn't make it this week. He's busy. Something on at school, apparently," replied Suzy, hoping there would be no awkward follow-up questions.

"Oh, perhaps Taylor will tell us about it. I'm sorry if you're disappointed, Darling. I know how much you enjoy learning French."

"Oh it's all right. I quite enjoy some of it. Bye. Won't be long. I'm just popping down to the corner shop." Suzy hurried out of the front door. She could feel tears forming again.

She planned to park her car near the junction at the end of her road, facing the oncoming cars. She parked in a suitable spot, close enough to one of the few streetlights so that Roddy would see her. She waited for nearly a quarter of an hour. Only one car passed her. She thought she recognised it as belonging to a neighbour; it certainly was not the Amport automobile. A few minutes later, a couple of large saloon cars drove by slowly, as if searching to locate an address. Could they be looking for her house to attend Gerald's meeting, she wondered? She turned to watch them over her shoulder. As she did so there was a sudden tapping at a side window. Suzy was startled as a figure was now standing close to the car. A face pushed close to the passenger door. It was Patricia Allbury accompanied, inevitably, by her canine treasure, Bruce, wrapped in his tartan coat.

Suzy leaned across to wind down the window.

"Hello, Dear. Are you all right. Not broken down or anything?" asked Mrs A. leaning in to see if there were any passengers.

Somewhat relieved that she was not about to be assaulted, yet irritated that once again the omnipresent Allbury had appeared at the wrong moment, Suzy gave a flustered reply. There was nothing wrong, Suzy explained; she was simply checking in her handbag to ensure that she had brought her purse with her....as she was about to go to buy some milk.

Mrs Allbury's sharp eyes, however, spotted the handbag, untouched and unopened on the passenger's seat. She made no comment. Instead, she apologised for disturbing Suzy. As she stood up and backed away from the car, she was framed in the headlights of a car which had just turned into the road. The noisy engine of an old Austin passed by.

Suzy turned, in time to see it heading along the road.

"B***er!" she exploded.

Mrs Allbury suddenly appeared to hesitate. Had she just heard Suzy's expletive correctly or had she recognised Roddy's car from last week?

By the time Edna Allbury and Bruce had moved on, Suzy had innocently executed a three-point turn without attracting further Allbury attention. Roddy had pulled up in the Johnson-Little's ample drive where Gerald's car had now been joined by two others. Unsure what to do, Roddy, nevertheless, got out of the car and walked hesitantly towards the door. What was going on? Whatever it was, it seemed likely to scupper any amorous activities planned by Suzy 'I'll Get You Next Time' Johnson-Little. He was not sure whether he was relieved or disappointed.

While he rang the doorbell, wondering who he was about to encounter, he did not notice another car arrive in the drive and park behind his car. Roddy waited but had to ring the bell a second time before the door was opened by Gerald. Gerald was in the process of uncorking a bottle of Burgundy. He recognized Roddy although he could not remember his name.

"Oh? Hello," he said in surprise, "Suzy's out at the moment. She said you couldn't come this evening. Said you were tied up at school. Something special on?"

Roddy was about to reply but the latest arrival was also at the door and was greeted by Gerald:

"Ah! Good evening, Ashley. Do come in."

Gerald nodded towards Roddy. "Bit of confusion here," he explained. "This young chap…"

"Roddy…..Roddy **Amport**," insisted Roddy who felt he was being introduced as if he were a ten-year-old.

"Er, *Roddy*, here, has come to give Suzy her weekly French lesson but she's out. She thought the lesson had been cancelled." Gerald added an after-thought: "Oh, and he teaches at Whitsborough."

"Whitsborough. Really?" replied Ashley awkwardly, giving Roddy a perfunctory nod as he edged passed him, keen to avoid further conversation. "Perhaps I ought to join the others?"

Roddy had a feeling that Ashley – was that his first name or his surname? – seemed slightly embarrassed.

Gerald, however, was more civil:

"I'm very sorry if there has been some misunderstanding – but I must look after my guests. We have a rather important meeting. I'm sure Suzy will be in touch."

Roddy managed to control a wry smile at the use of the word 'touch'.

"Please tell your wife that I apologise if there has been some misunderstanding. Shall I try again next week?" asked Roddy innocently.

"Oh yes do! I'm sure she will be disappointed to have missed you. I'll be staying in London….as usual…at my club," confirmed Gerald.

The door closed and Roddy returned to his car. He was obliged to execute a rather difficult manoeuvre as his Austin had become sandwiched between two of the guests' cars. One of these, a large foreign car parked behind Roddy's, bore the number plate: 'AS 777'. This, Roddy assumed, was Ashley's car and in avoiding it he was compelled to leave the imprint of two of the Austin's tyres on one of Gerald's flower beds; one recently planted azalea would not now be flowering the following Spring.

Had it not been for a small grey van, which had just drawn up near the entrance to the Johnson-Little drive, Roddy would have spotted Suzy, waiting for him in her car. The van, however, obscured his view. Suzy had planned to flag Roddy down when his car emerged from her drive.

She was about to jump out of her car when the grey van had unexpectedly pulled up right in front of her car. The driver, a small, Oriental gentleman, got out, walked back to Suzy's car, knocked on her window and bowed. He thus prevented Suzy from opening her door. She had to wind down her window to answer the driver's barely intelligible questioning. It transpired that he had come to deliver a Chinese meal but could not locate the exact house.

While Suzy attempted to explain that the van was in her way and that the house lay almost in front of him, Roddy pulled out of the drive and drove past, not noticing that the J-L huntress was lying in wait for him, her car partially hidden by the grey van. Suzy shouted at the delivery man as she produced copious tears of frustration.

Roddy settles for a quiet pint?

Roddy drove back to Whitsborough trying to decide whether he was relieved or disappointed. He was completely foxed by the fact that Suzy had, apparently, fabricated some sort of strange story about him being busy at the school. Having insisted that she would 'get' him next time, he realised something significant must have upset her plans. He could only guess that Gerald had returned unexpectedly.

He came to a familiar road junction where he intended to turn right. But, below one arm of the old signpost, there was a wooden sign with a pointing arrow.

It read: 'The Huxton Arms.'

The thought of a pint of bitter was immediately appealing and the Austin seemed to make the decision for him. Five minutes later, Roddy was standing at the welcoming bar ordering himself a much-needed pint.

There were only a few customers, mostly locals, and he chose a comfortable table near the hearth where a large, solitary log glowed softly. He picked a magazine from the pile on the nearby shelf but as he turned the first page, a familiar voice said,

"Well you can put that away. I'll have a pint, too. Since you ask."

"And mine's a…."

Roddy turned to see two familiar faces.

"…Gin and tonic, yes ok", interrupted Roddy with a half-smile.

He ordered the drinks and tried to think of an excuse to explain his presence, alone, at the Huxton Arms. He expected some awkward questions. Resisting any determined interrogation meted out by the combination of Angela and Drinkall would be difficult. He carried their drinks back to the table. 'Name, Rank and Number only' were the words which occurred to him. He wondered how long he could hold out under stiff interrogation. Why was he here alone, they would ask. He prepared for the worst.

Rather surprisingly, it was Angela who launched into conversation; she could not wait to tell Roddy the latest gossip. She was bursting to tell Roddy exactly how the dialogue at the Common Room supper had developed after he had left. Drinkall endeavoured to staunch her monologue before it began but Angela had no intention of missing such a golden opportunity. Drinkall was therefore obliged to sip his pint while Angela imaginatively described the events at supper in detail.

She colourfully described how Miss Lilliford, the visiting piano teacher, had led Drinkall on…further and further… up the garden path. Miss Lilliford, it seemed, had become increasingly enthusiastic about the possibility of buying the car which Drinkall was so eagerly trying to sell. Joyously, everyone else at the table shared the joke, suffering paroxysms of suppressed laughter as the apparently naïve Miss Lilliford sought evermore irrelevant information about the provenance of the car and its one, former owner. Angela located a tissue in her handbag and wiped tears from her cheeks as she tried to remember the exact questions fashioned so wonderfully by Miss Lilliford:

"Has the car ever been serviced by a man with a lisp?" and "Was the previous owner, by any chance, fond of curry?"

"Ok, Angela. Enough. So I was 'had.' Even the greatest salesman occasiona.."

"Salesman!!" exploded Angela.

"….*occasionally* makes a mistake," continued Drinkall defensively.

Roddy wished he had been present for the full performance. He would now view Miss Lilliford in a different light as, indeed, would the rest of the Common Room. All members would undoubtedly soon learn of the great Drinkall 'wind-up'.

"Ok, Angela. Enough? And I'll go and buy another round," offered Drinkall.

"Enough," agreed Angela, handing over her empty glass and wiping tears from her eyes. The wooden table showed signs of some miniscule spots of gin and tonic which had recently been expelled at a high velocity. Angela rubbed a tissue over the area with little effect.

"D.D. seems to have taken it reasonably well," remarked Roddy.

"Well, he hasn't got much choice. Not many members

of the Common Room have escaped his sharp tongue. This is payback. Big time!"

When D.D. returned with the drinks, Roddy thought the attention would now be focused on him. Where had he been? Why was he here, on his own? But Drinkall was determined to use the occasion to question Angela. He had gamely suffered from the banter, now he wanted a reciprocal response from Angela.

Drinkall was convinced that she had knowledge of the school's reputedly precarious financial position. He took a sip of his second pint.

"So what's going on behind the scenes, Angela? What's are the Pipes up to?" he asked, leaning forward conspiratorially.

Angela paused before answering.

"I am afraid, *Mister* Drinkall, that I haven't a clue what you're talking about." She stared back at him.

"Oh come on, Angela. You know exactly what I am talking about. There are rumours flying everywhere. Old Les Kent has picked up gossip in the town."

Angela stared at him once more.

"I repeat. I do not know what you are on about."

D.D. was about to argue the point but Angela volleyed, just in time:

"And even if I did, I most certainly would not be telling you."

"OK. Ok" Drinkall raised his hands in surrender. "It's just that it seems there is a strong rumour that the school is in trouble. Financially."

Angela replied defensively.

"Oh, well, there's always pressure on numbers in a small school, especially when there are boarders' places to fill. Philip has been living with that problem for years."

Drinkall tapped his heart several times: a significant gesture.

"Look, he's had a slight heart problem for ages," Angela explained. "It's under control and, before you interrupt, things are looking up, numbers wise. There have been some good signs recently. A number of positive enquiries. That's all I am going to say!"

It was clear to Roddy that this line of conversation was over. He feared the next line of questioning would be directed at him. He therefore explained that he had some preparations to complete for one of tomorrow's lessons. He moved quickly to avoid further conversation and the embarrassing possibility of having to give Angela a lift back to school.

Suzy has tears - but she uses her ears

The fact that Suzy had failed to 'get' her man yet again was a source of great frustration. Gerald's decision to hold his wretched meeting at their house was annoying. But the fact that the stupid Chinese meal delivery man had prevented her from intercepting Roddy was doubly maddening. She had already exhausted her reservoir of tears as she entered the house having had to park her own car in the road outside as there were now several large cars blocking the driveway.

She dutifully, but briefly, exchanged pleasantries with a couple of Gerald's mafia friends before disappearing into the downstairs study where she consoled herself with a large glass of sauvignon blanc, a box of tissues and a familiar video starring Cary Grant and Audrey Hepburn. Although she was well acquainted with the plot, she had to leave the film near the end to go to the kitchen to fetch some more tissues; her tears were flowing once more as the character played by Audrey Hepburn appeared to be in a critical state after the famous road accident scene.

It was while she was returning to the study that she stopped and overheard a little of the discussion from the drawing room. She caught a few snatches of the conversation about 'fifty new houses' and '…. yes, but Pipe would never…' This sentence was never completed because a voice interjected forcefully:

"Just let *me* handle the Whitsborough issue." Gerald emerged from the room at this point to fetch another bottle of wine.

"Are you all right, Darling?" he asked, spotting the tissues and tears.

"Yes. Thanks. It's just that the film I'm watching is rather sad."

"Why on Earth you watch those weepies of yours…?" He shook his head and moved past her, giving a weak smile. When Suzy returned to the study, she sat and thought for several minutes before returning to Audrey Hepburn's hospital bed.

What *were* Gerald and his cronies up to and why did their furtive meeting involve Whitsborough? This secrecy worried her. Their son was at Whitsborough, of course, but he wouldn't know anything. She would have to confront Gerald about it although she guessed that he would simply dismiss her questions.

CHAPTER 16

Kate goes filming: Fee to the rescue.

The pace of Kate McNally's life was moving fast: too fast. The break–up with her husband, the move to the country, finding a suitable school for Miles and then the sudden necessity to go abroad filming at short notice were all pressures she would rather have avoided. She felt that she could have coped – if only there had been time in between each of them. And then there was Roddy: any pressure from his direction, however, would have been welcomed. .

Because Miles would be joining the school in the middle of the term, there was little time for preparations. School uniform, sports kit, rugby boots and all the paraphernalia of pyjamas and wash-bags had to be obtained. This necessitated trips to the nearest town's clothing outlets as well as a visit, with the school secretary's help, to the school's second-hand clothing store.

To her great disappointment, Kate did not bump into Roddy while she was at the school. When Kate and Miles returned home, there was a telegram pinned to the door. It was from Kate's agent, Thelma.

"Plan changed. Flight Heathrow BA 9307.   Saturday: 1840hrs. Imperative!"

"Bugger!!" exploded Kate.

"Mum!!" Miles pretended to be shocked although Kate had occasionally used this word before.

"It looks as though there's been a change of plan. I'm going to have to leave for Athens on Saturday instead of Monday. Blast! I'm sorry, Darling. I'll have to ring Granny and Grandpa. You'll have to stay with them on Sunday night as well as Saturday and they can take you to school on Monday morning. Will that be awful for you? I'm so sorry."

Miles took the news stoically:

"I'll manage…I suppose."

Kate gave him a huge, smothering hug.

"I'd better phone Thelma to check the details and then just hope that Granny and Grandpa are available…and in a good mood." She gave Miles a consoling smile and he disappeared into his room to return to the inviting pages of his latest Hornblower adventure.

It was only after she had contacted her apologetic agent and then spoken to her mother on the phone, that Kate had a moment to gather her thoughts: Roddy? She had invited him to supper. How could she contact Roddy to tell him the situation and cancel their assignation? She dared not visit the school yet again and leaving him a phone message was risky and out of the question.

Later that afternoon, the phone rang. It was her old friend, the irrepressible Fee, Kate's closest and bounciest friend. Fee disclosed that she had found herself 'spare' at the weekend. No one had asked her to a party or out for supper. Being lonely in London, she moaned, was a miserable way to spend a weekend. Kate informed her of her own predicament. A crazy thought suddenly struck Kate. Was it a stroke of genius or a touch of madness?

"Fee, you know how much you like cooking? The supper you produced at my party was an international sensation. Well, as you're so keen to get out of London, why don't you drive down here on Saturday and cook supper… for a mystery man? I'll leave a key and you can stay as long as you like."

Fee was intrigued: the cooking would be no problem but who was the mystery guest? Fee giggled and said that she would only come if the man was good-looking, desirable, available, and, she added, preferably..under sixty. Yes, he was certainly all of those things said Kate who then misled Fee by saying that she was not *exactly* sure of his age and that if he was a touch over sixty then he certainly did not look it. Fee was hooked. But, of course, she demanded to know the name of the man.

Was he, Fee wanted to know, as dishy as Roddy, the chap who banged his head? Ah, well, Roddy was rather special stated Kate; there weren't many Roddys around. The man who was coming, however, was definitely a suitable substitute and certainly worth cooking for. .

The details and a hiding place for the key were agreed and Kate promised that there was plenty of wine. Fee was excited. She insisted on providing the food and then immediately phoned her hairdresser.

"How many drips make a shower?"

Saturday proved to be a busy day for Roddy. He had a full teaching programme and was on duty during the various breaks. This meant supervising 'Biscuits' during morning break, checking that the boys were sensible during lunch and that there was acceptable behaviour in the changing rooms before and after 'Games'.

This was the last Saturday before the Poppleford match and Roddy had to admit to a quiet glow of satisfaction as he watched the boys play. Edwin continued to be an inspiration although his engine had seemed to be noticeably quieter in recent practices. Roddy had commented on this.

"Don't worry, Sir. Just saving fuel. You wait until next Saturday!" Edwin explained.

Wesley, who had restricted his efforts to the odd burst

of speed and unselfish passing, commented that, "Preparation for an important game requires more than just the physical effort, Sir. The mental approach is equally important. Inner tranquility and composure – the calm before the storm – often produces the best results." Roddy wished that Wes had delivered the pre-match talks when he had been a boy in school teams.

Changing Room duty, Roddy believed, was the worst part of the day. The boys were instructed to shower after games, removing all traces of mud and sweat. The master on duty was supposed to keep an eye on this activity but the water was, according to the boys, often too cold. Excuses were rife.

On this particular day, Roddy engaged in a forthright and challenging discussion with Richard Hughes in the changing rooms. He had felt obliged to challenge Hughes about whether he had, in fact, showered 'properly.' Hughes replied that if Mr Amport would be kind enough to define his terms, then he would be able to provide an answer. In essence, Hughes wanted to know how many seconds he needed to stand underneath a shower in order for it to be deemed 'proper'. Two seconds? Five? Seven?

And then, of course, there was the question of the force of the shower. Did *five* seconds under a dripping shower fulfil the term: a *'proper'* shower, more than *two* seconds under a shower with a much greater force?

The discussion began to attract the interest of a number of other boys who were also changing in this corner of the room. Malcolm Elliot, who was in the top set for Maths and therefore possessed 'boffin' status, introduced the notion that it was all about the number of 'drips per second'. Roddy agreed that this was a concept worthy of further investigation but he declined Hughes' invitation to enter the shower room and actually attempt to count the number of drips falling over a given period of time. Roddy wrapped up the argument with a grin by noting that there were rather too many 'drips' in the changing room already.

As intended, the boys took mock offence to this insult and feigned outrage. Hughes led the protesting group out of the changing rooms with the words:

"Sir! That is a cheap and unworthy insult. You will be hearing from my solicitor in due course."

There were grins and waved fists as the group left. It was light-hearted exchanges like this that Roddy found particularly agreeable.

It was not until after six o'clock that he had any time to himself. Having returned to his flat, he stepped into the shower which ran into his bath. He observed wryly that it delivered such a feeble volume of water that he could almost have counted the number of drips per second – on just one hand.

Just as he reached the bottom steps outside his flat and walked towards his car, Budget suddenly appeared and wandered towards him with his tail wagging. Roddy bent down and gave him a few firm pats on the back.

"Saturday evening. Going out to play, Mr Amport?" called a familiar voice.

Angela walked towards him.

Why, he wondered, did Angela always have to spot him when he was about to meet another woman? Was she telepathic?

Angela delayed her final question until Roddy was entering the car:

"And who's the lucky lady?"

She *was* telepathic!

"I'll bet it's the girl who came looking for you last Sunday afternoon?"

Roddy did not reply. Angela had got that bit wrong so perhaps she wasn't telepathic after all. Which, bearing in mind his plans for the evening with Kate, was just as well.

No Kate?

Roddy drove down the narrow, twisty lane leading to Kate's cottage. His 'duty' day had passed satisfactorily and he was now looking forward to the evening's activities. He subconsciously rubbed a hand over his forehead.

Where the lane opened out into the meadowland opposite the cottage, a barn owl flew low in front of the car. It disappeared somewhere behind the cottage. The lights inside the cottage offered a warm glow and he thought he could see the outline of a figure moving near a downstairs window.

When he got out of the car, he could smell cooking, something roasting, perhaps? He had not eaten anything at all since lunch time and was certainly hungry. He walked towards the front door and was about to knock when the door flew open.

"Roddy!" was the delighted exclamation that greeted him.

"F...!" Completely surprised, Roddy nevertheless managed to avoid the use of an expletive.

"Fee! Oh good! You remembered my name.... from the party last week." Fee took two steps towards the dumbfounded dinner guest and gently smoothed her hand across his forehead.

"And that certainly looks a lot better than the last time I saw it."

She reached up and gave Roddy a gentle peck on the cheek. She then took his hand, led him inside and instructed him not to speak before she had poured him a large drink. She would then explain all. She thrust him into an old armchair.

Fee soon re-appeared, carrying a powerful gin and tonic. She handed it to Roddy and sank into the chair opposite. She took a substantial gulp from her own glass and then began to explain about Kate's enforced change of plan.

She informed him that Kate was mortified but simply couldn't risk contacting him again at the school to cancel. "To say that she was disappointed......" Fee's summary tailed off and she shook her head from side to side.

Roddy responded with several slow nods.

"Ah…so Kate's been summoned to film…?" said Roddy

Fee interrupted: "She *had* to go. There was no choice. Fortunately she had already made arrangements with her parents – about looking after Miles."

"Oh yes. Of course. He must be starting at Whitsborough on Monday," observed Roddy.

Fee took a deep breath:

"So the thing is – that you've got me – as a replacement - for the whole evening. Kate hoped you'd understand. But I have cooked supper."

"Do you mean you have come all the way - from the excitement of London – just to cook supper… for me?" asked Roddy.

"Well, yes. I suppose I have," replied Fee as if it were a surprise to her.

Roddy stood up, put his glass down on a small drinks table, paused and then bent over Fee and gave her a gentle kiss – on her forehead.

"Thank you. I'm feeling ravenous. I can't wait to sample your wonderful cooking again."

Fee stood up, took a gulp of gin – she had not mixed it with much tonic – and felt much relieved.

"Right. Now you just relax while I get on in the kitchen."

The roast lamb proved a huge success with Roddy who tended to rate food in terms of quantity rather than quality. Fee's cooking, however, rated highly in both departments. On Kate's instructions, Fee made full use of the wine available and she was keen to keep Roddy's glass topped up.

Time passed quickly. Conversation ranged easily over schooldays, families, films, university experiences and Kate's success. Roddy suspected that Fee had seduction in mind so whenever she entered the kitchen to fetch another dish or bottle, Roddy tipped his regularly replenished glass of wine into Fee's glass. Thus, Fee became evermore giggly and sozzled as the evening progressed.

It was after eleven when Roddy stated that he would go

into the kitchen and make some coffee while Fee deservedly relaxed. He guided her into a deep arm chair but she held onto his arm.

"Give me a big kiss first, Mr Amport. A proper one this time," begged the inebriated chef.

Roddy obliged with a momentary but generous commitment of his lips. He then moved smartly away and Fee seemed to be temporarily satisfied.

"Mmmm. That was good. Jush you wait 'til you come back," mumbled Fee.

However, Fee was soon fast asleep, making a series of odd nuzzling noises. Roddy placed the washing-up in the dishwasher, found some paper and wrote a note of thanks. He said that he looked forward to seeing her again - *with* Kate (!) Thankful that he had not had too much to drink, Roddy drove back to school. He half expected to see a light on in Angela's flat but was relieved to observe that there was no sign of activity there.

A meeting with Rosie?

There was, unusually, evidence of an intruder having visited his flat while Roddy had been with Fee. A large sheet of paper was pinned beneath some exercise books on the table in his small sitting room. Scrawled in Angela's distinctive writing was a note:

"A friend called Rosie phoned. Please contact her urgently (phone number below) either late tonight or early tomorrow morning."

Angela had added a note: "She sounded rather upset."

Angela's additional comment was, Roddy felt sure, her way of letting him know that she was keeping her penetrating eyes on him.

It was late now and using the school phone in the Common Room would have required a trip through darkened corridors, possibly disturbing sleeping boarders. He certainly liked Rosie and she had acted as a considerate and capable nurse. He rubbed his forehead thoughtfully and decided to phone her early in the morning. He set his alarm for 7.15 am and planned to phone her as soon as he was dressed. Even Angela, he felt sure, would not be in the Common Room so early on a Sunday morning.

The noise of a door slamming somewhere along the corridor woke Roddy five minutes before his alarm was due to go off. He dressed quickly and decided to shave after he had made his phone call. He could hear a few boys talking quietly in their dormitory as he scurried past.

The Common Room was empty even though he had half expected to find Angela there on some spurious pretext. Rosie answered the phone almost immediately.

"Roddy, thank you so much for phoning back. How are you now? Your head was looking ghastly when I saw you."

"I'm fine, thanks but I now tend to duck instinctively whenever a plane flies overhead."

"Well that's a relief," giggled Rosie.

Roddy thought she did not sound at all upset and decided that Angela had over dramatised Rosie's earlier phone call.

"And how are *you*?" asked Roddy. "How is your new job?"

"Oh, that's going quite well. I come into contact with lots of different people. It is just learning all their names, what their roles are and who to ask when I don't know something...all fairly inevitable in a new job...but it takes time."

The conversation flowed easily. Rosie asked questions, listened to the answers and responded to Roddy's enquiries thoughtfully.

After several minutes Rosie informed Roddy that she had phoned him because she needed to talk to him, face to face. It was an important matter which she did not wish to discuss on the phone and which she had decided not to mention during his 'sore head' episode. She wondered if Roddy was free to meet the following weekend. Roddy explained that next weekend he was on duty all day on the

Sunday, and that on the Saturday there was the Poppleford match. He explained to her how important this was. Rosie quickly grasped its significance.

Roddy now detected disappointment in her voice. Was she upset, he wondered? He recalled how kind and sympathetic she had been the previous Sunday.

"Look," said Roddy, "if this is so important, I could probably meet you today for a little while. I have promised to show the boarders a film at 4.00 pm and I must not let them down. But if you could drive to…"
Rosie interrupted.

"Oh, no! Damn! I've lent my car to Melissa for the weekend. It'll be in Norfolk!" said Rosie, sounding downhearted.

"What about catching a train?"

"I could do that." Rosie perked up.

"Suppose I drove to Newbury. I think that's on the London line…," suggested Roddy.

They arranged to meet at midday for a couple of hours. They would find a pub for lunch and Rosie could then raise the 'important' subject in relaxed surroundings. Roddy could almost detect the relief in her voice when he suggested this arrangement and he wondered what she wanted to talk about. He guessed that she wanted some sort of advice from someone outside her family; her flat mate, Melissa, may not, he guessed, have proved a very reliable source of wisdom. On the other hand, he surmised, this might just be Rosie's excuse to see him. Whatever the reason, Roddy found himself looking forward to seeing her again.

The hurried meeting with Rosie

Rosie was both excited and nervous. She bathed and washed her hair but the active butterflies in her stomach prevented her from eating any breakfast. She caught a tube to Paddington but then found that she had to wait half an hour for a train to Newbury. It would not reach Newbury until 12.15 pm. She was sure that Roddy would wait for her but, nevertheless, felt nervous and agitated.

Roddy encountered Philip Pipe after breakfast just as Philip was about to take Budget for a stroll around the fields. He informed Roddy that a drive to Newbury should only take an hour at the most; on Sundays the roads would be quieter. Having made himself look fairly presentable, Roddy left his room and soon encountered Edwin who was carrying a rugby ball.

"Just going outside for some practice," Edwin smiled. "All the other boarders in the team are coming too."

"An excellent idea, Press-up. But no tackling practice, please. That's how injuries occur."

"Don't worry, Sir. None of us would want to risk missing the match through injury. And we are looking forward to the film this afternoon, Sir. It'll be good to take our minds off the game."

"Right. I'll see you later," said Roddy.

As Philip had guessed, the roads were not busy but he still managed to take a wrong turning at a badly signposted roundabout. The result was an unplanned tour of Andover before he was relieved to spot a sign to Newbury.

An unexpected excursion

By the time Roddy had found his way to Newbury Station, Rosie had been waiting for nearly a quarter of an hour. Rosie, looking gorgeous, was standing near a well-dressed gentleman in his early seventies. She waved as soon as she saw Roddy's car and gave a beaming, inviting smile. .

Almost as soon as Roddy had stepped out of the car, she had wrapped her arms around him. He enjoyed this embrace and responded warmly.

"I'm really sorry I am late. I managed to discover more of southern England than I anticipated. Poor signposting!"

"Roddy, I promised Mr Bradstock, over there," she nodded towards the elderly gentleman nearby, "that we would give him a lift home. It's only a few miles away apparently but the last taxi was taken just as we came out of the station."

Roddy looked towards the gentleman who doffed his hat as they exchanged glances.

"He was terribly kind to me on the train when I spilled some items from my bag on to the floor: nothing very important except the silver fountain pen Daddy gave to me on my thirteenth birthday. Mr Bradstock helped search and found it for me lying in a gap between the seats."

"In that case we must certainly give him a lift but," Roddy hesitated, "I must warn you that I have a group of excited boys expecting me to show them a film at four o'clock. I simply mustn't let them down."

Rosie looked a little disappointed but Roddy took her arm.

"Come along. We must give Mr Bradstock his lift," he said, "then we can find somewhere for lunch…..and you can tell me what this 'important matter' is all about".

Mr Bradstock's 'few' miles turned out to be much closer to eight miles and these were mostly along rather twisty, wooded roads. Roddy was concerned about the time. Eventually, Mr Bradstock, who had been chatting politely, directed Roddy to turn into a drive. There was a substantial Edwardian house standing about thirty metres from the road, surrounded by uncut lawns.

Mr Bradstock now insisted that Roddy and Rosie should come inside with him where his housekeeper would provide lunch for them all. In spite of their polite protests, Mr Bradstock proved a forceful but generous host. His wife had died some years previously and he had eventually found an excellent and good-natured housekeeper. By the time they had finished the dry sherry thrust upon them, the handsome dining room table had two additional places laid out. Mrs Kryzykowski, the housekeeper, hovered nearby, smiling warmly.

The two reluctant guests were powerless to refuse this generosity. They raised their eyebrows in mutual submission and Roddy was impressed by Rosie's good-natured conversational efforts.

By the time they had completed the lunch, Rosie was aware that Roddy was regularly looking at his watch but she was also desperate to speak to him privately. "Thank you both for making my day. I don't have many opportunities to entertain now ......without my dear wife," said Mr Bradstock.

Roddy used the ensuing pause to explain that they must leave because he was expected back at Whitsborough. He explained the importance of his promise to show a film to the boys.

"In that case," answered Mr Bradstock, "I have the answer. I believe your school lies almost directly south of here and if you turn left out of the drive, you will soon meet the main road, which leads south. It will save you over twenty minutes of driving, and I will drive the delightful Rosie to Newbury station. My old Rover will enjoy a drive. She rarely goes out," he chuckled.

"That's very kind of you. It's an excellent idea," said Rosie hoping that she sounded sincere, although she was fighting a desire to burst into tears.

Rosie noticed Roddy looking at his watch once more.

"Roddy, you must go. I don't want to be responsible for making you late," Rosie insisted.

"But didn't you want to ask me about something?" he asked.

"Yes...but not now." Rosie was fighting back tears. "I'll be in touch. Please go."

"I do apologise.   I...er... I have been so selfish," pleaded Mr Bradstock. "I haven't allowed you any time to yourselves. I am so sorry. Please forgive me."

Rosie waved Roddy towards the door and forced herself to say, "Go!!" while she reached for a tissue from her handbag.

CHAPTER 17

THE WEEK OF THE POPPLEFORD MATCH

Monday: Rugby practice. Miles McNally's speed.
There was a different atmosphere on Monday afternoon before the 3rd XV's rugby practice. It wasn't exactly the calm before the storm but there was certainly tension. Edwin approached Roddy as he arrived at the pitch, carrying the sack of rugby balls over his shoulder.

"Well, Sir. This is it. The big one. The final week." Edwin paused. "Do you think we can do it?"

Several other boys gathered around, some kneeling while tying their boot laces.

"Well, we have one great advantage," replied Roddy.

"SURPRISE!" he roared with a threatening all-round stare. A couple of boys jumped back, startled. Roddy then issued a re-assuring smile.

"Poppleford Court will come here expecting to gain an easy victory. As you know, they have thrashed us for about the last ten years." He stared slowly round at the spellbound faces: the Chief with his braves before the battle.

"But they are going to be in for quite a shock,"

continued Roddy.

Wesley offered his considered and respected support:

"The concept of surprising one's enemy is hardly a new one, Sir, but within the framework of an inter-school rugby fixture, I believe that a ploy of this nature could, indeed, have a significant impact."

Roddy nodded his appreciative agreement although many of the boys exchanged puzzled frowns.

"Can you take us for a warm-up, Sir? My engine's keen to start," called Edwin and added a few 'Broom, brooms' before setting off on a jog towards the rugby posts.

Roddy was about to follow when one of the boys spotted a lone figure appearing from the direction of the changing rooms.

"It's the new boy. McNally, Sir. Looks a bit lost," said Hughes.

"OK. I'll go and see what's up," said Roddy. "You lot can go and grab the balls now and practise passing in fours. I won't be long."

Roddy had only come across Miles once before – when he first visited the school. He felt a little uneasy but was pretty sure Kate would not have mentioned their 'friendship'. He walked towards Miles.

"Hello. It's Miles, isn't it? I'm Mr Amport,"

"Yes, I remember you. You showed us round," and then hesitantly added, "Sir."

Miles had evidently changed into his games' kit but his 'shadow' – the pupil deputed to look after him during his first days – had disappeared on to another games' field.

"How old are you, Miles?" asked Roddy.

"I was eleven in August."

"Ah, so you are old enough for Senior Games. Good. Well, you'd better come and join my game. Played rugby before?" Roddy asked as they walked towards the pitch.

"A bit. We played soccer at my last school. I wasn't very skilful but I used to play mini-rugby on Sunday mornings. My coaches used to think I was pretty fast."

"Ah, good," grinned Roddy, "speed is always useful on a rugby field."

Roddy did his best to make Miles feel welcome as he introduced him to the others. Miles looked down at his feet but had to look up when Wesley moved forward with his hand held out. Miles shook the large Wesley paw with a half-smile. Several others said hello.

"Right, Miles. Put that blue shirt on and you can play on the wing. Know where that is?"

"Yes, by the touch line. Left or right, Sir?"

"Er, left," said Roddy.

The game began. However, there was a curious reluctance to tackle as forcefully as usual. Roddy felt that this was because no one wanted to be bruised or injured before Saturday. He stopped the game after about ten minutes and called them all round.

"Look, everyone. Bad practice is worse than no practice. Avoiding tackling is a bad habit. Now I want you all to play for fifteen minutes – flat out – and then we can stop. We can finish with 'end to end *he*' if you deserve it."

This popular incentive produced the required results and Roddy stopped the game after about fifteen competitive minutes. Miles had already shown one promising burst of speed.

The game of 'he' was, as usual, riotous fun as boys tried to run from one end of the pitch to the other without being touched by those who were 'on'. There was much dodging and chasing. After ten minutes and much shouting, the speedy Miles remained the only boy who had escaped capture. He was, therefore, expected to make a suicidal 'chicken run'. Inevitably, the 'hounds' surrounded Miles and finally dragged him down. Three boys then sat on him, the prostrate chicken. When Roddy called the hounds off, Miles stood up with a huge, muddy grin on his face. Kate's son had made a fine start and earned the respect of his new peers.

Monday: Suzy J-L discovers some alarming plans.
Inside Suzy's pretty head, an inquisitive little bee had been buzzing throughout the weekend. Just what were Gerald and the golf club Mafia up to? She tried asking Gerald how the meeting went and what they were all discussing so secretively but, as she expected, Gerald responded in his usual patronising way with responses like:

"Oh, nothing that would interest you, Darling" and "Just 'man talk'. Business, finance – all very boring."

Frustrated by these meaningless rebuffs and her failure, once again, to snare her prey, Suzy decided that she would have to embark on a little devious detective work. Why, she kept wondering, had 'Whitsborough' been mentioned during Gerald's clandestine meeting? If the results of her investigations provided her with an excuse to contact Roddy, the risk was worth taking.

Suzy therefore formulated 'Operation Whitsborough.' It required very little planning and was remarkably simple to put into effect. Entry to Gerald's study required no skeleton keys, gelignite or detonators; the door was usually left open. The regular cleaning lady, Vicky, dusted and hoovered the room once a week. It was a room Suzy rarely entered.

The filing cabinet was locked but Suzy recalled once seeing Gerald place a set of keys beneath the handsome silver cup on the mantelpiece. Gerald had won it at the golf club on a February day when it was so cold that only four people completed the eighteen holes.

Lifting the keys carefully and glancing about as though cameras were everywhere, Suzy found the correct key and opened the cabinet. Sandwiched tidily amongst various files with headings such as: 'Insurance'; 'Car'; 'Medical' and 'Mortgage' was a file marked 'New Housing Dev. Stilton.' Checking over her shoulder first, even though Gerald was in London, Suzy removed the 'Stilton' file. She closed the drawer, placed the keys in her pocket and took the file to the dining room table.

She nervously began to leaf through the letters and documents. At one point, she felt that she should be wearing rubber kitchen gloves in order to avoid leaving finger prints. Perhaps that was unnecessary? Dreading the return of Gerald at any moment, she decided that crime was not her forte; seduction was more her 'scene', even though in this she had, frustratingly, not yet achieved success. Amongst the thick pile of papers, there were letters and figures, and minutes of meetings. She recognized a few names on the headings but most of the details were meaningless.

It was not until she came to the bottom of the file that she discovered something which she could understand. Unfolding a precisely drawn and colourfully shaded architect's map, she finally discovered what Gerald and his gang were up to. She recognised the mapped area immediately. Only a few miles from her own house and not far out of the town, a large expanse of farmland had neat diagonal red stripes running across it. Next to this area was another area, criss-crossed by a series of brown stripes. In the middle of this area was written 'School.' The outlines of the school buildings were drawn in black. Faintly written beside them was the word: 'Whitsborough.'

Suzy experienced an immediate and powerful sensation. Was it anger, shock or guilt? She told herself that she should not feel guilty; that was what Gerald and his Mafia friends should feel. No, it was anger she was experiencing. Whitsborough was where Taylor was at school; where he seemed to be quietly happy. She read a few notes in the margin about the number of 'units' which could be built in the various shaded areas. Listed next to 'Whitsborough' was written '40-60 units'. So, she deduced, Gerald and his gang were involved in a big scheme to incorporate Taylor's school in a large housing development. She was horrified.

Suddenly, she thought she heard a car outside and quickly moved into action. She had to cover her tracks, return the file to the study and then decide what to do next. It transpired that there was no car outside but Suzy was unable to relax until she had replaced the file and was seated in front of the huge dressing table mirror in her bedroom.

She needed to think and then talk to someone. Confronting Gerald would be useless; he always seemed to win any argument. He would probably just spin out a clever lie or deny that there was any threat to Whitsborough. He would also be furious to discover that she had looked into his private files. Even if she protested on the grounds of the threat to Taylor's education and happiness, Gerald would dismiss this by saying that there were plenty of other suitable boarding schools he could attend;

"After all," he would say, "we pay the fees."

Angry, frustrated and depressed, Suzy did not know what to do next. She simply could not let Gerald and his mob build houses all over Whitsborough. She wondered who to turn to. Taylor's future was in jeopardy. Once more, her thoughts focused on Roderick Amport. Could this, perhaps, represent another excuse to contact him?

Wednesday: The Pipes and Wesley's father's plans.
Seated at the well-worn desk in his study, Philip was checking some figures which Fiona had produced concerning the finances for the following financial year. He hated planning: it required making decisions months in advance, based upon all sorts of possible variables and eventualities. He considered himself to be an imaginative person: he was an accomplished public speaker: he wrote entertaining reports on the pupils and lively articles for the school magazine; he had even written and produced a number of school plays. However, when it came to planning for future contingencies – and therefore requiring decisions in advance - he acknowledged his own weakness.

Fortunately, a distraction released him temporarily from

his torment. Dottie entered the study and immediately noted that Philip was looking tired and frustrated. She was not sure how he would respond to the news she was about to give him but at least, she thought, it would take his mind off future financial issues. Budget had followed her into the study and had wandered over to Philip to receive a friendly welcome.

"Fiona has just had *one* of Wesley's father's secretaries on the phone. Apparently the possibility that Mr Berkshire might fly from Abu Dookah – or whatever the place is called - is no longer just a possibility. He really is going to fly over in order to watch Wesley play against Poppleford Court."

"The big match?" said Philip, relieved to talk of something that actually interested him. "I gather that we might even avoid our usual thrashing. Even to narrow the margin of our defeat would be quite a coup for Master Amport."

"Well," continued Dottie, "it sounds as though Mr Berkshire of Abu Whatsit is a very big fish. He will even have his own team of 'security men' with him. Some of them will arrive before he comes. Probably to make sure you are not going to shoot him, dear."
Philip smiled.

"Just as well. My eyesight is not as sharp as it was!"
Dottie moved across the room to put a loving hand on Philip's shoulder.

"But it is all 'hush-hush.' You mustn't warn the Common Room until the morning of the game – and it is supposed to remain a complete surprise for Wesley, too."

"Well, it's certainly going to be an interesting day. Perhaps, if he is so rich, we could persuade him to donate a cup or some money for some new library books?"

Dottie smiled as she left Philip to his dreams. Philip then took Budget's head in his hands and looked him seriously in the eyes.

"And you, my furry friend, must forget everything you

have just heard."

Wednesday: Norman Stevenson is still on crutches.
It was over a week since Norman had suffered his accident while 'coaching' Edwin in his garden. His follow-up hospital appointment at the orthopaedic department was something he had been keenly anticipating for over a week. His wife's driving caused the journey to take at least fifteen minutes longer than usual to reach the hospital. It then took a further twelve minutes circling the hospital car park searching for a parking space. Cecilia usually avoided driving Norman anywhere as he was a particularly awkward passenger. His criticism of his wife's driving – and the drivers of other cars – was delivered all-too readily and loudly.

Although, he knew his knee had not completely recovered, he desperately wanted reassurance that he could attend the Poppleford match without the aid of the crutches. Norman imagined that everyone would know that he had injured himself while attempting to coach Edwin. This would have been too embarrassing to contemplate. Navigating his way slowly between wheel chairs and hospital trolleys, Norman reached the orthopaedic department in time for his appointment scheduled for 11.10am.

Still seated and waiting at 11.45am, Norman's fuse was burning increasingly close to the explosives. Cecilia did her best to calm him down, pointing out that many of the patients who had been summoned by the doctors appeared to be in greater pain and discomfort than he was. Several, heavily encased in plaster, looked as though they had been in an argument with tanks or articulated lorries. Norman did not like being reminded that he had been injured by a six stone boy on a garden lawn.

He was eventually summoned to see the doctor by a

large nurse who looked as though she would have made short work of a plate of pizzas. Norman was ready to speak his mind to the doctor about his fifty minute wait. He did not, however, expect to be greeted by a diminutive and delightful young woman with a broad, warming smile. She examined him carefully and told him that the ligaments appeared to be mending well. She recommended several gentle exercises for him to try. She stressed that, *provided* he avoided placing too much weight on the leg and continued using his crutches, he could attempt normal walking in about a fortnight. Firm but charming, she stood and dismissed Norman who hardly had time to question her. The large nurse held the door open for him and that was that.

Wednesday: Roddy's note from Suzy

It had been a busy and varied morning and, during the final lesson, Roddy had spent some time marking essays. The boys had been engaged in a grammar exercise about 'identifying parts of speech'. This lesson was punctuated when several boys asked what abstract nouns were. This allowed Roddy to explain and then offer a £5 note to any boy who could physically give him an identifiable abstract noun, such as a quantity of 'anger' or 'misery.' There were many enthusiastic but vain attempts to achieve this as volunteers struck or pinched Roddy's outstretched palm. No one was, of course, able to place a physical lump of *anger* or *misery* or *sadness* or any other abstract noun on it.

"What about *love*, Sir? Is that an abstract noun?" asked Wesley.

"It is indeed, Wesley," Roddy agreed.

"In that case, Sir......," said Wesley, rising slowly and beginning to walk towards Roddy with a threatening grin on his face, "perhaps I could give you some lo..?"

'*Love*??' Roddy repeated as he seized the moment for some theatre.

He gave Wesley a look of horror, and held his hands out

as if to repel an attack. It seemed that Wesley was about to pretend to offer Roddy some *love*. Roddy therefore backed towards the door as if genuinely threatened by Wesley's emotion. The class erupted in laughter as Wesley showed a gift for comedy timing and continued to advance towards Roddy.

"Enough!" cried Roddy as he stumbled back into a chair.

Smiles and a handshake ended the brief performance, accompanied by noisy applause and a wolf whistle which Roddy sincerely hoped would not have been heard outside the classroom.

After the lesson, Roddy returned to the Common Room where he noticed a typed and rather formal looking brown envelope awaiting him in his 'pigeon hole'. The postmark said 'Wellsford', a town about fifteen miles away. When he opened it, he discovered a short note apparently in a woman's handwriting. A glance at the final signature: 'Love, Suzy' confirmed this.

The letter initially explained that the envelope was posted in Wellsford in order to disguise the identity of the writer. Her main point was to confirm that Gerald would definitely **not** be present on Thursday evening and that she MUST see him. She had some VERY IMPORTANT information concerning Whitsborough.

A post script added: "It is imperative that you come!!!"

Roddy wondered what she really meant by this. He was not sure whether he would be able to continue resisting her very obvious and tempting advances.

That afternoon, during the 3rd XV's warm-up session, one of the boys collided with a rugby post. Nursing his wound, he was escorted up to see Matron by Wesley. Miles McNally, therefore, took his position for the rest of the afternoon. Twice, Miles demonstrated considerable speed and it occurred to Roddy that Miles might prove to be a very useful reserve for the Poppleford match.

Thursday evening: A 'proper' French lesson

At about 7.30pm, Roddy rose quietly from the Common Room supper table. He had waited for a moment when he was not involved in the conversation. He eased his chair back and moved quietly towards the door. Unfortunately, he caught Angela's eye. She gave him one of her knowing looks and glanced at her watch.

"Seven-thirty," she said with a wry grin. "Must be Thursday."

Roddy gave her an uncertain smile. Why, he asked himself, should he feel guilty about helping a parent to learn French?

When he arrived at the entrance to the Johnson-Little drive, Roddy was relieved to see only Suzy's car in the open double garage. He carried a couple of French text books although he somehow doubted whether they would be used during the next few hours. The door opened as he was about to press the bell.

Suzy, rather surprisingly, was dressed as though she was a respectable mother. There was no suggestion, as in earlier meetings, that she had naughtiness in mind. She gave him a perfunctory kiss but there was no hint of any excitement to come. Roddy immediately noted this change of approach. There was no coldness but Suzy's usual obvious desire for intimate activity was absent. Roddy was surprised and even a little unsettled. Had he, he wondered, done something wrong?

Suzy sat Roddy down on the sofa, poured them both a large glass of wine and then seated herself next to him but not as encouragingly close as on previous occasions. Roddy found himself feeling oddly disappointed. Suzy's blatant flirting had always been flattering. Temptation had certainly provided stimulation.

Roddy decided to play Suzy's game - whatever it was - and so he opened the pages of a French textbook. Suzy reached over, removed the book from him and placed it on the low table in front of them.

"Roddy…" she then paused, "I have some important information for you – about the school."

"Which school? You mean… Whitsborough?"

"Yes, of course Whitsborough, idiot," she replied giving him a playful slap on the thigh but her hand remained there for a second or two. Roddy noted this subtle, unspoken message. He found it reassuringly encouraging.

"It is really important, confidential news and I am not sure what you can do with it. But I must speak to someone about it."

Roddy sat up and turned towards Suzy. For a moment, he felt like an older brother about to advise a younger sister.

"OK," said Roddy, nodding his head slightly. "Try me."

Suzy looked at Roddy coyly.

"Well that's exactly what I have been intending to do for the last few weeks!!" said Suzy, giving him a long, inviting look.

Roddy thought for a moment. There were several interpretations of this situation but Suzy swiftly clarified her position by continuing to look into his eyes.

"I have some vital information concerning the future of Whitsborough. It could certainly affect you and poor Taylor."

"Well…???" Roddy awaited the details.

Suzy looked away for a moment.

"The thing is…there's a price for this information."

"A price?" Roddy was puzzled. "How much?"

"Not money!" Suzy sipped her wine, looked back at him and then towards the hall. "The payment can be negotiated…upstairs!"

At last Roddy understood the message.

"But that's…that's blackmail!!" exclaimed Roddy in mock horror, "...or is it bribery?"

"I don't mind which it is," smiled Suzy after a moment's thought, "but it could be fun!"

Roddy took a large, thoughtful gulp of wine.

"And you say this information is really important?" queried Roddy, whose eyes had now connected with Suzy's. She knew, at this moment, that she was about to land her prize fish.

"Yes. *Really* important."

She stood, took Roddy's hand, leant towards him to give him an affectionate kiss and led him towards the stairs.

"Right, she said, "Now let's negotiate."

Approximately thirty minutes later, the exposed label of an item of Suzy's black underwear lay on the carpet. Nearby was an ink-stained text book, entitled: 'A Modern French Grammar' -by J.W.Gillette. Half a metre above, the crescendo of amorous activity had subsided. Suzy had just engaged in twenty-five minutes of wild and abandoned physical exercise. She had enjoyed Roddy's performance considerably more than her irregular sessions of marital cohesion with Gerald. She also felt that her finely honed body had, for once, been really appreciated. Gerald's definition of making love depended entirely on how many glasses of claret, whisky or brandy he had consumed before he engaged in physical union. Usually his pre-coital alcoholic intake was considerable and his lovemaking was concomitantly disappointing.

In a gesture of comforting post-coital contentment, Suzy inspected the curved scar she had noticed on Roddy's otherwise pristine body. Her gently probing index finger teased the scar and she was about to question its origin when the warm touch of Roddy's right hand pleasantly distracted her as it sought a comfortable position along her thighs.

Was Roddy initiating Round Two – already?

"So….What's the big news about Whitsborough? I've kept my part of the bargain," stated Roddy.

Suzy affected disappointment and edged a few inches away – although she was pleased that his hand remained in situ.

"Is that what you have just been doing?" Suzy asked. "Just keeping your part of the bargain? I got the impression that you were rather enjoying yourself."

Roddy grinned, moved towards her and gave her a kiss which betrayed a good deal of affection.

"Mmmm. That's better, Mr Amport." Suzy moved a little further away from Roddy to take a good look at him. "That was all…really…" she sighed, "rather delicious!"

Roddy smiled and raised his eyebrows expectantly.

"Ok. Business now," she moaned and sat up. She rested her back against the headboard and clutched a pillow modestly to her chest. This, Roddy slowly and firmly removed as she began to explain the Whitsborough situation. Suzy paused as Roddy completed the manoeuvre and she gave him a look suggesting that he was a naughty child. Roddy grinned innocently back at her.

She began to recount what she had gleaned about the previous week's meeting of Gerald's local Mafia. She explained how she had overheard some of the meeting. It was when she mentioned the name of Ashley Stilton that Roddy also sat up; he had heard the name mentioned at school on a number of occasions.

He was surprised, but also impressed, by Suzy's nerve when she confessed to her raid on Gerald's private filing cabinet. Housing developments, shaded maps and secret planning schemes were subjects about which Roddy knew very little but, he agreed, Gerald's scheming could only be disturbing news for Whitsborough. Suzy was worried for Taylor. She told Roddy that he was perfectly happy at the school but Gerald had always heartlessly maintained that there were other schools where Taylor would be happy

"We pay the fees, so we can pay who we please," was Gerald's mantra.

"He just thinks happiness can be bought. The pig!" Suzy explained.

There were signs of tears in Suzy's eyes and Roddy put his arms around her once more. Suzy snuggled up to him.

"Thank you for telling me. I'm not sure what to do about it but I'll have to let Philip Pipe know," said Roddy.

Suzy suddenly realized the implications:

"Oh no. But…"

Roddy hushed her.

"Don't worry. I certainly won't betray the source of my information…or the fact," he added with a smile, "that I had to pay to get it."

Suzy was not quite sure if he was teasing or not. She looked worried.

"Well as I am paying…………" he moved close again so that both bodies touched each other from shoulder to toe. "……..how about……" - his left arm explored Suzy's firm stomach… "Two for the price of one?"

Suzy pretended to be shocked although there was delight in her eyes.

"You obviously like getting value for money, Mr Amport," and with that she wrapped her arms around him once more.

As the highlight of Suzy's evening ended, she was in a triumphant mood. She even made a couple of jokes about having just learnt a few things from Roddy which were not, she giggled, anything to do with French grammar. Fortunately, as she was dressing and tucking in her blouse, she noticed the French book on the bedroom floor.

"Phew!" she said as she picked it up. "Good thing I spotted it. I wouldn't want Gerald to find that in here."

"Would he have hit the roof, if he had?" asked Roddy.

Suzy thought for a moment.

"Possibly not. He has his own little excitement in London, I believe."

"What about if Taylor had found it?"

Suzy grimaced: "Now that would have been much more serious!"

When she was giving Roddy a final wave as he entered his car, and was brushing a lock of dishevelled hair away from her forehead, she suddenly remembered another sliver of Whitsborough gossip. She signalled furiously, instructing Roddy to wait. She ran over to the car and Roddy eased the driver's window down.

"Roddy, I almost forgot to ask you." She seemed quite excited. "I heard some more local gossip from my hairdresser. It, too, concerns Whitsborough."

Roddy wondered what else Suzy had discovered.

She paused, as if she were about to reveal a surprising secret.

"Have you," she asked, "ever heard of a film actress called Kate McNally?"

Friday: Roddy tells Philip the disturbing news

Soon after his return from Chateau Johnson-Little, Roddy was asleep. He had enjoyed the evening and had been amused – and somewhat flattered – that Suzy's eventual success in luring him into her boudoir (or, to be more accurate, a spare bedroom) had caused her so much satisfaction. However, he was rather surprised to find himself experiencing a period of wakefulness in the middle of the night.

The Whitsborough issue worried him. His own future might be affected by a housing development. Furthermore, he respected and liked the Pipes and was also concerned for them. Dottie could be dragon-like at times but her heart was in the right place. The teachers were, by and large, an agreeable bunch and the pupils were mostly pleasant boys although there were, inevitably, a few rogues. How, he wondered, could he explain the threat to the school and account for possessing such 'confidential' information? He found himself tossing and turning in his bed, almost as if Suzy had joined him for Round Three.

By the time he was eating breakfast at the Common Room table, he had made up his mind. He would have to tell Philip, and the sooner the better. He asked Angela her advice about when best to speak to him. Angela advised him to consult Fiona, when she arrived and, inevitably added a comment:

"Why? You're not handing in your notice already are you?"

Roddy had expected a comment of some sort. He briefly contemplated a riposte referring to Angela's recent self-styled and questionable 'appointment' as Deputy Head, but he managed to resist it.

Fiona proved helpful and sympathetic when Roddy explained that he needed to see Philip in private on an important matter. Fiona's wisdom and experience determined her advice: she was aware that Dottie had a habit of being present when members of the Common Room would prefer to speak to Philip when he was alone. Roddy realised that it would certainly be easier if Dottie was absent – just in case he was obliged to divulge the source of his information.

A time was arranged and Roddy therefore knocked on the door of Philip's study five minutes after lunch had ended. Philip asked Roddy to sit opposite him in an old wing chair. Philip began by complimenting Roddy on the impact and contribution that Roddy had already made to Whitsborough. He added that he had a fine future at the school and that he hoped Roddy was not about to tell him that he had already been offered a headship somewhere else.

Roddy smiled and thanked Philip for the amusing compliment.

"Thank you very much, Sir, but I...."

"Philip, please. I do like members of the Common Room to use my Christian name."

"Philip. Yes. Sorry." Roddy paused and hoped he could manage to produce the information clearly. "I've discovered some alarming information about Whitsborough – and its future. But the thing is: I can't really divulge the source of the information although I believe it to be completely genuine."

Philip looked concerned but said nothing. He waited.

"I believe there is a plan, or scheme or whatever, to build houses on the farmland around the school."

Philip sat up and lowered his eyebrows. He was about to speak but Roddy continued.

"And I believe that there are plans to involve Whitsborough in some way. Perhaps even building on our land."

"What! Build on school land? They can't do that. It's not possible." Philip's pulse began to accelerate. He could feel anger brewing in his chest.

"I understand that someone called Ashley Stilton may be involved," added Roddy.

"But he's the Chairman of the Governors. He'd never allow any building on…" And then Philip halted and thought for a moment. "Unless, of course, as you say, he really is *involved*."

The door opened and Budget waddled in, followed by Dottie. Roddy stood up but Dottie waved him back into his chair.

"Roddy has just given me some unpleasant news, dear."

"Ah, I saw that he had arranged to see you. Your diary was open on Fiona's desk," Dottie explained with apparent innocence.

"It seems that there may be plans to build near the school and Whitsborough may be included in the plans."

Dottie was stunned. Philip paused and then sighed.

"And it is possible that Ashley Stilton may be involved," he added.

"That bloody shark! I've never liked the man and I told you that he should never have been made a governor – let alone Chairman!" Dottie seamlessly moved into anger mode.

"He's given me some useful financial advice over the years," said Philip defensively. "He's helped us with cars, mini-buses… and finding a builder to do the school roofing."

"Oh, yes," agreed Dottie, "but I bet he received a backhander or whatever it's called. He'll take advantage of any chance to line his own filthy pockets."

Philip tried to clarify matters:

"Roddy, you say you cannot tell me the source of the information. Is that right?"

"Pub talk at the Huxton Arms? Some of Derek Drinkall's cronies?" suggested Dottie rather aggressively.

"No. My source has actually seen some of the plans – although I think I did once hear someone in the pub say that there are rumours locally of a big housing development somewhere nearby."

Dottie looked gravely at Roddy. Roddy felt like a naughty child being told off by one of his mother's oldest friends – which, indeed, was not far from the truth.

"Would your late evening journeys, by any chance, have anything to do with the 'source' of the information?" she asked.

Roddy felt awkward. He felt as though he had been accused of cheating in a school exam. However, he told himself that he was an adult whose private life was nothing to do with the school. He briefly thought of how he had succumbed to a parent's guile and attractions. Was that the school's business??

"Only indirectly," replied Roddy who thought this sounded suitably misleading.

Philip, who was sympathetic to the requirements of young masters' extra-curricular impulses, intervened. This prevented Dottie from engaging in any more detailed interrogation.

"Well, I must speak to Ashley. The sooner the better. I haven't seen him for some time…and that in itself is rather unusual."

Dottie gave Philip a sharp look. She wanted to know more about Roddy's 'activities' but Philip had heard enough.

"Right. Thank you for informing me, Roddy. If you 'hear' anything more about it I trust you will let me know."

Roddy nodded.

"Right. Off you go. And good luck with the Poppleford match tomorrow. I hear you might give them a surprise."

"A surprise? Yes, I hope so. But a victory? Well, we'll do our best."

"Oh. One last thing. I take it you won't mention this to anyone else," said Philip, glancing at Dottie. "There are several gossips in the Common Room."

Dottie understood immediately that this directive was also for her benefit. Philip was instructing her not to inform Angela.

"Don't worry, I can keep a secret," said Roddy, managing to avoid Dottie's eye as he left the room.

Friday afternoon: The final team practice.

There was a rather unreal atmosphere as the 3rd XV gathered for their final session on Friday afternoon. During the warm-up, no one seemed to know whether to try extra hard or whether to 'save themselves' for the following day.

Roddy soon sensed the uncertainty. He called all the boys round him and told them to treat the session as if it was a normal Friday. He then told Edwin to perform sixteen press-ups – one on behalf of each member of the team – and one for Roddy. This caused a good deal of laughter and Edwin was delighted to provide an impressive performance.

Having completed his task, Edwin made a suggestion.

"And now it's your turn, Sir. Seventeen! My sixteen and one for luck!"

"But I haven't done a press-up since," - why did Suzy spring into his mind at this point - "since…since…ever!" More laughter ensued.

Wesley stepped forward.

"In that case, Sir, allow me to act on your behalf."

No one had seen Wesley attempt a press-up. His power and (when he chose) his speed were, of course, already well known.

After several theatrical arm stretches and deep breaths, Wesley bent down and performed twenty perfect press-ups. This drew appreciative applause. Roddy then dropped to the ground nearby, positioned himself and then executed ten press-ups – before collapsing (this was not acting) and receiving enthusiastic praise.

With the tension broken, Roddy allowed them to play rugby for about fifteen minutes. They were soon all involved and the game was being enjoyed by everyone. Miles McNally produced one dazzling burst of speed before running into Wesley who was playing for the other side. Fortunately, Wesley merely embraced Miles firmly, enveloping him in his powerful arms. Roddy wished that Miles had arrived at the school earlier as he would have been an invaluable member of the team and not just a reserve. While everyone was enjoying the game, Roddy blew the whistle.

"A good move, Sir – psychologically," commented Wesley, evidently impressed by Roddy's team management skills.

"Is that it, Sir?" said a disappointed Edwin.

Roddy smiled:

"Let's save the best for tomorrow."

"I'm not sure whether I'll be able to sleep tonight," confided Edwin.

"Sir?" called Clesham, "You haven't told us who's going to be captain."

This observation immediately caused wide interest. Roddy had never really divulged his thoughts on this issue. He stopped and scratched his head in a deliberate manner.

"Well, there are two obvious contenders."

"Edwin," called a voice.

"Wesley," called another.

Roddy was about to disclose his decision but Wesley spoke first.

"My friend Edwin, here, has been at the school for many

years, Sir. I, on the other hand, only arrived at the beginning of this term. Edwin's conduct and example has been an inspiration to us all. It would be an honour to be led - into battle – by him."

Wesley shook Edwin's hand, offering a brief, deferential bow. All the faces now turned to Roddy to see how he would react. Timing his response to perfection – a considered and thoughtful pause - Roddy then smiled.

"Well put, Wesley." He then turned and held his hand out to Edwin.

"Congratulations, Captain!"

Wesley had made the decision that Roddy, himself, had intended to make.

CHAPTER 18

THE DAY OF THE POPPLEFORD MATCH

Philip Pipe summons Ashley Stilton

Although Roddy endeavoured to conduct his morning's teaching as routinely as possible, there was a tangible sense of excitement in the school. The two senior teams were due to play away matches at Poppleford Court but all the remaining boys would be allowed to watch the 3rd XV's much-anticipated battle. The fact that Edwin Stevenson was the appointed captain added a piquancy to the occasion because the school's 'Honorary Motorist' had become a popular figure with the other boys.

Philip Pipe, however, had a different feeling about this Saturday morning. Following the information that Roddy had provided about possible building developments, Philip had immediately contacted Ashley Stilton's secretary, Glenys, and had arranged a meeting with him at short notice. To say that Ashley Stilton was formally 'summoned' to see the Headmaster would suggest that Ashley was a wayward pupil. Whilst this was not, of course, strictly accurate, Philip's heart was nevertheless beating furiously. Dottie did her best to calm him but

Philip was incensed.

"Don't pre-judge the issue, Philip. Be calm. Roddy may have got the wrong end of the stick."

"Well, I'll give Stilton some stick all right," was Philip's response.

Ashley Stilton eventually arrived at the school almost a quarter of an hour late, a fact that did little for Philip's temper. Stilton was at a considerable disadvantage because Philip had not informed Glenys the reason for calling this hurried interview; Philip had simply told her that it was a matter of immediate importance. As far as Stilton was concerned, he was expecting a friendly chat. Philip might, perhaps, need help in sorting out some minor financial difficulty or dealing with a troublesome parent. He was certainly not prepared for the nuclear tirade Philip was about to unleash.

Thus, Ashley Stilton, who had once been a Whitsborough parent, and who had always had great respect for Philip's old-school values, found himself standing in Philip's study, his offered hand shake rejected.

Before even being directed to a seat, Philip launched his missiles. He told Stilton how he had supported the idea of making him a governor and how he had, several years later, persuaded the other governors to make him Chairman, even though there had been some opposition to this idea. Philip never disclosed the exact source of this opposition – Dottie. But now, Philip continued: he had stumbled upon a plot – there was a traitor in the camp, a double agent. The future of Whitsborough was under threat.

Stilton was still perplexed. It never occurred to him that the building scheme had been discovered; only a handful of people knew about it. Philip, having landed his troops successfully on the beach with a surprise attack, now embarked upon the second wave of his assault. More artillery was to be fired and Philip's heart rate reached record levels. Ashley Stilton's character was subjected to further dissection. It was some minutes before Philip eventually mentioned the reason for this brutal character assassination.

Philip revealed his knowledge of the proposed housing scheme nearby and the possibility of Whitsborough being a part of it. This disclosure was a huge shock to Stilton. Although he had not been the instigator of the scheme, he had been invited to participate in its development and was well aware of the tempting financial rewards. Matters had been treated with the strictest secrecy. He was dumbstruck and acutely embarrassed now that Philip had exposed him.

In a feeble attempt to vindicate his involvement, Ashley protested that he was concerned about Whitsborough's financial viability. Numbers had declined rapidly in recent years, money needed to be spent on the school's ancient plumbing system and many of the school's facilities required upgrading; they were falling behind those of rival schools – like Poppleford Court. There was no proper assembly hall, sports hall or even a swimming pool.

Philip dismissed this argument, asserting that Stilton's interests only lay in lining his own pockets. He was also pleased to inform Stilton that future school numbers were looking more promising. There had been a marked increase in interest in the school recently, particularly from 'the London Market.' One new boarder had arrived in the previous week, the son of a well-known actress, a set of twins was due next term `and this was already generating more interest in the school.

Philip threatened Stilton, saying that any underhand involvement Stilton had in planning to build houses on Whitsborough land would be investigated formally by his solicitors. Furthermore, Philip stated that he suspected Stilton had gained financially and improperly when organising a local firm of builders – friends of his, no doubt - to renew the school's roof. Stilton looked uneasy and embarrassed.

Meanwhile, not far away, a dark blue Rover was turning

off the lane in front of the school and crunching slowly up the drive. It drew up not far behind 'AS 777' - Ashley Stilton's expensive saloon car. Being an observant individual, the driver, wearing a well-worn grey suit, subconsciously noted the vehicle's personalised registration number. As he climbed out of his car, he straightened his tie and entered Whitsborough's wide open front door. He was about to knock on the door opposite when Fiona emerged from her office, carrying the day's post to the Common Room.

The man introduced himself, apologised for the intrusion and asked to see the Headmaster. It was rather important he explained, showing her his identity card. Fiona led the visitor along the corridor towards Philip's study. They passed two boys struggling to carry a pile of large atlases to a Geography lesson. Fiona smiled at one of them.

"Good luck this afternoon, Edwin. The big day has arrived."

The visitor was a little puzzled by the boy's unusual reply: it sounded like a car's engine revving.

Outside Philip's study, Fiona could hear the sound of an angry voice. She looked at the visitor, who nodded, indicating that he nevertheless wished to be shown in. Fiona hesitated briefly before she knocked and entered.

Philip's tirade was coming to an end; he had nearly used up all his ammunition.

"......and if this building scheme involving Whitsborough goes any further, I shall ensure that my legal advisers speed into action and that the Police, if necessary, are involved."

"The Police?" Stilton was shocked. "Don't be ridiculous. It's nothing to do with them," he added taking an inadvertent step backwards just as Fiona entered right behind him. He managed to avoid knocking into her but in so doing accidentally shoulder-barged the grey-suited gentleman with her.

"I am sorry to interrupt, Headmaster, but this gentleman says that he needs to speak to you. Urgently".

Philip looked irritated but Stilton appeared grateful for this pause in the battle. The visitor stepped forward, holding out an identification card.

"I'm sorry to interrupt, Sir. It's Allen. Detective Sergeant Allen. Wilsford Police."

Stilton twitched involuntarily.

"I've come to look round the school grounds and the surrounding fields, if I may."

Stilton gave Philip a nervous look, suggesting that Philip had laid a trap for him. Fearing the worst, he seized upon this opportunity to make a quick exit. Surely this policeman could not have been summoned by Philip already. However, he did not want to stay a minute longer. He must leave immediately and warn his fellow conspirators.

While Philip read the card Detective Sergeant Allen handed to him, Stilton neatly side-stepped Fiona giving her an embarrassed nod. He mumbled something about Philip being 'obviously busy' and slipped hurriedly out of the door. When he reached his car, he paused to take a number of deep breaths, executed a hurried turn and then sped back down the drive spraying gravel onto the lawns. When he reached the lane at the end of the drive, he had another worrying moment. A lone, helmeted police motor cyclist stood by his motorbike as if on guard. The impressive radio aerial at the back of the bike looked threatening. Stilton drove slowly past, fearing that he was now under police surveillance.

As Detective Sergeant Allen clarified the reason for his visit, Fiona began to nod her head. All the long-distance phone calls from Abu Dookah about Wesley Berkshire's appearance in the Poppleford match were now making sense. Mr Berkshire had, as seemed likely, decided to fly over specially to watch Wesley play. Although Philip had been told about all the phone calls from Mr Berkshire's many secretaries, he had not, until now, paid much attention to them.

"But why," asked Fiona, "does Mr Berkshire need a policeman here?"

Philip had seated himself at his desk in the hope that his heart would recover from his recent rant.

"Security, Madam," explained Det. Sergeant Allen. "And there's another of my men stationed at the bottom of the drive. This afternoon, Mr Berkshire – as you refer to him – will be accompanied by men from his own personal security force. I have just come to do a brief recce, before they arrive. With your permission, Sir."

Philip was beginning to recover and asked,

"But why is Mr Berkshire so important? Having his own guards is a little unusual, surely?"

"Not in Abu Dookah, Sir, where the political situation is highly volatile. The gentleman you call Mr Berkshire is, I am informed, one of the richest men there…in a country where rich means rich!! His real name is Barq Sheah,"

Philip looked puzzled:

"Barq Sheah?? But I don't….."

Fiona suddenly understood:

"Of course! Now I've got it. **Barq Sheah** has been anglicised - as **Berk-shire!**"

Philip shook his head in mystified disbelief.

Detective Sergeant Allen asked Philip's permission to have a look around the school and particularly the whole area where the rugby match would take place. Philip, willingly agreed and shook his head once more, wondering how on earth the violent enmities of the Middle East could be of relevance on the playing fields of Whitsborough.

Before the match: 1.30 pm

As the lunch was ending and the dining room was filled with the sounds of plates being scraped clean and then stacked, a large black car drove along the drive. Four Middle Eastern looking men in dark suits stepped out and quickly headed towards the playing fields behind the school. One of them was intercepted by Det. Sergeant Allen and the two men spoke for several minutes while Allen pointed to various significant features of the field.

About ten minutes later, Edwin and his team emerged noisily from the school building. They were not yet changed for the match but Edwin had organised a brief team gathering of his own. For the last couple of days, Edwin's active mind had thought of little other than the match and he had an idea. He was not sure whether Roddy would approve but when he told his team, they laughed in agreement. Miles McNally was now an enthusiastic member of the group because Roddy had said he should be ready on the touchline in case anyone was injured.

2.00 pm: The spectators begin to arrive.
Although there was half an hour to go before the match was due to start, Norman Stevenson, was determined to savour the whole occasion and he arrived early. Not a minute was to be missed. Not only was his son representing the school – and had therefore, at last, achieved 'sportsman' status – but Norman himself had an additional reason to be proud; he was, after all, the father of the team *captain*. Consequently, he had every intention of commanding the prime spectating spot on the half way line. Here, he would have the best view of the game but would also, he felt, receive the respect and admiration of the other parents. It was a late autumn afternoon and Norman had spent some time dressing for the occasion. He would like to have sported a club tie but had to wear the only striped tie he possessed, that of his stamp collecting society.

Unfortunately, he still required the use of his crutches. This frustrated him enormously and he prayed that no one would ask him how he had sustained the injury. Cecilia was forbidden from attending because, Norman insisted, 'only men should watch a man's sport.' In reality, however,

Norman was terrified that Cecilia might betray the truth about the cause of his injury.

He limped, slowly and self-consciously, round the side of the school to the pitch. This perambulation took him rather longer than he anticipated and he was annoyed to find a number of pupils already gathering to watch the match from his selected spot. However, there was no one standing by the half way line on the opposite side of the pitch so he hobbled across the grass to the other side. Before long, other parents appeared but they seemed content to spectate from the side nearer the school.

2.20 pm: Ten minutes to go. Wesley's father arrives with his entourage

Having finally secured a satisfactory vantage point, Norman was feeling a little breathless. Soon the first members of the Whitsborough team began to appear from the changing rooms. Alarmingly, there was no sign of Edwin. Norman double-checked but still there was no Edwin. His internal alarm bells began to ring.

Across the pitch there was a burst of activity. A group of five men appeared, accompanied by a woman wearing a grey and white fur coat. One of the men was dressed in what Norman perceived as 'Arab gear' and he was clearly the focus of attention. A gaggle of spectators scattered as this group moved imperiously to the central position on the touchline in front of the main school building.

Norman began to twitch nervously. He simply could not understand what had happened to Edwin. He hopped about, like a poodle on a pogo stick. Where was Edwin? He had to raise one of his crutches almost to a horizontal position as he attempted to prevent himself from over-balancing. Suddenly, he felt a hand grasping his shoulder firmly. He turned and found a face right beside him.

"Allow me, Sir," said the face in a foreign accent. The man supported the trembling Norman while examining the crutch.

"One can never be too careful," explained the foreign voice. Further close examination revealed that Norman's other crutch was not a disguised rifle either.

"My apologies, Sir. Enjoy the game." The face delivered a professional smile and moved further along the touchline.

Unnerved, embarrassed and mystified, Norman was finally relieved to catch sight of Edwin. He was performing his captain's duties by leading the opposing team from their changing room to the pitch. Norman experienced a moment of pride when he saw this but the experience proved only transitory. About a dozen Poppleford parents arrived and walked to Norman's side of the pitch. Many of them took up positions on either side of him, the lone limping Whitsborough representative. Norman felt intimidated.

A Poppleford mother gave Norman an insincere smile:

"I don't think I've seen you watching the matches before. Is your boy in the team?"

"Yes," replied Norman, "he's over there. He's the captain." This was perhaps the proudest moment of Norman's entire life.

"Really?" questioned the mother, rather surprised.

Norman pointed to Edwin who was now walking over to join his team.

"Oh!" cried the woman, "so you're a Whitsborough parent." She made this assertion sound as though he carried a dose of rabies. This time she gave Norman a more genuinely insincere smile before moving away.

Two men, who gave the appearance of being engaged in friendly conversation, emerged from the school. The younger one was wearing a blazer and the other, middle-aged, sported a well-worn tweed jacket. When they reached the pitch, they shook hands and parted. Each then walked to his team. Norman had not seen Roddy before but identified him immediately. Though not particularly large or heavy, he looked fit and athletic. He certainly looked like a rugby player and Norman realised that his own coaching expertise may, perhaps, have been a shade inferior to that of 'Mr Amport'.

Having watched Roddy address his team, Norman was pleased to see him walk in his direction. On his way, Roddy exchanged a few words with the referee, Derek Drinkall, who enjoyed refereeing and being the centre of attention. Although soccer was D.D.'s preferred game, he was, according to Michael Briton who coached the 1st XV, a competent rugby referee 'although he rather likes the sound of his own whistle.' Roddy was simply grateful that he would not have to referee his own team and would therefore avoid any possible accusations of bias.

While the Poppleford boys seemed content to warm up by just tossing a few rugby balls around amongst themselves, Edwin was quietly conducting an impressive series of jogs, sprints, stretches and press-ups. This raised a few raised eyebrows amongst the Poppleford supporters. Roddy smiled and chose to watch from a spot near the gentleman on crutches. Norman could not resist introducing himself and turned to Roddy.

"Excuse me, but am I right in thinking that you are Mr Amport?" he asked.

"Yes, that's right," replied Roddy.

"Well, I have heard a lot about you. I'm Norman Stevenson," he paused and proudly added, "Edwin's father!"

Norman only just managed to resist his desire to add that his son was the Whitsborough captain; he realised that Roddy probably knew that. Norman smiled warmly and held out his hand.

"In that case, I am honoured to meet you, Sir. Edwin has been an inspiration to all of us and if we do well today, it will be largely as a result of your son's example."

Norman glowed with pride.

"I understand that you gave him a lot of help during the summer holidays - fitness training, I believe?" added

Roddy.

This praise transported Norman upwards, towards the heavens. Furthermore, Roddy insisted that Norman should address him by his Christian name.

2.30 pm: Edwin's team 'drive' to their starting positions

Edwin had won the toss and had chosen to start at the end where Poppleford had been warming up. He had gathered the Whitsborough team at the side of the pitch and allowed the Popplefords to cross to the other end. He then signalled to his team to follow him onto the pitch and move to their positions for the start. The unusual aspect of this action was its vocal accompaniment. The school's Honorary Motorist instructed his team to 'drive' to their starting positions on the 'grid'. Thus, with a variety of engine noises the team moved to their positions for the kick off. Edwin and several others even held their arms as if gripping steering wheels.

This combination of revs and purrs proved remarkably effective. The Poppleford team looked around bewildered and the Poppleford parents were flummoxed. The Whitsborough pupils and teachers, however, simply chuckled knowingly.

The incensed Poppleford captain marched towards the referee to protest. Drinkall, however, was smiling and rather enjoying the humour of the moment.

"Oi, Ref. They're not allowed to do that!"

Whether it was the '*Oi*' or the '*Ref*' which incensed D.D. is not clear. If the complaint had been couched in more gentlemanly terms, all might have been well. "*Excuse me, Sir*," would have been perfectly acceptable and would have been received sympathetically, but the aggressive tone of this twelve-year-old offended D.D. This fact was hardly likely to be of benefit to Poppleford. Thus, D.D's reply to the complainant was brief and to the point:

"Nothing about it in the rules, old chap."

The Match

When the game began, two features soon became apparent: Poppleford were used to playing as a team of fifteen whereas the Whitsborough boys had usually only been able to practise in teams of seven or eight. However, the spirited tackling and defence of the Whitsborough boys was a revelation. Edwin provided an inspirational example to his team and Poppleford only managed to score twice in the first half. In previous years, Poppleford had often scored half a dozen tries at this stage.

At half time, Roddy gathered the team round him at one end of the pitch. Team spirit was still high and there was a feeling of optimism. The boys were becoming used to the fifteen man format and Roddy made two positional changes designed to ensure that Wesley would receive the ball more often and could then use his speed and power.

Half time: Wesley's father speaks to Philip Pipe

On the touchline in front of the school stood the commanding figure 'in Middle Eastern' gear. It was Wesley's father, Barq Sheah. He appeared to take little notice of his wife, Chuselle, who had met him in the school drive. He had instructed one of his guards to identify and locate the Headmaster. Philip had, in fact, been standing only a few paces away from the Middle Eastern magnate. He had been surprised, and impressed, by the supportive shouts of encouragement emanating from the mouth of this eminent parent.

When introduced, Barq Sheah addressed Philip with charm and respect. In excellent English, he told Philip how much he was enjoying the match and explained that he had been sent for two years to a famous English boarding school when he was fifteen. He had loved rugby and played successfully in school teams until he broke his ankle while on a cross-country run. As D.D. summoned the teams for the second half, Barq Sheah mentioned to Philip that he would be honoured to make a grateful and appreciative contribution to the school: his son, Wesley, had written to him, praising the school and the masters. Philip 'only had to ask.' Both men then turned their attention back to the game but Philip's mind, still disturbed about the Stilton situation, began to wonder what Barq Sheah really meant by 'a contribution'.

Norman Stevenson had been totally involved in the first half. The intensity and vigour of his vocal support had not passed unnoticed by the Poppleford parents. At half-time, while Roddy was speaking to his team, Norman stood alone. Some of the Poppleford parents were only too keen to air criticisms loudly enough for Norman's ears: the engine noises at the start; how the referee may have missed certain infringements and how certain Whitsborough supporters seemed to be yelling fanatically. This last criticism was clearly aimed at Norman – although, naively, he interpreted it as a compliment.

The second half: Wesley is inspired

The second half began with some Whitsborough fireworks. A misguided kick by one of the Poppleford players landed close to Edwin. He managed to pick it up and ran forward with it for a few paces before being powerfully tackled. The force of the impact caused him to spill the ball onto the ground behind him. Wesley grabbed the rolling ball and set off into enemy territory. He displayed the speed and determination which had not been revealed during the first half. Two brave, attempted Poppleford tackles simply bounced off Wesley, whilst the third and final tackler made little more than a gesture. Wesley's try under the posts was greeted with deafening Whitsborough cheers.

Norman raised both arms in delight, forgot his need for his crutches, and was only saved from falling spread-eagled on the touchline by Roddy's swift reactions. Norman thanked his saviour and asked why Wesley had not been so dynamic in the first half. Roddy pointed a surreptitious finger across the field in the direction of Barq Sheah's entourage.

"That man – apparently one of the richest men in the Middle East – is Wesley's father. He has flown over specially, just to see his son play today," explained Roddy. Norman gasped to think that he was in the company of such important people.

Roddy continued:

"It was a complete surprise for Wesley who did not notice his father was here until just now – at half time. I think, as a result, he will now be striving desperately to impress his father."

Roddy gave Norman a conspiratorial smile.

Just as play re-started, Roddy felt a tug on his arm. Miles McNally, who had been instructed to stay near Roddy in case he was needed to replace an injured player, had spotted movement on the other side of the pitch.

"Sir, sir. It's my Mum. Over there," said Miles, surprised and excited. "Can I go and see her?"

Roddy looked across the field and noticed a few nudging arms and strained necks. Kate McNally had obviously been recognised by some of the Whitsborough spectators. She was standing alone and Roddy subconsciously rubbed his forehead. She must have flown home unexpectedly and had no doubt been recently surrounded by photographers at the airport.

"No, Miles. I need you here – in case there's an injury. There's only another twenty minutes. The team comes first."

A disappointed Miles seemed to understand.

Norman Stevenson's accidental intervention!
Wesley's inspirational try had lifted the standard of Whitsborough's play and Roddy's half-time positional changes were also beginning to work. A promising passing movement resulted in the ball ending up in the hands of

one of Whitsborough's fastest runners. The boy, James Early, avoided a tackle, and sped diagonally towards a vacant area near the touchline. He then raced along the edge of the pitch, close to a line of shouting spectators. As he reached top speed, he was almost directly in front of Norman. Norman was so animated that he had moved forward and was virtually standing on the field of play. He was cheering wildly. Such proximity suggested that an alarming collision with James Early suddenly looked likely. However, a nearby spectator reacted quickly and hastily pulled Norman out of the path of the speeding boy. Unfortunately, one of Norman's crutches did not react so quickly.

The sudden tug on his shoulder caused Norman to lean back and raise one crutch to knee height. It was now horizontal and it protruded onto the pitch, just in front of James. The speeding boy, who was concentrating on avoiding Poppleford tackles, hardly expected to be torpedoed by the trailing metal crutch of a 'home' supporter. Thus, the unfortunate James found himself somersaulting out of control as he tripped over Norman's crutch and crashed painfully to the ground.

Referee Drinkall immediately blew his whistle to stop the game. Brave, but clearly in pain and badly bruised, James was in no position to continue playing. Angela, who often acted as First Aid Officer, hurried across the field from the far side, carrying a small medical bag. She helped the limping James back to the school where ice was applied. When D.D eventually re-started the game, a very excited Miles McNally was brought on as a replacement and an embarrassed Norman Stevenson was made to stand, like a naughty child, a full five paces back from the touchline. Injuring a member of Edwin's own team had not featured in Norman's recurring dreams of victory.

On the far side, in front of the school, Dottie used the injury hiatus to extricate herself from the unwelcome company of several Whitsborough mothers. They had insisted on complaining to her about trivial school matters: one mother wanted to know why the school tie now cost an extra shilling; another complained about the dates of the half term holidays. Dottie therefore strode along her side of the pitch and joined Kate McNally. Kate was grateful to be greeted so warmly by the Headmaster's wife. A wise old bird, Dottie knew that chatting to a film star would serve as a snub to the complaining mothers.

Dottie explained the reason for the presence of the security guards and surreptitiously pointed out Wesley's father, Barq Sheah. She drew Kate's attention to his wife, (or *one* of his wives!), Chuselle. Dottie had observed, and seemed keen to point out, that Barq Sheah appeared to be ignoring her. However, further Dottie gossip was abruptly interrupted. The game had restarted and the shouting increased as Wesley had started ploughing his way through the enemy once more. It took three Popplefords to bring him to the ground but Wesley managed to release the ball so that Edwin snapped it up and almost scored. Only a desperate Poppleford tackle prevented Whitsborough from equalizing.

The noise increased as the Whitsborough supporters sensed that there was the chance of an unforeseen victory. The Poppleford parents, conversely, began to fear that defeat was now a possibility. Barq Sheah had become progressively more vocal and, much to the concern of his guards, had paced along the touch line to question Philip about certain aspects of the play, the names of certain players (Edwin had certainly impressed him) and he wanted to identify Mr Amport, who was often mentioned in Wesley's letters.

An anxious Suzy appears

With only fifteen minutes remaining, an anxious looking Suzy Johnson-Little appeared on the touchline. She was clearly agitated and was hoping to find a moment to speak to Roddy. She wanted to make absolutely sure that no one had been told that she was the person who had found out about the building development. Ashley Stilton's unexpected arrival at her house that morning had deeply unnerved her.

Ashley had evidently driven straight from his meeting with Philip Pipe to speak to Gerald. Suzy did not know Ashley very well but she was nevertheless convinced that he was in a state of shock. At first, Gerald did not seem too alarmed when Ashley told him about his meeting with Philip Pipe; he suggested that Ashley needed to calm down. But Ashley wittered on about being a fool for allowing himself 'to be involved in the blasted scheme.'

He claimed that he had never really been happy about it and now realised that he was letting both Whitsborough and Philip Pipe down. Gerald only became concerned when Ashley announced that 'and now the Police are involved.' Gerald doubted whether this was true but Ashley explained how a senior 'plain clothes' policeman had arrived unexpectedly, wanting to look over the school and, significantly, all the playing fields.

Suzy pretended that she was completely ignorant of the whole scheme. She sat down with the two Mafia rogues and managed to get them to tell her the full story. Ashley said that he would, of course, have to resign as Chairman of the Governors immediately. Gerald pointed out that as the scheme would now soon become public, there would be huge local opposition to such a large housing development. The scheme had been, effectively, scotched. They simply wondered how it had been discovered. This was what worried Suzy and was the main reason that she wanted to speak to Roddy; for once it was not for another, more pleasurable, purpose.

A close game. Barq Sheah's excited promise

Screamed on desperately by their parents, Poppleford had launched several threatening attacks and only the inspirational tackling of Edwin and others had prevented the opposition from scoring. One of these attacks was brought to an abrupt end when a smaller Poppleford boy carrying the ball ran into Wes. Wes did not really tackle him; he simply enveloped him in his powerful arms. The ball was dropped and it rolled in its unpredictable way towards the replacement, Miles McNally. Miles picked it up smartly and evaded the nearest Poppleford player, who was slightly off balance. Miles then accelerated, dodged and sidestepped his way towards the other end of the pitch. Poppleford's only defending players were unable to match Miles's remarkable speed. Roddy felt a glow of pride as Miles scored the equalising try. He glanced across the pitch and saw Dottie being hugged by Kate in celebration.

With the scores now equal, the noise of the rival supporters reached new levels. Whipped into a frenzy of excitement, several of Barq Sheah's guards now began to shout and this added even greater intensity to the Whitsborough support.

Derek Drinkall was finding the pace of the game quite a challenge as the action became more frenetic. The sound of his whistle was almost drowned by the supporters. Norman, unable to restrain himself, had again moved close to the pitch and only the restrictions imposed by his crutches prevented him from hobbling up and down the touchline, level with the action.

Perhaps the loudest voice of all the spectators belonged to Barq Sheah. He had stayed close to Philip who, like many others, was also moving up and down the touchline following the play. In the excitement of the moment, Barq Sheah said:

"If we win this game, Mr Pipe – I'll...I'll build the school....a swimming pool." Seconds later, as the Whitsborough team surged forward, he leant towards a dumbfounded Philip and quickly added, "No! A sports hall!"

Philip was quietly bewildered and assumed this was just

a touchline jest. With only seconds to go, after an inaccurate Poppleford pass, the ball bobbled temptingly on the grass. Wesley found the ball in his hands and he spotted a large gap in the Poppleford defences. There were now only two Poppleford boys who could prevent him from scoring. With Wesley's speed and power now a known threat, a try – and victory – looked possible.

The two Poppleford defenders knew this was their last chance. The result was in their hands as Wesley pounded towards them. One of them, the full back, had already proved himself to be a brave and determined tackler. Wesley's momentum proved too great for the first defender but the brave full back executed a potentially match-saving tackle by flinging himself at Wesley's legs. He latched on to Wesley's left knee and simply refused to let go. Even with his considerable power, Wesley's speed was restricted. The determined Poppleford defender held on, like a sub-marine mollusc. He simply would not let go. Wesley was brought to a virtual halt. But from behind came a screaming voice:

"Here, Wes. Here!"

Once more, Miles McNally's sprinting ability had proved invaluable. Miles had overtaken the Poppleford defenders and he managed to appear by Wesley's side at the critical moment. In spite of the efforts of the courageous Poppleford limpet, who remained firmly attached to Wesley's knee, Wesley was able to lob the ball to Miles. Miles produced a juggling catch and then ran the last few paces to score the winning try.

D.D. blew the final whistle while the Whitsborough spectators whooped and applauded. Norman jumped up with delight and then down again in pain; he had overlooked the necessity for holding on to his crutches.

Remembering his duties as captain, Edwin led his team with 'Three cheers for Poppleford'. These joyful Whitsborough cheers were interspersed with several revs and engine noises which earned a few amused parental smiles.

Tea, cake and small chat

The school dining room was soon crammed full of parents. There would have been more room to move on an Underground train in the rush hour. Moving through the throng to obtain a cup of tea was a challenge not for the faint-hearted. As hosts, Angela, Dottie and Derek Drinkall bravely poured cups of tea from behind their barricade of trestle tables. The noise prevented civilized conversation. Barq Sheah accepted this all in good spirits and was briefly forced into close proximity with his wife, Chuselle. Dottie wondered just how many other wives Barq Sheah possessed. However, Barq Sheah soon abandoned Chuselle having exchanged only a few words with her. He now squeezed his way towards Philip and had to stoop slightly to speak in Philip's ear.

"I meant what I said, Mr Pipe. I promised a building... if we won...a sports hall. And we won! I hope it will be built in time for my younger sons to use it."

Philip moved back to look at Barq Sheah's expression. Barq Sheah simply looked straight into Philip's eyes and nodded slowly.

"After I broke my ankle when I was at school in England, I spent much time in the school's sports hall, recovering and exercising during the cold English winter. A sports hall would be good for this school, don't you think?"

Philip was speechless. Could this really be true?

Elsewhere, Kate thought she had managed to exchange eye contact with Roddy but could not be certain. Near one of the doors, Suzy, was also attempting to locate Roddy. Frustratingly, she found herself trapped in conversation with a chatterbox Whitsborough mother who lived near her.

Wisely, Norman Stevenson did not even attempt to join the chaos. Having limped across the field, he found a wooden bench outside the dining room. It looked out over the rugby pitch and Norman was happy to sit and quietly recall the glorious events of the afternoon. He had never felt so proud. Roddy had offered to obtain a cup of tea for him but Norman just smiled as he declined the offer. He just sat and wondered if he could ever be so happy again.

Eventually, the spectators drifted out of the dining room to be reunited with their sons. The Poppleford parents wandered away, somewhat subdued but many Whitsborough parents remained, chatting. Edwin and several others, including Wesley and Miles, dragged an embarrassed Roddy away from the remaining spectators in order to thank him. However, Roddy insisted that it was he who should be thanking them.

Barq Sheah, his fine robes sweeping along the turf, once more assumed the role of Most Important Guest. He moved forward to congratulate Roddy and shake his hand. They exchanged a few words and Roddy explained how Wesley had been a mature and forceful presence in the team.

With the excitement now subsiding, Edwin was on his way back to the changing room when he suddenly stopped, turned and walked back towards his father. He strode up to his seated parent, held out his hand for a handshake. Simply and sincerely he said,

"Thanks, Dad. All your fitness training paid off." He then nodded deferentially, delivered an awkward smile, turned and then strode towards the showers. If he had remained a moment longer, he would have observed several tears rolling slowly down his father's cheek.

Roddy became the centre of attention of another group of grateful parents just as Suzy J-L was easing hesitatingly towards him. She felt particularly awkward because Taylor had not been playing in the match. However, she had been worrying all morning and desperately wanted Roddy to confirm that he had told no one how the building plans had been discovered. Barq Sheah passed close behind her as he and his men were about to leave.

"I am a man of my word, Mr Pipe. You will have your sports hall," promised Barq Sheah as he left. "One of my secretaries will be in touch with you very soon."

Philip was glowing with pride and relief. A new sports hall would attract more parents and Whitsborough's financial future would be much brighter. He would make sure there was a report on the match, and the planned sports hall, in the local paper.

They shook hands and Philip watched Chuselle follow behind Barq Sheah as he departed. She turned to wave goodbye to Wesley. Barq Sheah's marital arrangements puzzled Philip but the day had been full of surprises.

An unexpected visitor

As the parents drifted away, Roddy was left alone for a moment.

"That was a most impressive victory, Mr Amport. I am glad my filming finished a day early so that I could be in time to see Miles play."

Roddy turned to see Kate who was now close to him. He gave her a warm smile but Angela appeared at this moment, striding purposefully out of the school building. She passed in front of Norman who was still sitting on his bench, inhaling the atmosphere.

"Roddy," called Angela. "Could I have word with you?" Angela signalled that this was not intended for other ears. Roddy gave Kate an apologetic smile.

"There's someone waiting for you – in a car – at the front. There was a phone call just after lunch. I didn't want to trouble you with it just before the game."

"Who is it?" asked Roddy. Angela seemed rather serious.

"You should just go… now!" replied Angela.

There was a note of urgency in her voice. Roddy could not imagine what this was all about. Philip emerged from a door at the back of the school building just as Roddy was about to enter. Philip, like Norman Stevenson, was clearly riding on Cloud Nine.

"Roddy, I simply cannot thank you enough. A wonderful, wonderful victory this afternoon. Incredible!"

Roddy was embarrassed but Philip had more to say.

"But it wasn't just the winning, it was the spirit and enjoyment that our boys...*your* boys...showed which was so impressive."

Philip held out his hand to give Roddy a warm handshake and leaned close to him. "And thank you for the 'tip off' about the building plans. I gave Ashley Stilton both barrels this morning and that, combined with the surprise arrival of the Police, gave him the shock of his life!" Philip chuckled, gave Roddy a pat on the back and then added:

"A famous victory, scotching Stilton's plans and an amazing promise from Wesley's father.......you've probably saved the school today, Roddy!"

Philip shook his head in disbelief but was then accosted by a grateful parent who was hobbling towards him on crutches.

While Roddy was entering the school via a fire exit, Derek Drinkall was approaching Kate McNally. He had not had time to change out of his refereeing kit but he had washed his face. He had combed his hair and put on a smart blue tracksuit top emblazoned with what he considered to be an impressive badge – a schools' football refereeing qualification: 'Grade Three.' Kate smiled and shook his hand.

Angela, however, observing Drinkall's fawning approach to Kate McNally, was determined to prevent any remote chance of him developing a casual acquaintance with her. She strode quickly towards them:

"Forgive me for interrupting, Derek, but there's a little too much noise coming from the changing rooms. It really needs a male teacher to sort it out."

Angela gave D.D. an empty smile as he backed away, having been checkmated.

"I am so sorry to interrupt, Miss McNally. I am Angela Bailey by the way. We met briefly once before." She was about to add 'Deputy Head' but thought better of it.

A surprise for Roddy.

When Roddy entered the school through a rear door, he spotted Suzy who was now hemmed in by a chattering group of Whitsborough parents. Several large dogs on leads waited patiently beside them. She pointed at him then carried out a 'zipping' movement across her lips, accompanied by a worried frown and a slight shake of her head. Would Roddy understand these gestures, she wondered?

Roddy understood the message. He 'zipped' across his own lips and gave her a smile and a nod with thumbs up. 'Message understood'.

There were still quite a few cars in the drive as Roddy emerged from the front entrance. A huge golden retriever stretched out in the back of one of the many estate cars. At the far end of the drive, parked away from the other vehicles, Roddy noticed Suzy's car, 'SJL 2'. However, near one of the large sycamore trees was a red Mini. The seated driver was waving to him. Roddy walked towards it and as he neared it, he recognised the driver who seemed reluctant to leave the car. Roddy opened the passenger door and climbed in.

Rosie threw herself across the front seat to give him a monumental hug. There was genuine warmth and comfort in this embrace. Roddy felt the delightful smoothness of Rosie's cheeks against his and there was a pleasant, natural smell of…softness. When she eventually pulled herself away from the hug, Rosie looked closely at Roddy's face.

"Well, I see your forehead has finally recovered. Hardly a mark there now."

"You were very kind to me when you came to see me. I never thanked you properly," said Roddy apologetically. He looked into her pale blue eyes affectionately and it was then he detected the first sign of tears.

"Roddy, I've something to tell you. I've desperately wanted to tell you before but even when we met last in Newbury there wasn't time. That lunch messed up my plan and I was **so** frustrated." The tears were now in free-fall.

"Yes, I could see that you were upset. I am sorry I had to rush back here," Roddy explained.

"Well, prepare for a surprise. I was actually trying to tell you the *first* time I came here to see you, a couple of weeks ago...but that time you weren't in a fit state."

Roddy could see that Rosie was about to unleash a Niagara of tears. He wondered what she could possibly be going to tell him. A new job? Flying off to work abroad? As he looked at her, he realised yet again how lovely she was and then he remembered how she had also acted as a very caring nurse.

"I phoned the school this morning and your Deputy Head – Angela? - answered the phone. She said that you had your important rugby match today but said that I ought to be able to speak to you afterwards."

Roddy found himself holding her hand as she seemed to be nervous.

"The thing is…" (there was a long pause)…"I'm pre…..." Rosie failed to complete the sentence. A family had just emerged from the front entrance and was passing close to the car.

"Pregnant??" questioned Roddy quietly after the group had passed. For a moment, he could think of nothing more to say. Rosie stared at him and nodded her head apologetically.

"It's all *my* fault," she added. "I just assumed it would be safe. Just the one time."

Rosie looked down as the tears began to flow. Roddy thought for a moment.

"Are you absolutely sure it's me. Just from that *one*...occasion, by the pool?"

"Absolutely. There hasn't been anyone else for ages. I'm

very choosy!" she added with the hint of a smile beneath the tears. "And, in spite of what you might think, I am not all that *'experienced.'*"

Roddy grinned

"Well, I got the impression that you knew exactly what you were doing….You must be a natural!"

Rosie gave Roddy a tearful smile. There was something very endearing and genuine about Rosie which Roddy now recognised once more.

"Have you had this all verified…you know…medically?" asked Roddy.

Rosie nodded.

"Yes. It's all been checked. The baby is due in May."

"The baby! Yes, of course," said Roddy with a mixture of surprise and pride.

"We've made a person!"

Rosie had envisaged this scenario over and over in her head. Somehow, Roddy's reaction was not at all what she had expected…but then she did not really know what to expect.

"In that case," said Roddy after a thoughtful pause, "there's only one course of action."

Rosie was dreading this moment. Roddy gently took hold of her hands.

"In that case", he said gently, looking directly into her pale blue eyes, "I think we should………."

CHAPTER 19

The end of term approaches
By the time Philip and Dottie Pipe had been informed that Roddy was going to get married, both sets of parents – the Amports and the Pitchworths - had recovered from the shock. Doctor and Mrs Amport were charmed by Rosie

within minutes of meeting her and could not believe that they were about to have such a delightful daughter in law, albeit in unusual circumstances. The Pitchworths, of course, knew Roddy from his attendances at the Cricket Week. He was a popular figure, one of the lads, but they were unsure as to whether he was ideal husband material yet.

Rosie's father, Mark, feared that Roddy's salary as a young schoolmaster would mean that he might struggle to provide adequately for his family's upkeep. However, his wife firmly forbade him from interfering and offering Roddy a lucrative job in the Pitchworth family's printing firm.

Plans

Roddy had made sure that he informed Philip about the marriage when Dottie was not present. Philip proved remarkably sympathetic. He predicted that Dottie would express alarm to start with, but would soon 'come to accept' it. He confided that Dottie had been unable to have her own children and might yet prove to be a keen babysitter and even a willing pram-pusher.

He would endeavour to provide Roddy with some more spacious 'family' accommodation at the school, or in the village nearby. He would certainly do his best but there was plenty of time to arrange this.

When Philip enquired a little more deeply about Rosie, Roddy, a little embarrassed that he knew so little about his fiancée's education, said that he believed she had read English at university.

"Perhaps she would like to do a little teaching - while Dottie baby sits?" grinned Philip as Roddy was leaving, "and thank you for telling me. I look forward to meeting your fiancée. She's a lucky girl."

The Open Evening

True to his word, Barq Sheah had already ensured that

Philip promptly received some initial sketches of a design for the sports hall. It was even more impressive than Philip could have hoped. Hired out to the public, it would provide a most welcome and significant additional source of income.

At short notice, Philip decided to hold an end of term Open Evening - a drinks party for all the parents during which he would reveal the plans for the sports hall. Uncharacteristically, it was Dottie, with a surprising eye for publicity, who suggested that they should ask Kate McNally to 'unveil' the architect's sketches. Kate gladly agreed and Philip then decided that this would be an ideal moment to introduce Rosie to the parents and formally announce Roddy's engagement. For weeks, this news had remained a well-guarded secret; the Pipes were the only Whitsborough people who knew of it.

Edwin and Wesley were invited to help hand round the drinks and canapés. Norman Stevenson, still in a haze of contentment, endeavoured to hi-jack Edwin's job and his plate of canapés. This was because no one seemed to want to speak to him as he had already unsuccessfully attempted to interrupt several groups of parents, engaged in animated conversations, with the opening line: "Of course, I'm Edwin's father..."

When Philip Pipe eventually asked for silence, he explained that he had two pieces of good news. First of all, he announced the engagement of Roddy and Rosie, which was a complete surprise to almost everyone. This earned both applause and a number surprised looks.

Philip then asked 'the distinguished actress – and parent,' Kate McNally, to draw back the curtain which concealed the sketches. Kate was stunned by the news of Roddy's engagement and she had to draw upon her innate acting skills in order to hide her feelings. Fortunately, the guests' attention was drawn to the impressive sketches as the drawings were revealed.

Dottie, who had been in full 'charm' mode all evening,

turned to find herself facing Mrs Berkshire.

"Hello, Mrs Pipe. I do hope the plans my husband sent are satisfactory. And do, please, call me Chuselle."

"Chuselle?" Dottie swallowed: the name still grated, but the gift of a sports hall would surely prove to be invaluable. "Chuselle. Yes, of course. Such a lovely name! I remember thinking that when I showed you round the school in the summer. I am **so** glad we were able to find place for your three boys."

Dottie could hardly believe that she could tell such an appalling lie. Chuselle smiled and Dottie half-expected to be struck a thunderbolt.

Having heard the news of Roddy's engagement, Suzy, struggled to withhold her tears; now she understood why she had not heard from Roddy for so long. Gerald, however, had been keen to attend the Open Evening. His thick skin enabled him to attend the party without embarrassment; no one, he felt, could possibly know of his involvement with the housing scheme. Suzy guessed correctly that Gerald really attended because he was keen to meet Kate McNally.

Angela was busy doing the rounds, topping up the glasses and had just arrived beside Gerald. He had just introduced himself to Kate and was about to tell her all about himself. Unfortunately, he felt a tap on his shoulder.

"And **I** am Suzy Johnson-Little," piped Suzy who then linked her arm lovingly round her husband's elbow. She smiled sweetly at Kate.

"Can I top you up?" asked Angela as she found herself part of this little group and was wielding a bottle of Muscadet.

"Oh, yes, please," gasped Suzy who thrust her empty glass forward. She felt that she needed several drinks having just heard Roddy's news.

"Mr Amport seems to be a very popular teacher," commented Kate. "Miles says he enjoys his lessons and he was grateful to play a part in the Poppleford match."

"Yes, a lot of boys like being taught by him," agreed Angela as she filled Suzy's glass whilst savouring her own private memories of Roddy at the beginning of the term.

"He is certainly good at what he does," she added.

Gerald turned his head and caught sight of Roddy who was now chatting nearby and holding his fiancé's hand.

"Of course! I *thought* I recognised him," exclaimed Gerald. "He's the chap who's been coming to the house and giving you French lessons, isn't he, Darling?"

Suzy cringed. She could feel her face turning red and prayed for the immediate appearance of a large hole into which she could instantly disappear. Angela's antennae were on full alert whilst Kate raised her eyebrows.

"French lessons?? Really?" remarked Angela, glaring at Suzy with unconcealed suspicion.

"Good looking young fellow like that….getting married so young..." chuckled Gerald knowingly. "I bet he'll leave a lot of women disappointed!"

The three women fell silent and avoided eye contact.

"Er...yes," agreed Kate, attempting to mask her feelings, "I rather think he will."

ABOUT THE AUTHOR

For many years, Colin Henderson taught at a well-known and successful school in Surrey. Previously, he spent a year teaching at a small, boys' boarding school which eventually closed in the 1970s. He always hoped to write a book, loosely based on his experiences there. None of the characters in this story is based on any particular individual although many are 'hybrids'. Schools such as these are richly endowed with memorable characters, whether teachers, pupils – or parents!

Printed in Great Britain
by Amazon

12837605R00147